MW01138923

MOTHER OF SHADOWS

THE CHOSEN: BOOK 1

MEG ANNE

Cover Design © Lori Follett of HellYes.design

Editing: Hanleigh Bradley

❀ Created with Vellum

For every girl that still carries a dream in her heart, this one is for you.

MOTHER

OF

SHADOWS

ELYSIA

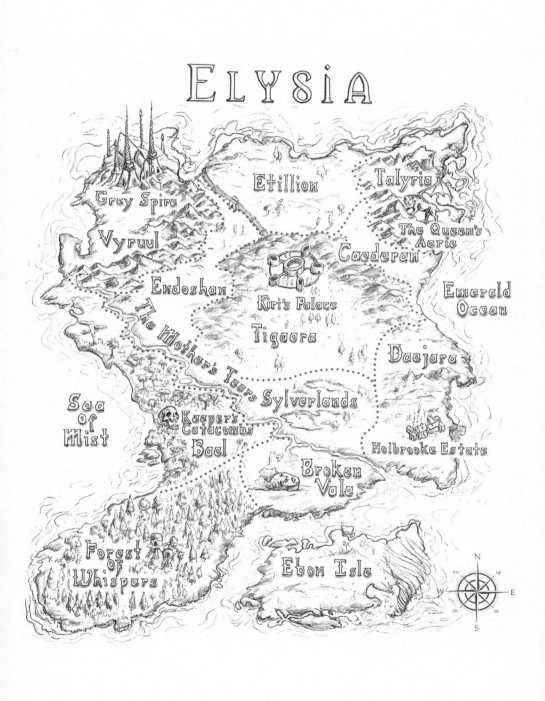

CHAPTER 1

*H*elena stretched a final time before sitting up in the behemoth wooden bed. *Have I already gotten used to this?* She ran her fingers along one of the glossy pillars before smoothing back the luxurious purple satin sheet and throwing her legs over the side. Bare feet met plush carpet, and she padded her way softly to the window; draping a silk robe over creamy shoulders and belting it loosely around her hips.

Peering out the large window she saw crowds of people already beginning to gather for today's festivities. A shiver of anxiety danced down her spine as a quiet knock sounded on the door.

"Enter," she called out distractedly, still taking in the gardens below.

"Good morning, Damaskiri," her maid, Alina, greeted cheerfully. Turning from the window, Helena offered Alina a nervous smile: the title still sounding strange to her ears. "Did you sleep well?"

Helena shook her head as she replied softly, "I was too nervous."

"Well, that's to be expected. I'd be nervous too if it were my life that was about to change so completely," Alina stated matter-of-factly as she opened the wardrobe and began to pull out the number of garments that comprised Helena's festival outfit.

"You'd think I would be used to that by now," Helena muttered with a wry smile.

Alina laughed as she moved efficiently around the room; stopping briefly to ask over her shoulder, "Would you like a bath drawn up, Damaskiri?"

Helena nodded in gratitude. "Yes, please Alina. Thank you."

With a wink, Alina smiled and sashayed into the bathing room.

The weak smile Helena had tried so desperately to keep in place began to falter as soon as the maid had left the room. Worry and doubt, Helena's constant companions in the last few weeks, were starting to creep into Helena's mind yet again. Numbly she folded herself into the soft velvet armchair and looked back toward the window. *How am I ever going to get through this? I can't possibly be who they say I am,* she thought desperately.

Apprehension had her stomach twisting in knots, and her back was stiff with tension. She ran trembling fingers through her chestnut locks while her mind raced through the events that had brought her to this moment. *Had it really only been a matter of weeks?*

HELENA SAT BACK on her heels, placing dirty hands on her knees and eyeing the flowers in front of her. After ensuring no weeds remained, she pushed herself to her feet as clumps of dirt fell softly from her simple blue work dress. She wiped the sweat from her brow and lifted her head to the warm kiss of the afternoon sun. A soft breeze stirred the strands of chestnut hair that had slipped from the knot at her neck. Smiling in contentment, her eyes roamed gently sloping green hills and the wide blue sky that surrounded her garden. Gardening was not easy work, but it was satisfying. It also was a far superior task to staying inside and washing dishes.

The familiar crunch of wheels on gravel had her spinning her head and shielding her eyes to see who was making their way to the little cottage. Recognizing the carriage that bounced and swayed down the path, her smile widened with joy. Helena began sprinting toward it.

The carriage came to a stop seconds before it would have crashed into her.

With breathless laughter, she waved in greeting. "Darrin! You've come back!"

A golden blond head preceded the tall, masculine body that unfolded itself from the confines of the carriage. Laughing green eyes took in the sight before him, and he walked toward his longtime friend with a smile.

Helena drank in the sight of him. She had not seen Darrin since he left to join the elite ranks of the Rasmirin, personal guards of the Damaskiri and her Circle. His sun-kissed skin still held its golden glow, and his emerald eyes had the same mischievous twinkle. He looked larger and more imposing than she remembered though.

"Hellion," he murmured with affection, using the childhood nickname he'd bestowed upon her years ago. She squinted her eyes in mock annoyance. "Been playing in the dirt again?" he continued in his lazy drawl.

She looked down at her dress and saw the smears of dirt in the soft blue fabric. With a helpless shrug, she responded, "What gave it away?"

He reached out a long finger and gently brushed the smudge of dirt her hand must have left across her face. She laughed, slapping his hand away.

"You've grown at least a foot since I saw you last."

She rolled her eyes at the exaggeration. "I was not a wee babe when you left, Darrin. It's only been a few years."

"Things have a way of changing," he said softly, his voice warm and deep.

"Will you tell me about everything? The Palace? The Chosen? The Circle?" she asked with excitement. Helena had always been curious about Tigaera's capital, Elysia, and its inhabitants. She felt worlds away from such wealth and luxury, not to mention the magic—since she was not one of the Chosen and therefore had no magical abilities herself.

He nodded, the warm glow in his eyes fading softly. "Yes, there is much to tell. But first, how is your mother, is she home?"

Helena's smile dimmed and wavered slightly. She tried to look down to hide the pain that lanced through her at the mention of her mother.

"Helena?" he questioned softly, tilting her chin up to meet his gaze.

"Mother passed last winter," she whispered, her voice hoarse with emotion.

"Oh, Helena," he murmured in sympathy, strong arms reaching to pull her to him. "Why didn't you write to me? I would have come."

"I didn't want to interfere with such important work. And there was nothing you could have done, besides." She held him tightly for a moment, accepting the comfort and strength he offered before stepping back, in control of her emotions again.

Darrin studied her a moment longer. "So it's just you then?"

She nodded. "Me and the horses. Anderson comes a few times a week to help fix things around here, and in return, I provide him with whatever extra food I can spare."

Darrin smiled at the mention of his grandfather. "I'm glad he has had you to look after him."

"Of course," she murmured in surprise. "He's family."

He shook his head with a chuckle. "Well, are you going to invite me in or make me stand out here in this blasted heat all day?"

"By all means," she said solemnly, gesturing that he should make his way into the cottage ahead of her.

"After you, Damaskiri," he said softly, earnest green eyes studying her.

She laughed at his game. "So I'm the 'Daughter of Spirit' now?" She shook her head in amusement. "You're setting your aim a little high for me, aren't you Darrin? I can hardly be the Damaskiri, especially seeing as how I don't have an ounce of magic in me."

The Damaskiri was the ruler of the Chosen, in very rare cases a Kiri or 'Mother of Spirit' might come into power, but it had been centuries since the last Kiri ruled. Helena's understanding of the Chosen was spotty at best, but even she knew that only a Damaskiri could call forth Spirit magic and only a Kiri could access all five branches of the Mother's magic equally.

He did not return her smile, nor did he make his way toward the door.

"A Rasmiri soldier never leaves his charge unprotected."

She raised an eyebrow at him and slapped him on the chest. "Maybe you have been in the sun too long, old friend. I believe you might be touched."

He scowled at her. "Just get inside, Hellion."

Confused, but still convinced he was playing one of their old games, she made her way into the cottage.

He followed closely behind her, and into the homey warmth of the cottage. It was too early for a fire to blaze in the hearth, but remnants of her meager lunch were still spread on the table.

"You never were one to pick up after yourself."

She shoved at him and threatened without heat. "If you are insinuating that my home is less than pleasant, I will skin you!"

He held up his hands with a laugh. "Not at all, merely appreciating that some things may never change."

She tossed one of her biscuits at him, aiming for his blond head. He plucked it from the air and devoured it in two bites. Smacking his lips in satisfaction, he asked for another. "Get them yourself, Rasmiri," she gestured to the basket on the table with her head. While he stuffed himself, she walked around the small room picking up discarded oddities in an attempt to tidy for her guest.

With a satisfied sigh, he sat back in the armchair his grandfather had gifted her mother when she first moved into the cottage. He ran his hands over the well-worn wood. She sat across from him on the similarly worn and faded couch, her fingers plucking unconsciously at the fabric. "So how long are you visiting?"

"I'm here on business," he corrected, leaning back in the chair and stretching his long legs out in front of him. She admired the bunch of muscles well displayed by, and encased in, the brown leather of his pants.

"What could the Circle possibly need to send you here for?" She asked, tilting her head inquisitively to the side.

The most recent Damaskiri had died suddenly only a few weeks ago without a new one being selected. The rituals and ceremony surrounding the rise of a new Damaskiri were mysteries to Helena, but she did know that when one came into their power, they would undergo a trial to test their magic. If they passed the trial, they would inherit the realm and claim the title. It was unheard of for a Damaskiri to die before her replacement had been found, which explains how that bit of gossip had managed to find its way to even her small cottage.

Reclining as he was, Darrin's face was covered in shadow. She felt a shiver of unease at the realization. "That's not an easy story to tell, Hellion."

"Perhaps you should start at the beginning then, Darrin," she snapped. She couldn't explain where the change in her emotion was stemming from, but she felt distinctly on edge.

He let out a long breath and seemed to weigh his words carefully before beginning. "Do you remember the stories we heard when we were children, Helena? About how the old masters had re-translated a prophecy?"

"The prophecy about the Mother of Shadows?"

Helena was very familiar with the story, if not the actual words of prophecy. It was foretold that a Kiri would rise, one whose magic would rival that of the First Born, the first of the Chosen. With her acceptance of the throne, the dawn of the Shadow Years would begin. A time when the Chosen would be tested, and those deemed unworthy destroyed.

He nodded. "The masters had discovered that their understanding of the prophecy was flawed. When the Kiri rose, like would call to like, and all of those found wanting would be destroyed."

Helena nodded. "Yes, the purity of her magic would destroy those that chose to corrupt it. The Shadow Years are to give rise to the rebirth of the Chosen; the promise of a new era. How is that flawed?"

"What do you suppose would happen, if the Kiri was corrupted?" he asked the question gently.

She scrunched up her face in thought. "Well, I suppose she would be destroyed too?"

He shook his head as he leaned forward. "Therein lies the flaw. 'Like calls to like,' remember? If she is corrupted, all those who remain pure will be destroyed."

Eyes wide, Helena's mouth turned into a small O of surprise as Darrin continued his tale. "The Circle and the remaining masters gathered that night and declared that when born, the prophesized girl would be taken away from Elysia. She would remain hidden, so as to be uncorrupted by the influence of those that would use her for their own purposes, until she came of age and it was time for her to inherit her throne."

"Imagine if we had known that growing up, Darrin! We would have spent many more afternoons pretending that we were searching for her instead of hidden treasure!" Helena snorted with laughter.

"Helena," he whispered, his voice serious, "It's not a story."

She shivered, suddenly cold; the chill that had found her earlier was now wrapping itself around her heart. "What are you saying?"

He shrugged. "She was hidden, her secret known only to those that sent her away. No one else knew where she was, until now."

The finality of his words stripped her of speech. A few of his earlier comments that she had dismissed as teasing came back to her. *After you, Damaskiri. I am here on business.*

"No," she whispered.

"I see you understand."

"But I have no magic, Darrin. How could I possibly be..." her voice faded.

He moved quickly to kneel in front of her. "I know that you are scared, Helena, but you needn't worry. Events were set into motion from the moment of your birth, and there are those that have planned for this. Your magic was bound so that you may lead a normal life so that it would be guaranteed to be pure. The binding will fade on your twenty-first name day when you come into both the throne and your power. There are people that have made it their life's purpose to protect you. *I* will protect you," he promised fiercely.

7

She felt as though he was speaking from a world away. "You're teasing me, surely?"

His warm hands wrapped around hers. "Be strong, Helena. Your people need you now, more than ever. We're entering a dark time, *Mira*, and they will need you to lead them. You were born for this."

The term of endearment made her eyes water. "I-I don't want this, Darrin. I'm happy here."

His lips flattened in disappointment. "Don't be a child, Helena."

Her body had begun to tremble. With each word that he said she could hear the faint hammer of a nail slamming the door closed on the life she knew. The ring of truth to what he was saying was too real to ignore, and she had never been one to abide lying. She refused to lie to herself.

"So, what happens now?"

He squeezed her hands in approval. "Now it's time to go home, Damaskiri. It's time to learn about your people and what you will need to do in the days to come."

Memories of stories she had heard as a child came back to her. "Isn't there a festival that's held when the Damaskiri comes into power?"

He nodded.

"Isn't she supposed to undergo some sort of trial of magic, to prove her worthiness before she can claim the title?"

"One of the things you will be prepared for and face upon your return," he assured her.

Struggling to take a deep breath, she looked him straight in the eye. "How long have you known?"

She noted the guilty blush stain his cheeks.

"Darrin," she said firmly, no longer asking.

"Since my tenth name day," he muttered, his voice pained.

Betrayal spiraled through her. She wanted to scream at him: *How could you not tell me? How could you keep this from me?* But she remained silent.

"It was the same day that I was told that I was to spend the rest of my life protecting you. I am to be your Shield, Damaskiri," he said, voice a fierce whisper.

"If I'm the one they speak of in this prophecy, why do you call me Damaskiri? Isn't she," Helena paused to correct herself, the tumble of thoughts racing through her mind making it difficult to focus. "Aren't I," she continued slowly, "fated to be a Kiri?"

"Yes, that is what the Circle believes, but since you have not undergone your trial any title is only honorary at this point. There's no title for 'next in line'," Darrin joked.

Helena didn't smile in response. More of the old stories rose to the surface of her memory. The Damaskiri has her own Circle of protectors. It is comprised of those that have been bound to her since her birth, loyal only to her. They have no mates or families of their own, and those they had prior to entering their service and training they must leave behind so that there will be no ties to bind them to any but her.

The Circle includes the Advisor, the Shield, the Master, the Sword, and the Mate. Each position is for life, if one should die in the midst of their service, a new one will rise to his place, except for the Mate. A Mate is for life, and there is only one.

Her eyes widened at what he had said. He was *her* Shield. Growing up he had been her best friend. Her confidant. He was either the one getting her into trouble or getting her out of it. They had grown up together, and she had never loved one as she loved him. She had always imagined that one day they would have a family of their own. Helena had never known anyone else, and could not imagine sharing her life with anyone other than him... even if they had never taken any steps toward such a relationship.

Noting her expression, Darrin nodded, his green eyes soft with understanding. He knew what she was realizing; it was the thing he had struggled with himself. He swallowed hard and averted his eyes before they could betray him further.

"Do you know the others?" she whispered, her voice sounding strange to her own ears.

He nodded again, still unable to meet her gaze. "All but the—

your," he corrected himself and cleared his throat before repeating more firmly, "your Mate."

She closed her eyes, feeling lost and afraid. "Yes, I remember. There is a ceremony of sorts, is there not? As part of the Festival where the Mate is chosen? They are bound on that day, rather than the day of the Damaskiri's birth, as with the others."

Green eyes searched aqua, seeking something. He saw her fear, and the battle to master it. Her skin had gone even paler than usual. Lips that were usually tilted in laughter were being worried by pearly teeth.

"Helena, I will be with you every step of the journey. You are not alone in this," he whispered his vow to her, begging with his eyes for her to understand. "If it could be any other way… if it could be me," he continued his voice hoarse with emotion.

She hushed him. "No, Darrin. We will not speak of it."

He hung his head, understanding that she was telling him that she did not blame him and that she forgave him. They sat there quietly for a moment, neither so much as moving. He shifted, to look back up at a face that had always been dearer to him than any other. He wanted to promise her so many things, but he remained silent knowing that such promises would only hurt her. It was his duty to shield her from anything that would harm her, including his own desires.

Color had returned to her cheeks, tingeing them a soft pink. She was still biting her lower lip, lost in thought, her brows creased with worry. Her laughing aqua eyes were clouded with the torrent of emotions she was sifting through.

He saw the exact moment that she controlled herself. Her eyes darkened, and the crease between her brows lifted. Her gaze met his, and she asked coolly, "When do we go?"

He sighed and pulled himself upright. "As soon as you gather whatever belongings that you would like to take with you."

She nodded, having anticipated his answer. She stood and made a move toward the back of the cottage where her room sat. "Darrin?"

"Yes, Helena?"

"I don't suppose we have time for me to say goodbye to Anderson?"

He felt his stomach tighten with emotion, and shook his head no. She nodded, resigned, and walked out of the room.

IN THE WEEKS THAT FOLLOWED, she had constantly been surrounded by people. Darrin was never far, but with all that she had to learn for the Festival, there was no time for the two of them to spend with one another. She was feeling the strain of many sleepless nights. Her emotions were raw, and she felt on edge. There were purple smudges under her eyes, which had not retained their laughing sparkle since arriving at the Palace.

"Damaskiri," Alina called. From the tone of her voice, it was apparent that this was not the first time she had tried to get Helena's attention.

Blinking rapidly, Helena pushed herself back out of the chair. "Yes, coming."

She walked into the bathing room quickly. Alina smiled at her; blonde curls pulled high atop her head, her cheeks flushed from the heat of the water. Helena closed her eyes and took in the heady fragrance of jasmine wafting from the water. The familiar fragrance helped to relax her.

"I remembered that you had mentioned your preference for this scent, Damaskiri. I hope it pleases you."

"Thank you, Alina. I think a nice soak is just what I need before the Festival commences."

"Would you like me to stay and wash your hair?"

Helena shook her head quickly. While it was nice having someone to take care of all the little chores she had always hated, Helena had not and could not get used to the idea of someone bathing her like she was a child.

Alina smiled a final time and walked out of the room.

Letting her robe pool on the floor around her feet, Helena stepped into the warm water and laid back against the cool marble tub. Trying to silence her mind, at least for the moment, she let her eyes close and hummed the old lullaby her mother sang to her as a child. She tried to ignore the pang in her chest at the thought of her mother, who was not actually her birth mother. It was one of the few things that she could not accept. Miriam had raised her, kissed all of her hurts, both real and imaginary. Miriam was her mother, even if it was only the mother of her heart.

Her hands fisted in frustration at her sides in the water, and a wave of longing for her old life washed through her.

After a moment, Helena took a deep breath and told herself firmly it was the last time she would look back. Rolling her neck, she let the water lap at her, willing it to help relax her muscles. Warmth suffused her strained limbs, easing the ache that had built up over the last few weeks. She let out a soft sigh of contentment. The stress ebbed, and she felt the first true sense of calm since arriving in Elysia.

It matters naught what you fear, or that you find yourself wanting. If you were born for this as they say, then you can do whatever is asked of you.

With a final deep breath, Helena stood from the now cool water and stepped from the marble tub. Despite her personal wish to remain safely hidden away in here for the foreseeable future, she knew that the only way to get through this was to meet it head-on. Determined to do so, she began the process of drying her body and hair.

There was a discreet knock on the door.

"Yes?" Helena called, quickly wrapping the towel around her body.

"It is time to get ready, Damaskiri," Alina's melodic voice floated through the door.

Steeling her shoulders and setting her jaw, she opened the door.

It's time.

*A*fter an hour of pampering, although she would argue the process of dressing was more akin to torture, she was declared a vision. Alina was beaming with pride at the Oohs and Aahs from other of the Palace servants. Helena blushed under the scrutiny and tried not to drop her eyes to the floor.

'*You must learn to control your emotions, Damaskiri,*' *Timmins had gently admonished.* '*One of the royal family would never shy away from any considered lesser than they. Furthermore, they do not waste time with public displays of emotion. To be ruled by your emotions is to be unable to rule justly and impartially. A Damaskiri must be both, and they must remain unyielding. You should never show that another has the power to affect your judgment.*'

If there was an etiquette lesson that was deemed most crucial, it had been that one. Her Circle's Advisor had been kind, but very insistent that her years away from the court would be the greatest detriment to her rule.

Conversely, Master Joquil had insisted her complete lack of understanding magic, and her questionable ability to wield it, would see her surely fail. She bit back a smile at the thought of the two older men arguing the point during her first formal meeting with the Circle.

It had been a relief to finally meet the men that would be responsible for her safety, education and overall well-being from now on. She had instantly liked them all.

Timmins held the position of Advisor. He was a tall, well-fit, older man with yellow hair that had begun to fade to white in the last few years. His blue eyes had crinkled with a warm smile when he shook her hand and spoke the vows that would formally bind his life to hers.

'I vow to uphold and obey your beliefs and take them as my own. I will be your voice, spreading your wisdom so that all may know your edicts. I will spend the rest of my days in service to you and your will, until such a time as the Mother reclaims me or the blade of war strikes me.'

Despite his age, she could feel his strength and the power that radiated from him in waves. He reminded her greatly of Anderson, she had thought with an all-too-familiar pang in her heart.

She had turned then to her Master. Joquil had studied her with cool amber eyes beneath thick black brows. He wore his raven hair, lightly flecked with gray, short; his close-cropped beard enhanced the firm set of his jaw. He was also tall, but slender compared to the others. He had spent years training in all aspects of magic and would be the one to teach her how to use her gift. His power had intimidated but also comforted her. He too had taken vows before her:

'I vow to uphold and obey your beliefs and take them as my own. I will be your light, teaching you the ways of the Mother and her Chosen. I will spend the rest of my days in service to you and your will, until such a time as the Mother reclaims me or the blade of war strikes me.'

Next came Darrin, more serious than she had ever seen him, with the candlelight reflecting in his bright green eyes. He had knelt before her, holding her hand tightly in his.

'I vow to uphold and obey your beliefs and take them as my own. I will be your shield, protecting your life and light from any that would seek to destroy it. I will spend the rest of my days in service to you and your will, until such a time as the Mother reclaims me or the blade of war strikes me.'

She saw him swallow and clear his throat before releasing her hand and standing. Her heart had clenched with affection at his promise. He had looked after her since before she could walk, and knowing that he would be by her side now was a constant source of comfort. She could find little to fear, other than worries of her own ineptitude, knowing that he would always be watching out for her.

Finally, she had turned to Kragen, her Sword. The sheer size of him was overwhelming. He was a solid wall of hard, sculpted muscle that towered several heads above the others. Each massive arm had a band of black symbols swirling around it which disappeared up into his shirt. She had made a mental note to ask him what they meant if she survived this whole fiasco. Unlike the others, he had no hair, opting instead for a skin lightly dusted with stubble. He had soft wrinkles near his eyes and mouth, showing that he spent most of his time smiling. Despite his size, she knew she would never have to fear him. If anything, he would tease her mercilessly and become an annoying older brother who always wanted to tell her what to do.

As if following her thoughts, he smirked and stepped away from the wall to move toward her. His voice had been a deep rumble as he unsheathed the weapon at his side and laid it at her feet:

'I vow to uphold and obey your beliefs and take them as my own. I will be your sword, exacting your vengeance and slaying any who would seek to harm you. I will spend the rest of my days in service to you and your will, until such a time as the Mother reclaims me or the blade of war strikes me.'

Mother help those who would seek to harm me, she had thought, imagining Kragen wielding the broadsword as he sheathed it. She had found herself feeling oddly emotional at the promises of these relative strangers, and tried to convey the depth of her feeling in her promise to them.

'I will strive to be true and just, worthy of the gift of service that you have vowed today. I promise to be a light in the dark days to come, using my power to protect and nurture, rather than dominate or destroy. I will be the exemplar of our people acting in their best interests, rather than my own. I further vow that I will never take for

granted your service to me, or what you give up, nor will I forget the gift you are to me. Above all, you are dear to me, and I shall seek to be worthy of your gift.'

Her voice had rung out over the stone walls of the room, and the four men in front of her had not so much as blinked while she spoke. No others had been allowed in the room for the ceremony, and so she was unaware the effect her words had had on them. She improvised slightly when she promised to seek to be worthy of them, straying from the traditional vows of the Damaskiri to her Circle. She understood the sacrifice they had made when they bound their lives to hers, and she wanted them to know that she likewise was bound to them.

Timmins shifted first, his eyes suspiciously shiny. Kragen cleared his throat, and Joquil seemed to lose some of the aloof superiority she noted when she first met him. Darrin alone was unable to contain his smile of approval. She had impressed them with her warmth and sincerity. She was a Damaskiri that they were proud to serve.

Making eye contact with each of them, she lifted the chalice that had been waiting on the table next to her and held it aloft, speaking the final words of the ceremony:

'Blood of my blood these four shall be, my voice, my light, my shield and my sword. I take them unto me, as my own, to cherish and protect as I would myself, until such a time as the Mother reclaims me.'

Each man, in turn, drank from the ceremonial chalice, which had been filled with wine—not blood as she had originally feared. As the ceremony concluded, she looked around the room at them and asked, "So now what?"

Kragen had thrown his head back in laughter, slapping Darrin's back. Darrin had flinched at the contact but chuckled too. Timmins and Joquil wore identical looks of surprise but eventually joined in. Feeling foolish, but knowing that they were not laughing at her, she laughed along with the rest of them.

"Now, Damaskiri, we prepare you." Timmins had smiled.

COMING BACK TO THE PRESENT, Helena fervently prayed that she would not let them down. Squaring her shoulders again, she forced herself to be still until the servants moved out of the room.

Head high she began her descent into the main wing of the Palace and through the doors that would lead her into the garden and the Festival. The torrent of information that had been forced on her in the last few days was swirling in her mind, and she was desperately trying to remember it all. There was so much she hadn't known, such as the fact that the Festival lasted a full seven days beginning at sunrise on the first day and concluding at sundown on the seventh. Nor had she realized that the selection of her Mate was intrinsically woven into the entire fabric of the Festival.

Helena had anticipated that she would be introduced to her birth parents upon her arrival at the Palace. However, she had been informed that neither her mother nor father had survived her birth. Helena found it difficult to mourn for parents she never knew but was saddened that she truly was without family. Timmins had been vague when informing her that their death was one of the essential elements of the prophecy that had come true, and no one else had deigned to enlighten her as to those other essential elements.

Luckily, this evening's ceremony was strictly a formal beginning of the event. She was only expected to greet the important guests and then, after a few from her Circle spoke, a formal dinner and ball in her honor would begin.

Forcing herself to focus on the present, Helena took in the surroundings of her new home. She had yet to have time to explore properly, but the Palace was comprised of five wings, each representing a branch of magic. The Wings met in the center of the structure but were also connected by walkways between them to symbolize how magic bound everything together. She had been told that each wing was decorated in the style of the branch it depicted. The Earth Wing was styled in neutrals and greens, enchanted to appear as though you were outside. Different rooms reflected different times of day or regions of the realm. Others were magicked to change according to the current time of day or season. It was there that all of the royal guests were kept.

The Water Wing was swathed in blues and grays, rooms enchanted to appear as though submerged, or to have streams flowing through them. Due to Water's ability to soothe, this was predominately where the healers and their families resided.

The Air branch was comprised of soft whites and golden yellows. These rooms were known for their vaulting ceilings and soaring towers. Each room had large outdoor areas connected to them with invisible walls so that when one walked out onto the balcony, they felt as though they were floating. This wing housed many of the Palace's libraries and ceremonial meeting rooms as well as the royal craftsmen and their workshops.

The fourth branch, Fire, was painted in the palest shades of rose to the deepest of reds. Fire was always a representation of passion; however, it was best known for its power to destroy, and as such this branch was where the Rasmirin resided. The rooms were generally stark, but not without beauty. Since the warriors required so much room for training and their barracks, the only times the females of the Palace would use this wing was for one of the annual festivals.

The final wing was for Spirit and was reserved for the Damaskiri and her Circle. Decorated in shades of purple and gold, it was associated with the force that animates and breathes life into all things. As the only one capable of tapping into this power and the strongest of all of the Mother's Chosen, the Damaskiri was the personification of this branch of magic. Helena had found it hard to associate herself with this role, but the unmistakable peace she had found in this wing, compared to all the others, was enough for her not to question it.

She let her fingers brush against a lavender bloom that was spilling down from a planter above as she made her way out to the garden.

She stopped suddenly, forgetting about the parade of people trailing behind her, and tried to take in the beauty that surrounded her. After only a few weeks, Helena was already certain she would never become immune to the splendor of the Palace. Its numerous towers met the sky and disappeared behind clouds, and the creamy marble sparkled in the sun making it appear to glow. It was surrounded on all sides by gardens specializing in the most beautiful flowers and trees from around the realm.

Helena's fingers were twitching with excitement at the idea of one day being able to explore them, and perhaps plant a few of her own favorites, but for now, she would have to settle with the glimpses she could catch as she was escorted by or through them.

Timmins chose that moment to rush to her side. "Is all well, Damaskiri?"

She nodded and gifted him with a small smile. "Yes, I simply couldn't help but enjoy the view. Doesn't it take your breath away?"

Timmins' eyes wandered over the scene before him, and he gave her an indulgent smile, but she could tell it didn't call to him as it did her.

She laughed softly. "It's all right, Timmins, perhaps it is merely in my nature to be impressed by such grandeur."

Eyes twinkling, Timmins replied, "I think you'll find, Damaskiri, that your nature will be the most spectacular beauty of them all."

She beamed at the compliment and held her arm out to him. "Shall we continue on, Advisor?"

He nodded, taking her arm and gently winding it around his own. "Do you remember what we discussed about the welcoming ceremony?"

Helena was slow to respond, "I believe so."

Patiently he repeated himself. "First, you will greet your people. You will wish them the blessings of the Mother and thank them for coming to celebrate your name day. Then you will greet each representative of the royal houses; you will give them the same welcome. Finally, you will present your Circle, and then the males who are of age who wish to declare themselves as prospective mates will step forward and present you with a traditional courtship gift."

She felt herself stiffen at the prospect. *What if no one came forward? Worse, what if none of them appealed to her?*

Helena struggled to quell the panic before it overwhelmed her. Her Circle had only briefly touched upon the process of her Mate's selection, but Timmins had assured her that a Mate had always been found. If Timmins' had noticed her brief hesitation, he did not mention it.

They continued their way through the Palace courtyard and to the platform that had been constructed for the Festival. Helena marveled at the beauty and simplicity of the display. The platform had been erected between a series of ancient trees whose branches were now heavily sprinkled with twinkling lights. In between the two main trees sat a massive throne. The dark wood was polished to a high shine, and its back was comprised of five wooden pillars which twisted up into the trees so as to appear as if the throne was made and anchored by them. The only other decoration was a lovely lavender cushion.

Helena's eyes drifted over the crowd intimidated by the sheer number of people that had traveled to bear witness to the ascension of their new ruler. She picked out a familiar coppery head and smiled.

Gillian, daughter of the previous Damaskiri, had become a fast friend. Helena loved her quick wit and admired how she was all dainty grace and femininity. In sharp contrast to her bright copper curls, Gillian had almost translucent green eyes and fair milky skin. Today she was a vision in an emerald green silk dress that clung to each of her curves.

Helena had initially felt gangly and awkward next to her when they first met, but Gillian had put her instantly at ease, despite being in mourning herself, and had winked conspiratorially, promising to tell her everything about everyone.

Gillian saw Helena and waved cheerfully. Knowing it would be unwise to do the same, Helena simply dipped her head in acknowledgment.

Smoothing down the soft velvet fabric of her own dress, Helena whispered softly, "How do I look?"

Darrin had moved to stand at her left side and overheard her. Leaning down to whisper in her ear, he answered, "You are a vision, *Mira*. Truly."

She smiled up at him and decided that the hour Alina had forced her to get ready was worth it.

"It's time, Damaskiri," Timmins said softly.

Helena ascended the stairs to the platform and made her way to the center. The crowd, which had been chatting excitedly, went quiet for a brief moment and then roared in approval at their first glimpse of their future ruler.

Helena's aqua gown perfectly matched the color of her eyes, which were also emphasized by thick, sooty lashes. The gown left her shoulders and neck bare, displaying a large expanse of her creamy skin. She wore no adornment, save for a simple gold pendant that was symbolic of the Mother. Alina had twisted her long hair atop her head into a riot of loose curls and braids that were anchored by beautiful pearls. As a final touch, Alina had lightly dusted her skin with a golden shimmer; which, under all of the twinkling lights, made her luminous.

Standing in front of her people, and hearing their approval, was the first time Helena had truly let herself believe this was happening.

"Welcome," her voice thundered, and she realized that they must have used magic to project her voice so that she may speak normally, but all could hear.

The crowd instantly settled.

"It is with great honor and privilege that I stand before you today. Thank you for traveling so far to celebrate my name day, and my return home." The crowd cheered loudly at that, and Helena mentally congratulated Timmins.

"May the Mother keep you safe, and bless your days with light and happiness," she continued.

"May the Mother protect you always and grant you her eternal wisdom," they chanted in response.

Helena turned toward the bowers that held the representatives of the royal families for the other six realms.

"Tigaera welcomes its sisters today, and thanks you humbly for gracing us with your presence. May the Mother bless your lands, as she has ours, and keep your days filled with light and happiness."

With those formalities concluded, her Circle moved to stand beside her. One by one they came forward, repeating the vows that they had made to her a few weeks prior. This time, however, she did not repeat her vows to them. When she had asked why Timmins had informed her that it would be a show of weakness of her part to make promises to those that served her. Helena had not understood and was still uncomfortable that she merely sat there while they proclaimed themselves bound to her.

Rising, Kragen and Darrin moved to stand on either side of her. Joquil and Timmins moved to the stairs greeting the eleven males that were making their way toward her to present themselves for consideration.

The crowd seemed to murmur in surprise at one of the suitors. Helena narrowed her eyes and tried to determine who it was that caused the commotion.

As with everything else related to the formal ceremonies during the Festival, Timmins had briefly explained the tradition of gift giving.

'It is a tradition that goes back to the days of the Old Ones, Damaskiri. A suitor must declare his intent with a gift of magic. It is said that while the Festival lasts for seven days, and the suitors will continue to vie for the position during that time, when she receives the gift of her true mate, a Damaskiri will know instantly.'

'How does a man know that he could be the true Mate?' Helena asked.

Timmins leaned back in his chair, pondering the question for a moment, 'Well, it would be naïve to think that all that declare themselves do so without thought of the power such a position holds. However, just as your Circle can be determined from your birth, like will call to like. The Mother creates perfect mates for her Chosen, it is why there is only one, and it is why the Damaskiri has always found hers. It is crucial that a Damaskiri finds that bond before she can truly understand what it means to rule.'

'Not everyone finds their mate though, Timmins.' Helena whispered, thinking of Miriam and those that forsook the potential of finding their mates to serve in a Circle.

'No, not everyone," he had agreed softly, sympathy and

understanding laced into each word. 'But the Damaskiri's magic is much stronger than the Mother's other Chosen; it would only make sense that her Mate's would be too.

'They were made to find each other, Damaskiri. It is said that the strongest and truest power is love...'

Timmins had trailed off then, but his words had left her unsettled for days. The idea of love happening so quickly seemed foreign to her, but then again, she had never been in love. She had pushed it out of her mind and had not thought about it again until today.

He had also insisted that she was to remain seated while they presented their gifts. Helena refused.

'But, Damaskiri, that would suggest that you consider them to be equals. Until your Mate proves himself and is selected, you cannot show such deference.'

'These men will humble themselves before me and their entire realm. I will not subject them to unnecessary displays of power or pride. It is my heart they are trying to claim, Timmins, and if that does not allow them to be my equal, then your ceremony is flawed and will be changed.'

He had stared at her in surprise, admiration glowing in his blue eyes. 'Very well, Damaskiri.'

She stood as the first suitor walked to her throne. His dark eyes widened in surprise, and the crowd's echoing murmurs seemed a dull roar.

She offered him a soft smile, and he closed the distance between them. He went to kneel before her, but she placed her hand on his shoulder and stopped him with a quick shake of her head.

Realizing that she would meet him face to face, as equals, he flushed with pleasure. He was younger than she was but tall. Given the state of his well-worn but sensible clothes, she would guess he came from a trade family, and that his gift of magic had been a surprise to them all.

Swallowing quickly, he uttered the formal declaration, "Damaskiri, may the Mother open your heart to me and allow our souls to find the one they were created for." He said the words with soft earnestness, sweat beading on his brow.

She noticed his hands trembling slightly as he removed the small globe that was concealed in his pocket.

"For you, Damaskiri," he said shoving it into her hands quickly.

Helena looked into the globe and saw that it had been enchanted to contain a miniature ball with the people twirling and dancing within. She held it up to her ear and could hear the soft strains of music. Delighted she studied him with a new appreciation.

"What is your name?"

"Teramos," he replied nervously. "But my friends call me Amos, Damaskiri."

"Thank you, Amos. It is beautiful."

His cheeks flamed with pride, and he quickly shuffled away.

The rest of the suitors were presented without much to distinguish themselves, with the exception of the last two.

She was trying not to fidget when she heard the crowd start to stir again. She felt, rather than saw him come forward. It was as if her body was equally hot and cold at the same time, and she shivered in response. He moved to stand in front of her, and she looked up, and up, to meet his gaze.

His hair was obsidian, smoothed back off his sculpted face. His face was all hard angles, and he had steely gray eyes which stared into hers without a hint as to the emotion behind them. His lips were full and inviting, but with none of the lines around them to suggest he was prone to smiling.

Her eyes continued their perusal, greedily drinking in the golden skin and heavy muscles of the man before her.

"Damaskiri," he murmured, his voice a low growl.

She felt an answering response low in her stomach.

"May the Mother open your heart to me and allow our souls to find the one they were created for," he continued, his gray eyes boring into hers.

At his words, her heart started beating more quickly.

His lips quirked as if he knew the effect he was having on her, and he raised his hand as though to touch her. She heard Darrin and Kragen shift in response and watched him still.

He looked over her shoulder, meeting the gaze of her two warriors. Looking back at her, he then looked down into his hand.

Her eyes followed his and saw a perfect white bloom resting in his palm. She had never seen a more perfect magnolia bloom in her life. The velvety petals were brilliantly white, and the fragrance heady.

"Magnolias are my favorite," she whispered, eyes shyly meeting his.

A dimple flashed in his cheek, and its appearance instantly transformed his face. "I know."

She laughed at his audacity. "How?"

"Would you believe me if I told you I have dreamed about you since I was a wee lad?" he asked, deadpan.

She tilted her head to the side, her laughter making her eyes twinkle. "No."

He shrugged, as though he had expected as much. "I may have bribed someone."

She laughed again in shocked amusement. "I'll bet you did. What is your name?"

"Von, Damaskiri," he replied in the same deep growl.

"Thank you, Von. I shall treasure it, since you did go to so much trouble to ensure I would like it."

He nodded at her, a small smile playing about his sculpted mouth, and with a last glance, he started away.

As he stepped away, she heard the hissing of the crowd. She narrowed her eyes again in disapproval. He must have been the one they were reacting to earlier. She was not pleased that they would feel they had the right to judge anyone who was presenting themselves to be her mate.

She studied the crowd with a frown. The hissing continued, and someone went so far as to throw something in Von's direction.

"ENOUGH!" she shouted, icy anger wrapping itself around her.

Von stopped mid-descent and looked back at her; black brow lifted in surprise.

"How dare you treat one of your brothers this way," she bit out, her voice a whip. "It is not for you to judge or determine the worthiness of another. The Mother and her Vessel are the only ones with the authority to do so. You will treat each other with respect and deference, especially those who humble themselves and their pride as they offer themselves to be *my* Mate."

The crowd was shifting, ashamed and in awe of the woman before them.

"I am to be your Kiri, and my Mate will be my equal; you will not," she paused, eyes singling out the troublemakers, "in *any way*, harm what is mine." Her voice had dropped to a ragged whisper.

With that proclamation, the entire assembly gaped. She had all but declared him as her choice, and she had spent less than three minutes with him.

Shaking with rage, Helena finally realized what she had done. Horrified at the display of anger, so unfamiliar to her, she looked helplessly over her shoulder at Darrin.

He was frowning at Von slightly and looked back toward her, green eyes glowing with some unnamed emotion. She turned her gaze to Timmins and Joquil, certain their reaction would help her gauge how terrible of a mess she had made. She jerked in surprise finding pride shining there instead of the twin expressions of disapproval she'd anticipated.

The final suitor approached her hesitantly, and she felt her lips curl into an amused smile. It was Gillian's twin brother Micha.

"That was some display, Damaskiri," he whispered, with a twist of his own lips.

Helena smiled ruefully into green eyes that were identical to his sister's. "I'm sure I just made quite a mess of things."

He was quick to shake his head. "No, Helena. You just showed your people the depth of strength that resides within you. You established, with a few words, what you expect of them and that you protect what is yours. They love you already."

She rolled her eyes. "So what have you brought me?"

He chuckled at her teasing, and continued lightly, "May the Mother open your heart to me and allow our souls to find the one they were created for."

He then held out a beautifully illuminated book. She accepted it with reverence, gently turning the pages. Each illustration moved, the characters literally coming to life on the page.

"Ooh," she whispered in wonder.

"It is a book of fairy tales. I figured since you grew up so far away from your people and our history, this might be a way for you to learn about your culture." His voice was soft and sincere.

Eyes glittering with tears she met his eyes. "Thank you, Micha, I have never loved anything more." She hugged the book to her chest.

He nodded, smiling in relief and made his way off the stage.

Suddenly, Helena felt exhausted. The weight of all those people staring at her, in addition to the emotions of the afternoon, were starting to bear down on her.

Joquil moved forward and released the crowd to the feast that would start in the tents set up in the gardens. As he spoke lights began to glow in the garden, illuminating the way.

Timmins hurried over to her.

"I'm so sorry," she whispered brokenly, "I don't know what came over me."

He shook his head, "No, Damaskiri, you do not apologize." His voice a soothing murmur.

Kragen placed his large hand on her shoulder. "You are our Damaskiri," he rumbled, "and sometimes that calls for a display of power. You are a natural, Helena."

She blinked up at him in surprise. He had never referred to her by her name before, and the purposeful use of it now could not more clearly reflect his admiration and approval. As she looked at the men around her, she could see that they all approved of her display of temper, and that knowledge brightened her mood considerably.

Darrin wrapped his arm behind her shoulders and squeezed, giving her a gentle hug. He let go just as quickly and took his place at her left.

With a deep breath, she met the eyes of the four men that were becoming so dear to her. "Well, now that we've cleared that up, shall we go eat?"

"I thought you'd never ask," Kragen quipped.

The others laughed and made their way to the main tent for the feast.

CHAPTER 3

*S*tepping into the tent, Helena paused in delighted awe. Centered in the Air Wing of the Palace, the tent had been erected in its courtyard. Where there should have been fabric walls, there were sweeping views of the six different lands, each scene fading and bleeding into the next. One moment you were viewing a vast ocean with waves crashing against the shore, the next an endless forest with the trees so tall you could not see where they ended. It was a perfect tribute to Tigaera's visitors.

Before any of her Circle could ask what was keeping her, she hurried to catch up with them. At the northern end of the tent, a long table had been decorated in purples and golds, with a countless number of candles ablaze and flowers spilling from their various vases.

Murmuring her approval, Helena took her seat in the center; her chair an echo of the throne she had sat in during the welcome ceremony.

Turning to her right, she asked Darrin, "Did you ever think we would end up at one of the royal feasts?"

His green eyes flashed with humor. "This is hardly my first royal feast, Hellion."

"I wasn't aware they let the Rasmirin attend the feasts. Aren't you lot supposed to be out protecting and defending?" she teased.

Straightening his tunic before looking at her from the corner of his eye, he smiled wryly and admitted, "To be fair, I never said I was an invited guest."

Helena's laughter rang out, causing many of the nearby guests to turn and see what had caught her attention.

Turning back to scan the room before her, Helena continued, "I just can't believe that only days ago I was at home at the cottage and now I'm here." As she looked about the room, her eyes scanned and cataloged the familiar faces.

In front of her and slightly to her left, Micha and Gillian sat and spoke animatedly with a gray-haired man she assumed was their father. Behind them, at another table, Von sat with a contingent of his mercenaries. She noticed the people around him were stealing glances and whispering furiously to their dinner mates.

As if feeling her attention on his, Von glanced up and caught her eye. He nodded and smiled slightly, but it didn't reach his eyes. Instead, his brows were lowered, as if puzzled.

Flustered, Helena looked away, trying to recall the names of the other faces her eyes stopped upon. She noticed Amos speaking to another of the men that had presented themselves to her... *Harris?* she guessed, embarrassed that she had already forgotten so many of their names.

The blond man had been very soft-spoken, and she had trouble hearing what he had said even standing directly before him. *His gift had been the...* she paused, searching her memory, *the bracelet, no... was it the music box?* She shook her head sighing in defeat, eyes now continuing their journey about the room.

Her scan stopped once more, her gaze colliding with a pair of coal eyes staring at her intently from a grizzled face. It was twisted in a scowl, but before she could place it, or discern the expression in those dark, calculating orbs, they were gone.

Suddenly cold, Helena shivered causing Darrin to reach out and touch her arm gently.

"Are you all right, Damaskiri?"

She nodded distractedly. Looking around, Helena could not find whoever had been studying her so closely.

"Maybe you should eat something?" he suggested softly.

Surprised, Helena noticed the food piled high in front of her. "How did that get here?"

Darrin chuckled around his own mouthful of food and simply gestured for her to eat.

SOMETIME DURING DINNER music began to play, but when she searched Helena could not locate any musicians. The center of the tent had been cleared and where tables once stood there was now a massive dance floor in their stead.

As the guest of honor, it was once again up to her to formally open up the evening's festivities. That was why, once her plate vanished without her notice, Darrin led her to the center of the room.

The music stopped, bringing the chatter to a halt as well, all eyes turning toward her and Darrin. After a few beats of silence, the first strains of a song started.

Helena and Darrin bowed to each other and began the first steps of the formal court dance. She was grateful that she remembered to pick up the side of her skirt to avoid any mishaps. The steps became faster, she and Darrin twirling around each other in time with the heavy beat of the drum.

Timmins and Joquil had told her this dance was the embodiment of the Mother's magic, each step representing the interplay of the elements. The solid stomps on the ground depicting Earth, while the gentler motions of the arms acting as Air weaving around them all. The growing speed of the steps, Fire's greedy inferno.

She had stopped them then, to ask whether the sweat dripping down her back was supposed to represent Water.

The two had laughed, recognizing they had perhaps pushed her too hard in their attempts to ensure her perfection of the dance.

Eyes still shining with mirth, Timmins had informed her that the flow of movements into one another was the representation of Water, while she, in the center of it all, represented Spirit.

Now, as the dance was coming to a close, Helena better appreciated the beauty of its movements. The bodies surrounding them on the dance floor were a blur as she continued to spin and weave around Darrin. Her skin was flushed and her head light as blood rushed through her body; her heart racing as it beat in time to the drum. Breathless laughter bubbled up in sheer joy as the dance came to an end.

There was silence in the room again before the crowd erupted in applause and cheers. Still smiling, Helena wrapped her arms around Darrin for a quick hug before stepping back.

Darrin let out a startled gasp as he looked at the floor below them. Everywhere they had stepped during the dance, was now softly glowing. The entire shape a replica of the necklace Helena was wearing.

"Oh," she breathed as she noticed what had caused the crowd to react.

Before she could do more than look back to Darrin, a voice was at her ear asking her to dance. Seeing Micha, her smile grew and as she nodded her assent, she was lost in the sea of bodies now moving around her.

PANTING, Helena stepped off of the floor. She had not stopped since her dance with Darrin over an hour ago. She had to turn down Nameless Suitor Number Four's offer so that she could catch her breath.

Fanning herself and leaning her hip against a nearby table, Helena smiled as Gillian made her way over.

"I seem to be lacking the equipment"—Gillian gestured toward her groin—"required to spend time with you at this sort of event."

Helena let out a surprised laugh. "I'm glad you have found a way to persevere despite that handicap."

Gillian smiled conspiratorially. "So are we to be sisters? Micha is quite taken with you."

"I'm not certain how such a sweet man can be related to you," Helena teased with a grin. "Although he is a lot of fun to spend time with."

"You certainly seemed to enjoy your dance together."

"Yes, definitely. A partner who doesn't step all over your feet, or let their hands wander, is much appreciated."

"But wandering hands is the entire point of dancing," Gillian said as she batted her wide, green eyes innocently. "How else are you supposed to know if you'd like to invite the man to your bed?"

Blushing, Helena could only shake her head in mute amusement.

"Seriously, Helena, the physical chemistry is the most important part of any relationship. That's a part of the process you know. You have to try out all your options before you know which one is the perfect," she paused as if savoring the word, "fit."

"I'm pretty certain that is absolutely *not* the point of this process," Helena concluded matter-of-factly.

Gillian simply shrugged and folded her arms across her chest. "Suit yourself, it's your potential lifetime of cold bed sheets. If I were you, there's absolutely no way I'd make *that* mistake! Forever is a long time to be miserable."

"Damaskiri," a gravelly voice she instantly recognized said at her shoulder.

Turning to Von, she offered him a warm smile. "Hello again. Are you enjoying the party?"

Frowning slightly, Von eyed the dancers nearest to him. "This is not generally the sort of entertainment I would seek out, but I suppose it has a certain appeal."

"I bet he lets his hands wander," Gillian muttered below her breath.

Helena blushed fiercely and spoke before Von could address the comment.

"And what sorts of entertainment do you usually seek out?"

It was Von's turn to look uncomfortable. "Erm, quiet ones."

Gillian let out a sharp bark of laughter. "If it's quiet you're doing it wrong, Holbrooke, but I get the feeling you already know that."

"I meant reading, my lady," Von said dryly.

"Hmmm," Gillian murmured, clearly not believing him.

"I love to read," Helena said quickly. "I've spent many nights curled up in front of the fire with a book."

"Mother you are hopeless," Gillian said throwing up her hands in exasperation. "Darling, you are the only one in this conversation actually talking about books."

Confused, Helena looked between the two of them before it registered. Wide-eyed she looked back to Von.

His eyes were narrowed in annoyance as he studied Gillian. He turned back to Helena and his expression instantly softened. "Shall we dance, Damaskiri?"

"Yes, that would be wonderful."

He offered her his hand. She hesitated before finally placing hers in his much larger one, anticipating the bolt of heat that rushed through her at the contact. His hand tightened around hers as he led her to the dance floor.

The music swelled as one song rolled into the next. He wrapped his free arm around her waist, its hand resting warmly against her back as he pulled her closer to him.

As they spun and wove around the other dancers, Helena was only aware of Von's body pressed close to hers. She felt his muscles bunch and shift against hers. Distracted, she missed a step and looked up apologetically.

Ignoring the misstep, Von asked, "Are you enjoying yourself, Damaskiri?"

"Immensely! This is my first ball; I'm pretty overwhelmed by it all. Does it show?" she asked in a rush, excitement making her aqua eyes glow.

"Not at all, Damaskiri," he responded with an ironic smile that was completely lost on her.

"Don't you think, given the circumstances, that you should call me Helena?" she asked thoughtfully.

"Under the circumstances, I absolutely do not think I should call you Helena. There are far too many people around for the familiarity to go unnoticed, and the last thing I need is more rumors. Or the attention of your Sword," he added as if in afterthought.

Hearing her name on his lips, even if not directed at her, lit the fire within her. Without thought, she blurted out, "I look forward to a time when such formalities will not be necessary between us."

Horrified at her boldness, she stared fixedly at his shoulder and began berating herself. *This is not a courtship, Helena. This is politics. Mother's teeth, you have ten other suitors! What is he going to think of you, if you keep throwing yourself at him?*

"As do I," he leaned down to whisper in her ear, "Helena." His lips brushed against her ear softly as his breath caressed her cheek and neck.

She shivered, aqua eyes meeting gray. They stared in growing silence, steps forgotten as they got lost in one another. She jumped when the voice spoke beside them.

"Damaskiri, I believe it is my turn to dance with you," Kragen cut in.

She offered him a smile, before stepping back from Von, eyes still searching his. Wordlessly, he merely nodded and offered her hand to Kragen.

And while his hand had not wandered, she still felt the blaze of its impression against her back as she watched him walk away.

CHAPTER 4

*V*on stared absently at the scene before him. His room was supposed to be comforting as it reflected his home landscape. Unfortunately, it only served to set him on edge. The rocky terrain and mountains were beautiful in an eerie and primal way, but there was no warmth in the vision.

Steel gray eyes shifted from the balcony scene into the interior of the room. On the large four-poster bed the curtains were parted slightly, revealing a sleeping woman. As if feeling his gaze on her, she shifted and stretched.

The sheet fell away from her naked body, long arms stretched above her head pulling her small breasts to attention, the dusky nipples tightening at the subtle change in temperature. Her back arched then, and her eyelids fluttered open.

Von watched the display with disinterest.

"Come back to bed," the woman purred, trying to use her body to tempt him.

When he didn't move, she stood from the bed and walked over to him slowly.

She tossed a head of long black hair off her shoulders, to give him a better view, her hands gliding up her body pausing at her breasts to rub and tease her nipples into rosy points before running them down over her hips.

Eyes half closed she bit her lower lip and bent down toward him, hand reaching between his legs.

He grabbed her wrist tightly before she could make contact with the evidence of his disinterest. "Attempt to touch me again, and I will cut it off," he warned, his voice icy.

She stood quickly in surprise.

"Leave."

He let go of her hand, and she moved to grab her gown from the floor.

With a final heated look over her shoulder, she moved to open the door and left.

Von let out a slow breath and closed his eyes. Not one to generally feel remorse, he was feeling decidedly guilty for accepting her invitation at the feast. He had been so overwhelmed by the intensity of his reaction to the Damaskiri that he had thought to exorcise her from his system with another willing female.

He shifted in his seat uncomfortably, a frown pulling down his lips. She was more beautiful than he had anticipated. Shining chestnut tendrils had fallen from their place in the intricate braids atop her head and down to her shoulders; her laughing aqua eyes, framed with thick black lashes, smiled up at him as they danced. Her slender body had fit against his perfectly, warm under his hands.

He felt his body stir in response to the memory.

Unsettled, his frown deepened.

Even more than her beauty, her spirit had surprised him. He remembered her words as the crowd had recognized him and responded with the usual uproar of disapproval.

'*...you will not, in* any way, *harm what is mine.*' Her eyes had darkened to twin navy pools, her voice a scathing warning. He had never had anyone stand up for or defend him. The thought was laughable; he was the first born of Darius Holbrooke, and the Holbrooke line had been cast out years ago after his grandfather's father had attempted to destroy the Kiri and her Circle.

He had not come to the Festival with the intention of actually claiming, or falling for, the Damaskiri. He had simply hoped to use the time that he was close to her to try to convince her to lift the ban that had been on his family for the last five centuries. His brother needed to see a healer, and none would come to them.

Memories of the broken and twisted limbs and his brother's pained smile as Von had said goodbye did much to dampen his ardor.

Even so, when he had looked into her eyes and spoken the words of intent, he felt as though his own soul had been staring back at him. Never had he felt so vulnerable or connected to anyone. He rubbed the back of his neck with a grimace; it was not a feeling he'd necessarily like to repeat.

The guilt and uncertainty unnerved him. He wasn't certain if the guilt was from forgetting that he was here to help save his family, or if it was from sleeping with a whore after offering himself as a life mate to another.

Scowling he stood and walked toward the balcony, willing the familiar peaks and valleys of Daejara's mountains to ease his tension. Such emotion was foreign to him. He learned a long time ago to rid himself of anything that would weaken him or distract him from his duty. Over the last seven years, he had gained a reputation as the fiercest and most brutal mercenary in Daejara. He and his band had roamed the realm, accepting any task if the money had been good. They had no scruples; they couldn't afford them.

Reminding himself of who he was, and of his purpose, Von felt some of his tension ebb. The reminder, however, didn't keep him from wishing, just for a moment, that he could be the kind of man that would be worthy of such a woman.

SHE HEARD the voices as she rounded the corner and moved toward the meeting that had apparently started without her. Alina had insisted that she dress according to her station, even for a meeting with her Circle, even though she would have to change again for this afternoon's ceremony.

Helena shook her head ruefully, but her smile faded as she heard the men more clearly.

"We cannot allow her to entertain his suit!" Darrin roared.

"Allow her?" Joquil had repeated with a laugh. "It is not for us to *allow* the Damaskiri to do anything. Did you forget your vows already, child?"

"He has a point, Joquil," Timmins soft voice stepped in. "You know who he is, who his *family* are. More importantly, you know what he has done. How can we protect her from evil if she is to bind herself to it?"

"He will not harm her," came Kragen's sure reply.

"It is our duty to protect her," Darrin bit out, "but there are times we will not be there, especially once she completes the binding and he becomes her Mate. She will be destroyed, and in turn, we will all be destroyed."

The men were quiet as his words sunk in.

After a moment, she heard Joquil say, "The Mate is the perfect partner for the Damaskiri. He was made for her, and she for him. They are one. It is not possible that the one she chooses will not be the one that she was destined for. She is to be the most powerful Kiri we have ever seen. All power is two-sided and who better to help her understand the darker side of her nature than such a Mate?"

She heard objections from the others, but Joquil continued, "She has to be able to understand the darkness in order to save us from it. Just because we have kept her safe thus far, does not mean she is prepared for what is to come. The Mother provides for her Chosen; she will not forsake us."

Helena's blood felt like ice. All the lingering joy from last night's festivities and the morning's frivolity faded. She was faced, once again, with the enormity of the burden that was placed on her shoulders. She could not afford to forget it. She pushed the door open and stepped into the Circle's Chamber.

The men were sitting around the table, a fire blazing beside it. Each face was lost in thought. She took note of the worry and concern on Darrin's and Timmins' faces, as well as the absence of both on Joquil's. Kragen alone seemed to be as he always was, she took comfort in that.

They looked up as she entered.

"Good morning, Damaskiri. Did you enjoy your ball last night? It was your first, yes?" Timmins greeted her warmly, all trace of doubt vanished, or at least well hidden.

"Yes, it was lovely," she murmured, pretending that she had not overheard their conversation.

Joquil stood and moved toward her. "We have a very busy day, Damaskiri. We should get started with your final training right away unless there is anything else you all need?" he addressed the other men.

They shook their heads.

Then, if you would excuse us," he asked the others.

They rose and made their way to the door with murmurs of support. Darrin gently touched her shoulder as he walked past.

"Let us review before diving back in, shall we? Tell me, Damaskiri, what do you recall about the five branches?"

Helena mentally shook herself, trying hard to dispel her lingering unease at the Circle's conversation and to project confidence that she didn't feel.

"Well," she began tentatively, "power can manifest in a number of ways, each unique to the user but generally tied to some common element within that branch. Earth, for example, generally provides the Chosen it's gifted with incredible strength, both of body and of mind. Those adept in the Water branch are most commonly healers, and they can influence the sleep or dreams of others."

Joquil nodded and motioned for her to continue.

"Those blessed with an affinity for Air can sometimes control or influence the weather and are almost always known for their speed; while any gifted with Fire can summon and manipulate that element at will."

"And what of Spirit?" he prompted.

"Spirit can only be wielded by a Damaskiri or Kiri. It is the power of self and allows for the manipulation or control of one's mind, including animals. The stronger one is, the more control they can have over another. In some cases, they can also foresee the future."

"And can a Chosen be gifted in multiple branches?"

"Yes, although it is extremely rare to be gifted with more than two branches and even more uncommon for someone to be considered a master of more than one branch. In most cases, a Chosen only has one or two abilities tied to a single branch of magic."

"Do you remember anything else about what happens when there's a dual or multi-gift?"

"The branches influence and work with each other. For example, if someone has both Fire and Air, in theory, they would be able to call forth a storm of Fire."

Joquil was smiling in approval. "Very good, Damaskiri. A Chosen generally does not learn the true potential of their gift until they are of age; in your case, it will remain to be seen how your gifts will work together and what your limitations are. Do you have any questions before we move on?"

"I did have one other question, and I apologize if it's silly—"

"You have been separated from your heritage your entire life, Damaskiri, it only makes sense that you would have questions," he interrupted, dismissing her apology.

She offered him a bright smile in return and continued, "Yes, well, I was curious why no one seems to be using their magic." She paused, trying to explain herself, "Everything, since I arrived here, feels so... well, normal. Are there some kind of rules dictating when magic can be used?" She finished with a shrug, feeling foolish.

It was Joquil's turn to smile. "Ah, I can see how you would think that, Damaskiri. It is not that magic is not being used, it is simply not being used in your presence."

"But, but why?" she asked, eyebrows scrunched in confusion.

"It's out of respect for you. As the future ruler of the Chosen, they did not wish to offend you by blatantly displaying a talent you are unable to use since your own magic remains bound —or was until very recently."

Helena laughed. "But that's ridiculous, isn't the ability to wield magic what it intrinsically means to be one of the Mother's Chosen? It would be as if a musician would not share his songs with his neighbor who could not sing. Just because someone has a gift does not mean they should hide it from one who does not!"

Joquil nodded in agreement. "You are wise to say so, Damaskiri. Your people simply do not wish to insult you. Shall I have Timmins inform them that you wish they stop concealing their magic?"

"Yes, please. I have always been fascinated by the idea of magic since I never had my own. I was looking forward to being surrounded by it when coming here, however, even during my practice with you, it has merely been a lot of talking and no magic."

He laughed at her teasing. "Perhaps we can begin to amend that today. Are you ready to start?"

"As ready as I'll ever be," she sighed.

He smiled sympathetically. "Today I will help induce the meditative state. You were so close to reaching the barrier yesterday that I think a little extra push may help you succeed."

"Have you been holding out on me, Joquil?" Helena lifted a mocking brow.

He shrugged prosaically. "What was the point of wasting good magic when you did not understand what you were doing?"

"I suppose you have a point." Her eyes narrowed playfully as she settled into the large gray armchair which had informally become hers.

Helena sat back in the chair and closed her eyes, beginning to focus on her breathing.

She felt Joquil's hands lightly touch her shoulders, and her breathing became more measured and slow. Her worry and tension faded, and her muscles slackened at the release.

Helena's head fell back against the chair with a contented sigh.

"Stay focused, Damaskiri," Joquil murmured. Helena was certain he was smirking.

She tried to pull her mind back to her, and begin the now-familiar process of seeking the magic within her.

Having one's magic bound was much like attempting to find buried treasure without a map or deciphering a code without a key. If you knew where to look, you could find it, but you could also go in circles for ages and never realize it had been next to you the whole time.

Now that she was used to searching for it, Helena could recognize the wealth of power within her. It felt like a still pool hidden within her very core. In her mind, she could see its black surface patiently waiting for her to dive in and explore its depths.

Under Joquil's patient, albeit smug, guidance she was learning to move closer to its placid shore each day.

There you are, she smiled as she came upon the dark shores within her.

"Call your power to you. Wrap it around yourself, as you would a blanket on a wet night," Master Joquil's low voice called to her as though from a distance.

It seemed as if the pool recognized her presence and was beckoning her, urging her to join it.

Helena moved forward. Each day she was pushing against the invisible barrier between herself and the water, but the closer she got the weaker she felt. Reaching the barrier, Helena felt as though she was straining with her fingertips to brush the edge of the water.

Just a bit further. She wasn't sure if she was attempting to motivate herself or if it was the inky depths before her, or were they one in the same? The thought had her pausing briefly. Mentally shaking herself, she refocused on her task; if she could only get a little closer, she would be touching it.

Bracing herself, she started forward again. Breath labored, Helena could feel her forehead beginning to pound. In her mind, she was now on her knees attempting to crawl to the lapping edge of the water. She could feel herself trembling with the effort.

Fingers were splayed against the wall, pushing so hard she could feel the barrier begin to crack and become malleable. *Yes*, she thought fiercely, *just a little further.* With a final roar, she pushed. The barrier gave way, ripping with a sigh before falling away completely. She pushed herself up and was now standing at the edge.

With a pleasured gasp, she reached out and touched the pool. She tingled from the contact, feeling the source of her power reach out to her, caressing her as it welcomed her.

It was as though she was an empty basin, and her magic was water seeking to fill her to the brim. The tingling turned into pinpricks, and her heart raced.

She heard shouting but did not know where it was coming from. Standing before the pool, she was watching it continue to drain, filling her beyond her capacity. What had initially felt like a pleasant warmth spreading through her limbs was beginning to burn. She cried out in confusion.

Stop, please... it's too much, she thought, limbs shaking and breath coming out in labored gasps. Suddenly, the power began to ebb away, swirling back to its pool.

As she came back to herself, she heard Master Joquil's frantic shouting, and awareness flooded her. Slowly she opened her eyes. When her eyes met his, he gasped and took a few teetering steps back.

She stood slowly, aware of her body in a new way. Each sense was heightened, and it was as if she was learning how to move her body for the first time. She flexed her muscles feeling the new strength within them.

Her eyes flitted to the unlit candles on the wall. Moments later flames leapt from the wicks reaching toward the ceiling.

Joquil, sat quickly, hands firmly gripping the arms of his chair. "Blessed Mother," he whispered in awe.

Helena walked toward the mirror in the corner of the chambers, studying herself in surprise. While the changes were mostly subtle, it was undeniable that her magic had changed her. Gone were the soft remnants of childhood, round apple-shaped cheeks giving way to sculpted cheekbones. Her skin had always had the dewy glow of youth, but now it was as if she was lit from within. Her hair, which had always been notably long, now cascaded down her back in shining waves. The biggest change was her eyes. Aqua eyes were now twinned iridescent prisms, catching and holding the light so that they sparkled.

She held out a hand to the mirror, letting her fingers run over her reflection.

"Are the changes permanent?" she asked curiously. Her eyes flared in surprise at her voice, which sounded like a harmony of voices rather than just one. As she turned her gaze to Joquil, each detail of the room stood out in sharp contrast.

She could detect individual fibers in the fabrics of the cushions and drapes and the flow of the wood grain in the chairs. She could also see with perfect clarity each strand of hair on the Master's head and the multitude of emotions which moved rapidly across the Master's face.

Master Joquil steadied himself before speaking. "I believe so, Damaskiri, however, you can use your magic to dampen the effects, so to speak."

She turned back toward the mirror and blinked slowly. When she opened her eyes, they were aqua again, except for a thin band of iridescent light which remained around her pupils. Her glow had also dimmed, and when she spoke, it sounded like one voice, although still more melodic than usual.

"Will it always feel that way?"

Joquil inclined his head. "I don't believe so, Damaskiri. Think of your body like a starving child. It would slowly die, yes? Well now imagine that you introduce that child to food. The child is starving and desperate, it will shove the food down as quickly as it can, and likely make itself sick in the process. Your body was much the same. When it found its magic, it greedily sucked in as much as it could, and the effects overwhelmed you. With more time, you will learn how to contain how much you take, and it should not affect you so."

Helena nodded in understanding and moved back toward her seat at the table.

"So now that we know I have magic"—her lips twisted in amusement—"how do I pass my trial?"

Joquil smiled with her and leaned forward. "The Damaskiri's trial is a test to gauge her depth and control of her magic. There is not much known about the specifics of the trial other than that it will test the furthest limits of a Damaskiri's power. Given what we have witnessed today that will surely be a substantial feat."

"You could say that."

Joquil chuckled. "You must remember to stay focused and the rest, as they say, will take care of itself."

Overwhelmed, but vastly pleased, Helena sat quietly for a moment. She could feel the waves of her newly discovered power lapping gently within her. With the awareness came the knowledge that she could call its waves to action with the smallest inclination. The pool stirred at the thought.

"Joquil?" she asked too innocently, not ready to face the tasks of the afternoon.

"Yes, Damaskiri?" came the wary response.

"Is there time for us to show the others?" Childlike excitement laced each word.

"I believe we can make time." He couldn't help but smile in response to her reaction and indulge her. "Do you have something in mind, or should I just call for them."

Helena's smile grew, and her eyes twinkled mischievously. "I may…"

He groaned and shook his head, muttering as he left the room. "I am going to regret this, I already know it."

Her laughter followed him out.

Standing quickly, she eyed the room looking for the perfect spot for her little performance. She chose to stand in front of the window, her back toward the door. She took a few deep breaths to help steady her emotions. She drew her magic to her, prepared this time as it flooded her. Before it could overwhelm her, she stopped it.

She heard the masculine voices approaching, and bit back a smile.

"Helena, what's going on?" Darrin asked, concern evident.

"Would you still love me if I never found my power, Darrin?" she asked, her voice small and wavering slightly.

She heard the men shift behind her, their worry and fear palpable at the thought of her failure.

"Perhaps all you need is more time, Damaskiri," came Timmins gentle response.

"No," she said as she started to turn, "I'm afraid that wouldn't help."

As one, each of the men's eyes widened, and their mouths went slack.

She had un-dampened the magic's effect so that they could all witness it in full force.

Kragen was gripping the back of a chair so tightly that it snapped under the pressure.

Her peals of laughter rang throughout the room and seemed to echo with phantom other voices.

Timmins was recovering most quickly, his gasp of surprise turning into an admiring smile.

Darrin was the last to respond, his golden skin pale and clammy.

"You don't like it?" she teased. "Perhaps this is better?"

She closed her eyes and let out a slow breath, feeling her body respond to her requests. Shining chestnut waves became gray gnarls, and supple limbs shriveled with the weight of age.

As one, the men gasped in awe. To cast such an illusion so seamlessly, and without conscious effort, was stunning.

Darrin chuckled, the playfulness of his friend helping him to recover more than anything else could. "No, I can't say I prefer the crone to the goddess, although to be fair both make me right nervous."

Helena shook her head back and forth, releasing the illusion and calling back her magic dampened state.

Kragen whistled. "Gentlemen, I believe we've found our Damaskiri."

"No, Kragen," Joquil said warmly, "we've found our Kiri."

Their cheers were deafening, and all she could do was laugh as they took turns spinning and twirling her about the room.

CHAPTER 5

The days continued to pass in a blur for Helena. It was a continuous cycle of dressing, changing and attending some formal ceremony at which she would smile and pretend to be vastly interested in conversations she couldn't remember, with people whose names she had already forgotten.

There were rare moments that stood apart from the others, but overall it was a tedious process.

She had thought that her greatest challenge would be awakening her magic. However, the real test was learning to control and contain it. It took constant effort for her to keep her power leashed, but oftentimes if she were distracted, it would find a way to sneak out.

At dinner the previous night, she was so engrossed in the storyteller's tale that her visions of the scene had begun to spring to life around him, much to the delight of the Palace guests. The poor man had been so shocked, however, that he had lost his place in the story and was unable to continue.

The day before that, she had been listening to another of Timmins' lectures regarding etiquette, wishing she could be outside feeling the sunshine and breeze on her face instead when a gust of wind whipped through the chamber upsetting all of Timmins' carefully laid documents. She had apologized profusely for the disturbance, embarrassed beyond end that her distraction had caused such havoc.

Now, in a welcome moment of solitude, Helena sat in the flower garden, her anxiety over her upcoming trial and the strain of controlling her magic wearing on her. She was so afraid of letting her Circle down, or humiliating herself further, that it was pure bliss being able to sit quietly and just be.

The last day of the Festival was almost upon her, and in mere hours she would finally face her trial. And then, assuming she succeeded, the final ritual which would bind her to her Mate would take place, concluding the Festival. Her mind sorted through her suitors, affectionately thinking about Amos and Micha, but knowing in her heart that the selection had already been made. She conjured Von's face in her mind, smiling unconsciously as she did.

She let out a heartfelt sigh and closed her eyes, tilting her face toward the sun. Appreciating her heightened sense of smell at the moment, she breathed deeply inhaling the scents of the flowers that surrounded her. In her mind, she was identifying each flower by its fragrance, and appreciating the mundane task immensely.

"Am I interrupting, Damaskiri?" a deep voice asked next to her.

Startled she jumped and twisted to the voice's source, surprised anyone had been able to sneak up on her when she was not actively trying to diminish her senses.

She felt her face flush and her heart begin to race as she stammered, "V-von, what, what are you doing here?"

His lips quirked in an amused smile. "You summoned me, Damaskiri."

"I, I did what?" she asked in surprise, eyes widening in embarrassed realization. With a groan, she closed her eyes and covered them with the palm of her hand.

Von moved to sit beside her, gently taking her hand and peeling it away from her face.

She looked up at him sheepishly.

"It's all right; I didn't mind. I hope I'm not intruding?" he asked again, steel eyes searching hers.

She shook her head. "No, I was just noting the flowers." She felt foolish as she uttered the words. She was supposed to be the most powerful woman her kind had seen in hundreds of years, and she was sitting in a garden daydreaming about a man she had just met a handful of days ago. She must amuse him greatly.

Sneaking a glance at him, she saw his knowing smile. She snapped her eyes shut again.

"It must be hard, having so many demands for your attention when you are used to being only responsible to yourself," he said simply.

Helena nodded, eyes opening to stare at the bright yellow roses in front of her. "Yes, it can be overwhelming. Especially when I'm not sure what I'm supposed to be doing half the time. Stick a shovel in my hands and point me in the direction of a garden and I could happily plod along for the rest of my days. Put me in a ballroom full of people wanting to dance and gossip and, and touch me," she said with an exasperated laugh, "and I am so far out of my element I feel like a floundering fish!"

He let out a surprised bark of laughter.

"I'm sorry," she said softly. "I shouldn't complain, I'm feeling a bit sorry for myself at the moment, which is utterly ridiculous."

He brushed a strand of hair from her cheek and electricity sizzled through her at the contact. "By all means, Damaskiri, I will happily sit here with you and let you unburden yourself."

She tilted her head and studied him, gray eyes shining with amusement and obsidian hair ruffled by the breeze.

He looked more relaxed than she could remember seeing him before. Then again, she had only seen him briefly during the various festivities and had never truly been alone with him until this very moment. Her cheeks flooded with heat at the thought. Timmins would surely give her an earful about the inappropriateness of such a situation when he heard about this. A stubborn voice inside of her questioned: *who's going to tell him?*

She smiled ruefully. "I must seem like a child to you, complaining about not only finding that I have magic, but that I am, in fact, the Mother's chosen Daughter."

He shrugged. "It's one thing to grow up knowing who you are and what you will do with your life, and then quite another having it all turned on its head. I think anyone would struggle with such change."

"And you?" she asked curiously. "Did you know what you would do with your life? Did you know that you would be here, sitting beside me?"

He laughed again, his laugh notably forced. "No. Decidedly not. I knew that I would be a warrior and that I would bring honor to my family on the battlefield. I never imagined that I would be a guest at the royal court fighting for the hand of the Damaskiri. Not my kind of battlefield at all," he finished dryly.

She arched an eyebrow in surprise. "Then why are you here?"

He sighed. "Do you know who I am, Damaskiri? Why those people taunted me during the declaration ceremony?"

She shook her head quickly.

"I am Von Holbrooke, son of Darius Holbrooke," he stared ahead of him, unflinching as he continued, "My ancestors were the ones who declared the blood war on Kiri Celestine Di'Cameron and her Circle. They were responsible for the slaughter of thousands.

"They almost succeeded, but they were eventually defeated and branded as blood traitors. My family line has been banned from Tigaera ever since. None will so much as trade with us, except by coercion, and we live in exile from our people and our birthright.

"I became who I had to be, to help my family survive: ruthless; cunning; a mercenary in every sense of the word. There is no softness in me, Damaskiri. I cannot afford the luxury. So no, I had not planned on ever being one of the declared suitors of a Damaskiri." He glanced down at her quickly, gauging her reaction before continuing, "Life, as you are aware, does not go according to plan. I wanted to bring honor to my family, remind the realms of our power and all that." He snorted dismissively. "Instead, I am ridiculed by those that see themselves as my betters and feared by those who recognize my strength. Yes, I've reminded them of our power, but still, they slight us."

His voice had deepened as he spoke. He had rested his elbows on his knees, hunching forward.

"So, you came here hoping to..." she trailed off, not wanting to finish her sentence, her heart aching at the thought that she was simply a means to an end.

He let out another wary sigh. "I came here to continue my task, Damaskiri. I need to restore my family's name; I need the ban lifted so that my brother can have a proper healer. But nothing goes according to plan," he stated again wryly.

Confusion was etched on her face. Was he saying that that wasn't what he was after anymore? Afraid to ask that question, she asked another, "What's wrong with your brother? Why will a healer not see him?"

"Nial was in an accident when he was younger. It was my fault." Von grimaced at the memory. "He had always been small, but he wanted so badly to be like me. I challenged him, told him to try to ride the new stallion that our father had just won. The stallion was pure temper, not the sort that would allow a rider anywhere near him, but my brother was determined. He vaulted on the stallion's back, and the stallion reared. He couldn't stay on, and he was thrown. The stallion trampled him as he rode away. Nial's legs were damaged beyond repair, they've never grown properly, and he's been confined to his bed ever since. That's no life for a man."

Helena could feel the misery and guilt rolling off Von in waves. *This is why he seeks you.* Despite her bruised ego, she gently touched his back, feeling him stiffen at the contact.

"No matter what happens tomorrow," she said softly, "I will help your brother. He will have a healer, even if I must go myself."

Von looked at her in surprise. "Even after I told you who I am, what my family has done, you would help him?"

She nodded. "I may not understand everything that you've done, nor agree with the decisions you have made, but everyone deserves to be judged on their own actions, not those of their ancestors. You have done what you needed to do to survive and to support your family; there is no shame in that."

He looked at her in wonder. "Is that why you spoke for me?"

Her eyes narrowed at the memory. "I spoke for you because it was the right thing to do, and because you are mine; whether you intended to be or not." Her voice was soft but unyielding. She was reeling from his confessions, his depiction of himself at complete odds with his tale about his brother. Her pride at war with her compassion. She couldn't help but feel like an utter fool for sitting there like a lovesick girl, while he had been strategically plotting, even if it was for a valid, albeit selfish, reason.

He sat unmoving for a moment before reaching his hand toward her. "Helena," he said softly.

She noted the use of her name with surprise.

Grabbing her hand, he continued to meet her gaze intently. "Things do not go according to plan. I told you what brought me here because you asked. It was not my intention to do so, at least not like that, but I would not hide it from you either. You should know who I am."

She remained quiet, uncertain of what he was saying.

He let out a breath and continued, "Helena, your soul calls to mine. I could no more deny that than I could my name. Just because it may not have been my intention at the start of my journey, does not mean that I am not pleased with the result, or that I will not do right by you and our bond."

He nudged her playfully with his shoulder. She bit her lip as she smiled, pleased to hear his admission. "You leave much to be desired in the way of wooing, Von."

He laughed, relief evident in the sound. "I did not realize you desired wooing, Damaskiri."

"Damaskiri I may be, but I am a woman first and foremost, Mate. You would do well to remember that." When she stood and looked at him, it was with iridescent eyes. Her hair danced in the wind, and she turned away from him, but not before watching the grin falter in shock from his face. Her laughter floated behind her as she walked toward the Palace.

He remained on the bench, stunned. He had known that she was whispered to be the most powerful Kiri his people had ever seen, and he thought he had an idea of what that meant. As he watched her hips sway while she walked away from him, he realized that he knew nothing.

Ah, that's where she's run off too. Gillian landed softly on a tree branch high above the flowering garden, leaves raining down gently from the contact. *And with him!*

This should prove very enlightening; she thought, jumping down a few branches to better hear their intense conversation.

From her perch in the trees above them, Gillian could overhear Von's story, shocked that he was so blatantly confessing his selfish motivations. Gillian had tried to use every spare opportunity she could to get closer to the young Damaskiri, and she had learned easily enough that the girl was a romantic. Growing up so far removed from court society had not prepared her for the reality and politics of royal courtships. Gillian was certain such a declaration would seriously bruise her tender feelings for her suitor.

Tawny feathers ruffling in the breeze, Gillian leaned forward, unconcerned with looking suspicious. If the two felt her watching them, they gave no indication and would only see a hawk if they did happen to look her way.

Gillian noted the strain around the girl's eyes, but it was not hurt making the aqua orbs glow, it was compassion. *Mother help her, she's falling for it, and for him,* Gillian rolled her eyes in disgust; *she's making this so easy.* Gillian was almost disappointed that the task ahead would not require her to use the true extent of her creative plotting. Almost. The sooner this was settled, the better.

'Your soul calls to mine...' the blood traitor was saying now.

Please! Gillian squawked in amused disbelief. *The warrior wouldn't know the sight of his blackened soul even if he had one, let alone admit that he actually had feelings for the girl.* Green eyes noted the softening of the girl's face at his words, and she winced in sympathy before catching the errant emotion. She could not afford to let herself feel anything for the impostor. She scoffed, *the fool believes him! He is practically doing the job for me.*

With a toss of her head, Gillian spread her wings and took flight, missing the sight of the girl as she stood, or the man's look of amazement as she walked away.

CHAPTER 6

*H*elena sat at the ancient sprawling vanity, fingers tapping a mindless tune on its shining surface. Alina was deftly twisting and pinning loose curls atop her head, using magic, instead of pins, to help keep the curls in place. Helena was glad for the shift, the sheer number of pins needed to keep her hair from listing drunkenly to the side of her head made her head ache.

She was wondering idly when she had begun thinking of the Palace as home, and her Circle and Alina as her family. Although it had been little over a month since she had moved here from the sweet cottage and her simple life there, this life, this world, was becoming more real to her than her years at the cottage.

It wasn't the grandeur of her new home, although she loved the soft femininity of her room decorated in its various shades of purple and gold which were both calming and lovely. She especially loved the deep armchair which sat underneath a large window with an unimpeded view of the main garden. And there was definitely something to be said for carpets that were so thick she felt her feet got lost in them. She scrunched her toes into the soft fabric at the thought and smiled, wrapping her lavender shawl more tightly around her shoulders.

Alina noted her mistress's smile, and couldn't help her responding one. "Thinking of someone, Damaskiri?" she teased lightly.

Helena blushed, she hadn't been thinking of Von actually, but at the suggestion, his image blazed brightly in her mind.

Her mind replayed their afternoon in the garden. She knew that she shouldn't be disappointed by his story, and she wasn't really, it was more of a deflation. Her coming back to reality and recognizing that it would be incredibly naïve of her to think all of the suitors had declared themselves because they had dreamed of her since they were children, or heard stories of her beauty and decided they must have her. And really, she chided herself, wouldn't that be worse? To be wanted as an object rather than a person.

Von had stated that he hadn't even anticipated the possibility that he would be selected as the Damaskiri's Mate, he was just trying to help his family. That was honorable in its own right, and she couldn't find it in herself to blame him for it. More than that, he was honest about it. He hadn't tried to hide his reasons for pursuing her behind false claims of emotion and feelings for her.

His honesty gave them a foundation to build from, and that's all you needed to start a relationship she decided. Not that she had been in one before, but surely it would be like any other, built on mutual respect and trust? She hoped that eventually, those would grow into affection and companionship since she had always wanted a marriage full of love and laughter.

She stared wistfully into the mirror trying to imagine Von gazing at her with love or bouncing a child on his knee, but entirely unable to conjure the image. He was too cynical, too... too male, she thought, to be placed in such a domesticated role. It was his maleness, though, that was causing the fluttering low in her stomach.

Well that, and the way his dimple would flash and his gray eyes would light up in surprise when she made him laugh.

Alina's laughter tinkled sweetly. "So that's the way of it?" she asked.

Helena grinned at her ruefully and stuck her tongue out at the girl through the mirror.

"You're very lucky, Damaskiri, to have such a strong Mate. He will be good to you."

Helena smiled at Alina. "You don't believe him to be a traitor then, as the others do?"

She shook her head, lips pursed as she concentrated on pinning the last few curls up. "No, Damaskiri. He's your Mate, which means that he was made for you. You're the most kind and warm lady I've ever met; I cannot imagine the other half of you would not be as passionate." Alina's eyes met Helena's briefly before she continued, "He may be less inclined to show that side of himself, but that does not mean it doesn't exist within him."

Helena was pleased with the thought. "You don't think that if he's the other half of me, he is the darker half?" she asked, repeating her Circle's explanation for the match.

Alina paused, considering. "He might be, Damaskiri, but aren't we all made of both shadows and light? Shadows cannot exist without light though, so you cannot have one and not have the other. Just because he may be that side of you does not make him evil."

"Yes," Helena responded, her smile blooming beautifully across her face, her eyes going soft and dreamy. "I think so too."

Alina chuckled at her mistress's obvious infatuation. "There, all done. You are ready."

Helena glanced into the mirror and studied the reflection that stared back at her. Chestnut curls were piled intricately atop her head with their ends falling softly to her shoulders. Her face was absent of any makeup; the effect should have left her looking fresh and youthful. However, her aqua eyes peered back sharply, the silvery ring around her pupils swirling like a mist of light creating the sense of all-knowing wisdom that belied any innocence. It was a captivating and stunning effect, for all of its simplicity.

There would be no elaborate dress to armor herself with this time. She would wear the traditional attire of the trial: a loose cotton robe, belted with a cord around her hips all in shades of tan.

Standing she turned in a slow circle.

Alina clapped with delight. "I can't think of a lady who has ever looked more beautiful," she whispered in awe, her smile lighting up her entire face.

Helena's lips twisted in a wry smile. "Liar, I see one standing before me."

The girl blushed in pleasure but waved away the compliment.

With a breath that was equal parts sigh and groan, Helena turned toward the door. "I suppose I have to go down there now. Time to get this over with, one way or the other."

Alina reached her hand toward her mistress, tentatively lest Helena should refuse her. Sensing no rebuke, she squeezed her shoulder infusing her gentle warmth and belief. "You will be amazing, Damaskiri. There is no question."

Feeling the soothing magic woven into the words, Helena couldn't help but smile. She was still learning much about magic, and the depths of her own vastly outweighed her maid's, but it was the intention behind the action that allowed Helena to wrap the girl's conviction around her.

With a last smile, albeit strained and lopsided, Helena moved out of the room and fell into formation with her Circle which had been waiting outside.

She could sense the current of their emotions around her, a heady mix of anticipation, confidence, and pride. Her Circle was more sure of her success than she was, but then again, they weren't the ones who had just discovered who they were mere weeks ago.

She felt, rather than saw, Darrin move closer to her. It was an unconscious display of support and protection, and she appreciated the gesture even if he didn't realize he had offered one.

The group took a hallway winding down into the deeper levels of the Spirit Wing where the ceremony chambers were located. Having grown used to the roar of the crowds during the Festival, the relative quiet of their steps was daunting. None but the Circle were allowed into the antechamber of the trial room, and only the Damaskiri was allowed through the gold door at the end of the room.

The decorations were more muted down here, the overall mood more austere and intimidating than warm or comforting. Following a dark purple rug into the antechamber, the group stopped. Helena turned to face her Circle, meeting each man's eyes briefly, attempting to communicate her appreciation for each of them in those few seconds.

There were no rituals to follow at this point, no ceremonial words to say. All that was left was for Helena to take the few remaining steps into the golden room and through the door. She opened her mouth as though to say something, but couldn't find any words. So instead she closed it and shrugged with a small smile. The men smiled encouragingly in return.

Turning from them she took the last few steps on her own and with a deep breath reached for the golden door. It was warm to the touch and surprisingly light for its size. Without a sound, it opened inwards, and she stepped through.

At first, there was only silence and mist; she could not see farther than an arm's length in front of her. Behind her, the door had vanished. She felt the familiar tingle of her magic being called to the surface, even though she had not beckoned it.

As her magic continued to flow, the tingle turned into a burn. She would have thought she was having trouble breathing, but she had not drawn a breath since entering the chamber. In fact, she couldn't feel her heart beating at all. The thought frightened her momentarily, but the drawing of her power had consumed her attention. It was all she could do to focus on keeping herself together.

"Ah, there you are," a voice whispered. It sounded as though someone was standing behind her speaking directly into her ear, but there was no one there.

The hair on her arms and neck rose in response.

"We have been waiting for you," it continued, although now it sounded like multiple voices speaking at once.

Her head began to pound at the intensity and amount of power flowing through her.

"The trial of a Damaskiri forces her to face her innermost self," the voice, singular and distinctly male continued.

"The darkest parts of self and its most hidden fears and desires," another component, discernibly female, took up where it had left off.

"It is your response to these parts of yourself that will reveal both the purity of your magic and your wholeness of self; a true Kiri requires both. The trial begins."

The last echoed around her as the mist swirled and revealed a bed with two bodies moving against one another. Eyes grew round as she realized what she was seeing.

Head thrown back in a carnal growl, Von turned to look at her, never stopping his thrusts. Her body responding to the image, she took a step forward.

A flash of blonde hair caught her eye and Helena looked past Von to see the woman below him. It wasn't her. As her eyes, mirroring her pain and confusion met his, he laughed, the sound a deep growling thunder that swelled throughout the room.

"Come join us, woman, perhaps you will learn something," he purred before giving her a feral grin and looking back to the woman arching up to meet his increasing thrusts.

Betrayal lashed at her like a knife, and she felt her fury wrap around her like an icy blanket. She snarled, and within her, the pool rippled.

Before she could act, the scene in front of her changed. She was now in the halls of the Palace, holding court over her people, every face reflecting their disappointment in her. The people murmured with distrust and unease. She watched her Circle turn their backs on her and walk toward the back of the room. She wanted to call out and run to them, but she was rooted to the spot. She did not know what she had done, only that she had failed miserably; her magic continued to twist and rise its way up and out of the deepest recesses within.

Now she was in the gardens of the Palace, but the sky was dark and the air filled with the acrid smell of smoke. Helena coughed and spun around in confusion, the intensity of the emotions evoked by the previous scenes still swirling within her and only adding to her disorientation.

The towers of the Palace were crumbling, and she could see the remains of fire blazing throughout the courtyard. Where there had once been rows upon rows of the flowers she had loved to get lost in; now there were only charred, almost skeletal, remains standing in their stead. Eyes flicking down, she saw that the ground below her was covered in seared and bloody bodies, or at least what was left of them.

Gasping, she dropped down to help them, and as she turned them over, she began to recognize faces. One after the other: Timmins, Joquil, Alina, Micha, Amos, Darrin... all those that she had come to love.

Body trembling, she stood and looked at her robe, now splattered with blood and ash; the warm liquid dripping down her fingers and onto Darrin's lifeless face. His blank eyes staring up at her unseeing. Beside him Micha's head began to turn, the one eye remaining in its socket blinking, while the bloody mouth gurgled as it tried unsuccessfully to speak.

An anguished scream tore through her throat, and an answering bolt of lightning struck a nearby tree, her magic's outward sign of its response to her terror. The still-smoking branches shuddered, unable to withstand the additional assault. With a deafening crack, the tree was rent in two, one half falling toward the pile of bodies below. The unearthly scream continued while her magic's answering storm rolled through the sky, its fury wreaking havoc on what was left of the land.

She knew with complete certainty that she was the one that had slain these people.

Shaking, she tried to move away, but the corpses began to grab her feet, moaning wetly in their attempt to pull her down. In fear, she felt her magic lash out, and the body that had grabbed her exploded, raining warm pieces of flesh upon her. It was Kragen.

"No!" she screamed again, tears falling from her eyes, blinding her. She was completely shaken, overwhelmed by the emotions within her: rage, shame, and anguish vying for her attention and calling her to action.

One by one the images flickered through her mind, Von laughing, remorseless at his betrayal, the backs of the men as they left her, and Darrin's face twisted in the agony of his death.

Sobbing, she fell to her knees. Around her, the wind rose whipping her hair around. Thunder growled in the sky, echoing her own screams.

Within, she felt the depth of her magic swirl through the pool as she pulled it to her, and released it. Her back arched at the intensity of the release and she felt herself come undone.

There was silence, the scene before her replaced again with silvery mist. She felt as though her body had no shape; she merely floated within the mist.

Eventually, the sound of Von's laughter brought her back to herself. Panting, she knelt on the ground; her forehead pressed into her one raised knee. Afraid to open her eyes, lest she sees more bodies or something even more terrible, Helena did not move.

"These events will come to pass, if you do not trust," the voice-of-many whispered.

She jolted to awareness, spine stiffening as though waiting for an assault.

"The eyes can see what the heart knows to be false. If you do not trust in yourself to know the difference, you will be lost," the female voice continued. The ends of her hair fluttered, as though a hand had run through them.

"He is you, and you are he. A betrayal of your bond can only occur if you do not trust," the last words whipped against her.

"A Kiri knows herself, the shadows and the light. To fear the shadow is to betray the light. Recognize the potential for destruction, but do not fear it and it shall not pass." The whisper faded away, leaving her.

Confused and trembling Helena stood. Was she done? How did that test her? She felt as though it had only tormented her. And then she knew.

Her test was to see if she could withstand the worst of herself. She was shown, in the most literal sense, what it would mean if she doubted not only her power, but her bond with her Mate. It all came down to that; it had always been about that. That was why it was such an integral part of the ceremony; he was the other part of her, and she had to fully accept and understand both.

To let that bond unravel would lead to a destruction of her people, the fulfillment of the prophecy so many had tried to circumvent. And in her uncertainty, she would be the source of their downfall. No matter what they would have done with her as a child, the end result would have been the same; it would always have come to the same end.

The door behind her opened. Muscles quaking in protest she turned toward the light filtering through it. She did not know how long she had been in the chamber; her sense of time was utterly gone.

She walked through the door back to the four men that had waited for her. As one they fell to their knees in fear and awe.

"It is done," said the layered voice that had whispered to her in the chamber, her magic's voice.

Helena stood in the doorway, her robe and skin still covered in blood and soot. Her hair tumbled down her back and shoulders in a riot of waves and her eyes iridescent and unfocused, their swirling depths seeming to hypnotize and see straight through to one's soul.

She opened her hand, and the pendant of the Mother dangled from her fingers, the simple knot in the center replaced with an egg-sized stone the same iridescent smoke of her eyes. As the men recognized the Kiri's pendant, Helena's eyes rolled back in her head, and she collapsed.

CHAPTER 7

*V*on heard the scream, its intensity and pain tearing through his body.

"Helena!" he shouted, coming to attention and reaching for the sword at his hips.

He looked around warily, eyes narrowed and trying to identify the threat. He crossed the room swiftly, feet silent as he made his way to the door.

Sensing nothing, he opened the door and peered outside. A servant was scurrying by with her arms full of fabric. Today's washing, he guessed.

She halted a few steps past him and turned. "Did you need something?"

He shook his head, and she continued down the hallway. After another few moments, he allowed his body to relax. Von could have sworn he'd heard Helena screaming, but if the Damaskiri was in trouble, the entire Palace would be in an uproar.

Releasing his sword, he brought his hand to his jaw and rubbed the day's beard thoughtfully.

Magic had always made him uneasy, his own source of power lending itself predominantly to his skills on the battlefield. He had never been quick to accept things that he did not understand or could not explain. This fit neatly into both categories. He caught a flash of movement out of the corner of his eye and went to grab for the sword again when he realized it was still in his hand.

His body was trembling like a green boy. *Magic,* he thought with a curse. Von knew he would not be able to relax fully until he had personally guaranteed her safety, and not just with his eyes. He was going to make damned sure that she was unharmed, and the Mother help the poor bastards that tried to stop him. Since he was all but the final member of the Circle he decided to go find Helena's guards, and demand to see her. He wanted to hold her. Von's steps faltered as he realized it was not merely want, but a bone-deep need to feel her safely in his arms. He took a shuddering breath to steady himself before resuming his ground-eating strides down the hall. He moved quickly, ignoring the curious stares he was drawing.

As he rounded the last corner, he saw the men he had been searching for walking toward him. They moved tentatively, Timmins and Joquil turning to look behind them often. There was a mix of emotions playing over the men's faces, but concern was most prevalent among them.

Before he could open his mouth to greet them, they shifted in formation and he was able to see the other two. The first thing he noted was the panic etched in Darrin's face. Following the man's gaze, Von's eyes were drawn to the woman being carried in Kragen's arms.

Her limbs dangled lifelessly over his arms, her head lolled back and allowed her hair to all but graze the floor.

In seconds he had reached them, his body on full alert and his senses primed with magic.

"Isn't your job to ensure her protection," he snapped, his voice low and deadly.

Timmins visibly flinched at the waves of danger he felt rolling off Von. He held his hands up and spoke softly, each word carefully measured. "We could not have anticipated this result, nor are we to blame for her collapse."

Not even remotely mollified, Von continued to scowl at the older man.

Darrin moved to speak, taking his eyes off of Helena only briefly, "She entered the door for her trial; hours had passed with nary a sound. When they opened..." he seemed to stumble over his words and Von could tell how the sight had affected him.

Kragen's deep rumble took up the story, "She was covered in blood. Before we could so much as blink she was falling to the floor. From what we can tell, she is unharmed, but the drain on her magic was too much for her."

"She is unharmed, but covered in blood?" Von asked, his lips curling in disbelief and eyes narrowed in censure. "Whose blood is it then?" he demanded, his voice still lethally soft.

"We do not know, my lord," Timmins shrugged helplessly.

"Before she collapsed, she showed us this." Joquil was holding out the pendant, a silver light emanating from the stone.

Von felt his body stiffen at the sight. *So she has passed, why then has she collapsed?* Ignoring his reaction, he continued, "You said you hadn't heard anything, but I could hear her scream from my room." The statement was an accusation.

Timmins shrugged again. "I cannot do much but speculate until she awakens and we speak with her, however, if I had to guess it would seem that the bond the two of you have already begun to cultivate has allowed you to stay connected to her during her trial."

"The books on the Damaskiri trial have always been unfailingly vague. We could not have anticipated that behind those doors she was doing anything other than meditating. We heard nothing," he emphasized.

Von frowned at the old man's words. Had he been connected to her? He knew that he had heard her, and he knew that he had not imagined the pain and terror in her scream.

He looked back at Kragen. "I will take her."

The warrior gazed back at him steadily, before inclining his head in agreement.

"The hell you will!" snapped Darrin, eyes wounded but fierce. "We are her Circle, you sir, have not yet spoken the vows that will bind you to her. You have no right," his voice shook with emotion, "no right to touch her."

"Darrin," Timmins said softly, quiet rebuke in the word.

"The Kiri has already chosen her mate, Shield," Joquil said firmly, his face void of expression. "Even you cannot stand in the way of that."

Von let the men speak, but Darrin would not move from in front of Kragen, and with Helena still limp in his arms Von wouldn't risk hurting her by ramming Darrin out of the way.

"Boy," Von sneered, with thinly veiled disdain, "stand down. You have already failed her once today, do not do so again."

The blond man flinched at the accusation but moved mutely to the side. Kragen stepped forward and set Helena with surprising gentleness into Von's arms.

Von allowed his gaze to sweep over the girl in his arms. Her usually luminous skin was waxy and purplish bruises were in sharp contrast to her eyes. He tried to dispassionately note the blood that covered her, used to seeing such scenes after his own battles. The blood itself did not bother him, it was the sheer amount of it, and that it covered *her*.

He felt a sharp tug in his chest at the sight and immediately snapped his eyes up before he could allow himself to be distracted by his emotions. He turned back the way he had come and started climbing the spiraling stairways as quickly as possible without jarring Helena.

"Joquil," he called over his shoulder, "Perhaps you should do something to ensure we do not draw unwanted attention to ourselves."

The man nodded in agreement, and Von felt the familiar tingle of magic race down his neck as Joquil began warding the passageway. His sensitivity to the use of magic was one of the most helpful skills he had acquired through his years of traveling and warring. It usually meant the difference between the life and death of his men and would signal a potential threat long before one materialized.

Without stopping Von slammed his foot into Helena's door, the door splintering and flying open with a crash.

Within the room, Alina spun around with a sharp cry, her eyes widening in shock at the sight of her mistress in his arms.

"Go grab a healer, quickly. Do not spread tales, and do not come back in this room until I ask for you."

Alina nodded, trembling fingers still pressed against her lips. She rushed quickly from the door, pushing past the four men still standing in the doorway.

Von turned to them, "Guard the door. No one comes in until I say," he said sharply, his voice still deadly soft.

"That goes for all of you," he added with narrowed eyes, sparing a final second to stare at Darrin until the blond man left the room. Joquil followed behind him, gesturing and murmuring under his breath as he sealed the doorway, ensuring privacy for the room's occupants.

Von set Helena down softly on her bed, finally allowing himself to fully catalog her injuries. A warrior by birth and blood, Von was not one to use his powers as anything other than a weapon or perhaps to bring some minor comfort to the otherwise stark living conditions of the road. His grandmother, however, was a noted healer in her time, and she had taught him a few things before her passing.

Closing his eyes, Von called the unfamiliar branch of magic to him, feeling the warmth rush through his fingers. He ran a gentle hand down her body, trying to sense any irregularities within her. He found none.

"What did you do, little one?" he asked her softly, easing himself down beside her.

With no apparent injury, Von could only assume that Timmins had been correct in his assessment that she had pushed her magic to its very limits causing a severe drain of her own vitality.

Not pausing to consider what he was doing, Von reached out to her again, resting his hand firmly on her chest over her heart. Driven by pure instinct he tried to share his own life force with her. He felt the drain immediately, tendons pulling sharply in his neck, and sweat breaking out on his brow.

It wasn't until he felt himself beginning to shake that he pulled away. Letting out a ragged breath he studied her again. The waxen quality of her skin had diminished, and the dark circles under her eyes had faded. She was still too pale, but now, at least, she looked as though she could be sleeping.

He heard her murmur, and his eyes snapped to hers willing them to open. She began to shift restlessly on the bed, a groan escaping her lips as though the movement was too painful.

His lips quirked despite themselves; it looked like his Mate was a warrior in her own way. He understood the fatigue battle could bring and the accompanying sense of frustration at your own body's weakness.

Her eyelids fluttered open, her eyes widening slightly when she saw him watching her.

"Von," she rasped.

"You gave us quite a scare, Kiri," he murmured.

"Kiri," she repeated, pleasure making her eyes glow brightly. "I did it?"

He nodded, returning her smile.

"Why do I feel like I fell from atop the tower then?" She groaned again as she tried to push herself up.

He placed a hand on her shoulder and gently pushed her back down, "I was hoping you'd be able to tell us that. Your Circle says you stepped out of the trial room, showed them your pendant and collapsed."

Her eyebrow furrowed in confusion. "I don't remember that. I, I don't remember much of..." she trailed off, and her eyes widened in horror as it came back to her.

He saw her beginning to panic and immediately began to murmur the nonsensical words one uses to soothe. She calmed quickly but flinched when he went to smooth a strand of hair from her forehead. He noted the reaction but ignored it.

Her eyes flickered up to his, and away again. He could tell she was weighing whether or not to share what had happened, and he knew from experience his patience would do more toward persuading her than any words.

"I saw you," she murmured finally.

He raised an eyebrow in response.

She swallowed and continued, "You were..."

He noted the blush. "I have a feeling I can guess what I was in the middle of. Did it make you nervous, *Mira*?" he teased.

She shook her head, smoky eyes narrowing fiercely. "Not nervous, furious."

He stopped his finger's lazy exploration of her cheek and jaw. "Furious? I've been told I make a woman feel many things during coupling, but that is a first."

Her lips twitched despite herself, and aqua eyes met his. "Perhaps if you had been coupling with *me*, I would have reacted differently."

"Ah." He shifted uncomfortably. "I dare say you would have."

"I didn't like it, Von. The sight of you with another woman..." As she trailed off her eyes searched his, her voice low and tense with emotion when she continued, "You are *mine*, I-I will not share you."

He grabbed her hand in response, ignoring another sharp tug in his chest. "I would not expect you to, Kiri. I would not share you either."

She smiled softly at his words. "I suppose I should warn you that I did not react well... to the sight. I did not realize I was a jealous woman."

He laughed at that, squeezing the small hand in his. "Noted."

Her smile faltered, and she related the other sights that she had seen, her eyes bright with unshed tears.

He felt his own tense response to her words, although how much of it was a fierce protectiveness of the beautiful girl that was lying before him and how much was fear at the possibility of such total destruction at her hands, he could not identify.

"It seems we both have been warned today," he said neutrally.

"Indeed." Looking back up at him and shaking off the final vestiges of her trial she added lightly, "I'm surprised they let you in here all by yourself. I'm not sure if I'm offended or relieved at the lack of people crowding around me in concern." She laughed, belying any possibility that she was offended.

"I did not give them an option," he said flatly.

73

Her laughter deepened, and she offered him a large smile. "I suppose thanks are in order then."

He shook his head, a small smile playing on his own lips.

"None is necessary, Kiri."

"You did more than just keep them away," she murmured, no trace of doubt in her tone.

He shrugged sheepishly.

"I can feel you," she whispered, tugging on his hand until he met her gaze. "I can feel you inside of me." Her other hand rested on her chest where his had been earlier. "It feels like you reached inside me and left a little part of yourself in my soul."

Her words simultaneously chilled and warmed him.

There was a sense of wonder in her voice. "Can I try?"

He blinked, startled. "I don't know if that's wise, Kiri. Your trial seriously weakened you."

She shrugged off his concern, pushing herself up to face him. Bracing himself, he warily watched her reach for him and rest her hand against his chest. She stared straight into his eyes, and he felt the warm pulse of her magic flow into him. He let out a startled gasp, feeling his own sense of awe.

He could feel her spirit swirling within him sweetly caressing his own as shy and playful as a kitten. He felt her very essence, a heady combination of youthful innocence and pure womanly fire and he knew, with complete certainty, that he would always feel her soul entwined with his own.

She went to move her hand, a satisfied smile on her lips, but he stopped her by placing his own hand over hers.

Slowly, so as not to scare her, he leaned down and brushed his lips against hers. She melted against him with a soft sigh.

Still connected he could feel her reaction to his kiss, his lips moving gently against hers. Her pleasure and curiosity lapping at him like a gentle fire. He felt his own body respond to her eager sweetness, so he pulled away, but not far.

Her eyes opened slowly, and she studied him with eyes now

darkened with desire. Just as he could feel her reaction to the kiss, she had felt his. She knew the effect her desire had on him.

He couldn't help the satisfied smile that lurked on his own lips.

"Mine," she said in a throaty whisper, wonder and desire swirling within iridescent eyes.

He inclined his head, not breaking eye contact.

"Yes, Kiri, and you are mine," responded the Mate, his own voice rich with promise.

He felt a final caress of her spirit within him as she shifted away. *You'll have to show me that again, later.*

He blinked in surprise at her voice in his mind. Before he could ask her what she meant, he heard Darrin pushing the remains of the battle-worn door open, his expression openly defiant.

With a groan, Von moved away from Helena. He pressed a soft kiss to her forehead, still ignoring the dried smears of blood. *It was too much to hope I could keep you to myself,* he thought.

He saw her lips twitch and realized that she could hear his thoughts just as clearly as if he had spoken aloud.

I think it's part of the Mating bond; she offered in response to the unasked question. *I think when you infused your spirit with mine, you showed your acceptance of the bond.*

He shook his head ruefully, his dimple flashing quickly.

He turned his attention back toward the angry man in the doorway.

"Did you not think to tell us that she had recovered," he bit out furiously, as he moved toward her side. "We have been beyond worried."

Von rolled his eyes. "Relax, puppy, she just opened her eyes a few moments ago."

Darrin bristled at the insult; green eyes narrowed in challenge.

"I wouldn't do that, if I were you," Von cautioned, all gentleness vanishing from his stance and expression.

Helena put her hand on Von's arm, and his eyes flickered toward her, warming slightly as they studied her. He nodded, tersely, and walked toward the door, but not without a final scathing glance at her Shield.

As Von left, Helena let her attention return to Darrin.

He stood tense by her side; she could sense the guilt and concern weighing on him.

"You are not to blame for this, Shield. It was not your place to protect."

"It is always my place to protect you, Kiri."

Helena shook her head at his pride. "Do you think so much of yourself, sir, that you could stand between a Kiri and her trial?"

Color stained his cheeks at her admonition. "Hellion," he whispered, his voice conveying all that he was not at liberty to say.

She opened her arms, knowing that he needed the hug more than she did. He moved swiftly, wrapping his arms around her and burying his head in her hair. She felt him breathe deeply a handful of times. With a final shudder, he pulled away, his mask of calm back in place.

He gestured at her torn and bloody robe. "So what did you do to deserve all that?"

It was Helena's turn to shudder.

"That bad?" he asked softly.

"Perhaps you should call the others," she said flatly, ignoring the question and readjusting herself against the mountain of pillows at her back.

He nodded curtly and grabbed the men from the hallway.

As her Circle entered the room, she felt each curious gaze as though the questions were spoken aloud.

"It is not my blood," she told them.

They nodded, but their relief at her admission was palpable.

"The Mother saw fit to warn me what my failure would mean. This is the cost." She gestured at herself. "I cannot fail."

"You did not fail, Kiri," Joquil reminded her.

She offered him a small smile. "Nothing is that simple, Master. My trial is not one to be overcome so quickly."

"But the pendant..." Timmins started in confusion, before stopping himself.

"Perhaps I should clarify. I passed the trial of the Damaskiri. My magic has accepted me, and I was gifted with the pendant of the Kiri.

76

Now I must face the trial of the Kiri; it is not a trial one can prepare for. It is not the trial written of in your history books, and I cannot rely upon your counsel to see me through this time."

Aqua eyes turned to smoke, and her voice blended with the harmony of many. "The Mother showed me what my failure would mean. I would be the destruction of us all."

The men shivered at the wind that whipped through the chamber at her words, but they stood firm.

The mountain of corpses and acrid smoke filled her mind once more.

"Then you will not fail, Kiri," Kragen said simply, pulling her back from the vision.

Iridescent eyes met his. "Pray you are right, Sword."

"Whatever the Mother sees fit to test you with in the future, you will be prepared, and we will be by your side. You will not face this alone."

She smiled at her Shield. "I hope that I am deserving of your faith in me."

Alina knocked on the door gently. "Kiri, may I allow the healer to check on you now?"

"Am I needed anywhere right now, Timmins?" Helena asked, her desire to curl into a ball and sleep at war with her duty to her people.

"No, you rest now. All that remains is for the Ceremony of Binding, but that can wait, it's just a formality at this point anyway."

Helena felt herself smiling at the thought of Von.

"I'll be outside if you need me."

"Thank you, Darrin, but you should rest as well. It seems it was a hard morning for us all."

"I'll be outside," he repeated.

She rolled her eyes. "Suit yourself."

Alina was followed into the room by Tanya, the Palace's most gifted healer. Tanya exuded competence and unflappable strength. She noted the blood without qualm.

"Are you hurt, Kiri?" she asked gently.

Helena shook her head. "No, merely a bit drained it seems."

She nodded, as though anticipating the answer. "I'll just give you a once over, shall I? And maybe a tonic to help you relax for a bit?"

"That sounds lovely."

Tanya smiled and set warm hands on either side of Helena's head. Her last thought before drifting to sleep was that Tanya's eyes were the exact color of her favorite armchair.

CHAPTER 8

"Why are they all naked?" she squeaked.

Gillian's laugh was a sultry chuckle. "Relax, Helena, they aren't actually naked, much to my endless disappointment. They have that scrap of cloth covering the most interesting bits, see?" She pointed toward the cloth slung low on the candidates' hips that tied off in a flimsy knot on the side.

"But, but why?" she asked again, desperation coloring her voice as she eyed the row of men standing on the dais. Heat flooded her cheeks, and she could not bring herself to lower her eyes past their chins.

The women in the crowd were cheering enthusiastically, calling out the names of their favorites and praying for the fluttering pieces of fabric to get caught in a strong breeze and fall to the floor.

Helena couldn't deny that the sight was a spectacular one, eleven males in their prime were all lined up waiting for her. More specifically, they were waiting for the Ceremony of Binding to begin, at which she would publicly choose her Mate.

"Well, I did warn you that attraction was part of picking a mate," Gillian teased bringing her back to their conversation, "you'll know you've found your mate because of how they respond when you run your hands over their chest—everyone will for that matter."

Helena's eyes went wide at the implication, and she looked at Gillian in panic.

Gillian's enjoyment of her distress was clear. "Relax, Helena; I'm teasing. Tradition dictates that when a Damaskiri rests her hand over the heart of her true mate, her soul will call to his and their heartbeats will sync as the soul is reconnected to its other half."

Helena recalled the other night with Von and the way that she could feel him inside of her ever since. She sent a tentative tug down the invisible tether she felt connecting her to him.

Blazing gray eyes met hers from his spot in the line-up. She couldn't even offer him a shy smile as she looked back toward her feet to avoid the feast of male flesh currently on display.

No one else had realized that the two had inadvertently completed their mating bond while alone in her room, but even if they had, there was no way to escape this final public ritual. Helena was glad that it happened that way, to have to experience that intimacy while thousands of people watched them would have diminished some of the magic in the moment.

Not to mention the reaction to the kiss that had followed. Helena felt her ears turning pink at the memory of that kiss; her toes curling in her shoes. Oh yes, she was thankful that she had been able to avoid that particular spectacle.

"I just don't understand how that requires them to remove all their clothing," Helena said through gritted teeth.

Sighing, Gillian rolled her eyes. "Helena, don't be such a prude. All of the men who are refused tonight will not be lacking sympathy or company for that matter," she added as her green eyes roamed the cheering crowd. "The entire process of finding your mate requires a complete surrendering of self. This is all symbolic"—her hand gestured to the men—"they are standing there to bare their souls to you, to show that they have nothing to hide and that they are willing to sacrifice their pride when needed, in order to best serve the realm. Granted the tradition might be a bit outdated, but the meaning is what matters. Besides, even you cannot deny that it's a little fun."

Helena brought her eyes back to Von. He stood among the others defiantly; his head tossed back—the better to stare down his nose at those standing below him. There was no shame in his stance, just confidence and a bit of impatience, as his arms crossed over his chest.

Helena had to look away. Standing on the other side of Von was Gillian's twin. Micha was built much like his sister, looking almost childish standing next to Von's impressive bulk.

Micha noticed her and winked, his lips twisting up wryly as if to ask *what can you do?* His pale skin was flushed from the attention of the crowd, but he too stood still, awaiting the beginning of this final test.

"If that's what this is all supposed to demonstrate, then why are they the only ones who are naked? Shouldn't I be as well?"

Gillian's horrified reaction was almost comical. "Helena, you are Kiri. The first Kiri in centuries. Of course you aren't going to parade around in the nude." Gillian made a face and seemed to struggle with her words before continuing, "You are the most powerful woman in the world, there is no reason for you to ever debase yourself. These men are seeking to be worthy of you, not the other way around."

Helena frowned at that, Gillian's words sitting uncomfortably. It just didn't make sense, this double standard, if mates were supposed to be two parts of a whole, how could one ever be seen as more than the other? Helena shook her head, causing her chestnut curls to dance. No, she refused to accept that. So long as she was the one being mated, she would never treat these men as less than equals.

Knowing that she still had some time before the sun made its final descent in the sky, Helena looked around for Alina.

The girl was standing off to the side chatting with the healer Tanya. Helena excused herself and started toward the girl.

Seeing her coming, Alina met her halfway.

"Is something amiss, Kiri?" Alina asked.

Helena quickly shook her head and then paused, trying to choose her words with care. "I need you to help me with something, but we don't have much time," she added as she looked back up toward the sky.

Alina was nodding. "Of course, whatever you need, Kiri."

Alina's eyes grew round as Helena explained what she wanted to do.

STANDING off to the side of the dais, Helena was wrapped in a cloak the color of the night's sky. It had a deep hood that was currently pulled low over her face, hiding her from the crowd.

Timmins had stepped to the center of the stage and held up his hands to get the crowd's attention. There were a few last hoots and cheers until finally, as one, the crowd fell silent.

"One of the Chosen's most beloved traditions is the choosing of the Mate. Tonight, our Kiri will make her choice, completing her Circle and formally beginning her reign as our ruler."

Timmins stepped back and swept his arm to the side, revealing Helena to the crowd.

There were low murmurings starting in the crowd as she stepped forward, the cloak parting to reveal the luminous glow of her skin as she moved.

Standing just to the left of the first candidate, Helena's hands trembled only slightly as she lifted the hood and then dropped the cloak.

The crowd was silent before letting out a giant roar of approval. Helena did not stand there naked, as it had first appeared, rather she was wearing a short flesh-colored shift. It hung loosely on her, but due to the un-dampened state of her magic, the glow of her skin emphasized the way the thin material caressed her curves. It emphasized the gentle swell of her hips and the more generous slope of her breasts.

This was the first time the Chosen had seen their Kiri's power unleashed. Her eyes swirled with iridescent fire, and she stood silently before them.

A small rustle of wind brushed her hair up until it seemed to float behind her; she was mesmerizing. The Chosen were entranced.

When she spoke, it was with the melodious voice-of-many, "The

Mother guides and her Chosen bend to her will. It is with her blessing that we are gathered here tonight to celebrate her ultimate gift: the mating bond. Once I join myself to the Mate, the Circle will be complete."

The crowd roared again, chanting for the name of their selected.

Helena turned her back toward the crowd and faced Amos. He could not contain his gasp as he stared at her. His heart was racing when she lightly rested her hand against his chest.

"Be at peace, Amos," she said softly, speaking only so that he could hear her.

Instantly the tempo of his heart steadied enough for him to take a shuddering breath. He blinked and brought dazed eyes back to hers.

"I release you of your promise to me. Your heart and your soul are your own, go forth with the Mother's blessing," Helena spoke more loudly, her voice still enhanced.

Amos nodded and stepped off the stage and back into the crowd.

One by one she continued down the line, each time quietly repeating the same words to the men as they stood before her.

Finally, it was down to Von and Micha. The Chosen were restless, and they shifted and watched to see which of the men would be selected.

Helena stood before Von, her hand steady as she lifted it to rest above his heart, covering the dark whorls of a tattoo that began there before flowing up and over his shoulder.

His skin was on fire under her hand, but his heart continued to beat in time with her own.

His lips were lifted in a small smile.

"Hello, Mate," he said in her mind.

Her answering smile was pure feminine joy. *"Mine."*

She could feel the way his body responded to her claiming. His eyes gazed at hers with a fierce hunger, the gray turning molten with desire.

"Shall we put on a little bit of a show for them?" Helena asked, tilting her head to the side.

Von lifted an eyebrow. *"What kind of show do you have in mind?"* he asked, the voice a seductive purr.

"Not that kind, Mate."

She felt the flickers of his disappointment through their bond.

"Von Holbrooke, do you accept the mating bond?" she asked aloud, her voice magnifying and rippling so that it could be heard across the entire crowd.

"I do," he answered, his deep voice warm and proud.

Closing her eyes, Helena called to the swirling pool within her. Letting her instincts guide her, Helena summoned a small ball of starlight and willed it to grow.

Starting from the place where her hand rested over his chest, the light began to swell and spread. There were delighted gasps from the crowd as they noticed the ball of light that was quickly expanding from where they were connected until there were wrapped in a cocoon of light.

Standing on her tiptoes, Helena pressed a sweet kiss to Von's lips, before falling back on her heels. She felt an answering growl and pressed her lips together to contain the giggle that threatened to spill forth.

Stepping away from him, she looked toward Micha.

He was smiling, but she could see the disappointment in his green eyes.

"Friends?" she asked him softly.

"Of course, Kiri."

Smiling, she repeated the words that formally released him and gave him a quick hug before turning back toward Von who swept her into his arms and spun her around until she was breathless with laughter.

"I have something for you," he declared suddenly, there was a playfulness in his gray eyes she hadn't seen before.

Fascinated, Helena watched while Von produced a crown of magnolia blossoms from behind his back, before unceremoniously placing it on her head.

"What is this for?" she asked, lifting a hand to set it in place.

"You told me you desired wooing, *Mira*. I figured I should probably start now."

"I suppose it's better than nothing, even if it is a little late," she teased, pleasure at his words bubbling up within her.

"I suppose it's a good thing that I can spend the rest of our lives making it up to you."

Helena's heart swelled at the earnestness of his words.

He brushed back a curl from her face, smiling down at her.

She had promises of her own she wanted to offer, but she could not find the words her heart wanted to speak, so instead, she kissed him and hoped that was enough.

CHAPTER 9

"V on?"

The whisper would have startled him if it hadn't brought the feeling of warmth and peace he was learning to associate with Helena.

"Kiri?"

"Am I disturbing you?"

"Well at the moment I am being lectured by Timmins on the importance of protocol. So, no, definitely not."

He felt, rather than heard her amusement. *"Finally, someone else is on the receiving end of one of his speeches."*

His lips quirked at her irreverence.

"This is no laughing matter, Von. I do not need to remind you what is at stake." Timmins stood in front of him, frowning, his arms crossed over his chest.

"I know the words, Advisor; you need not continue shouting them at me."

"You're getting me in trouble, Mira. Is there something you need? Preferably something that requires my attendance far away from your Advisor?"

"Not at the moment. I seem to be at the mercy of Alina's

ministrations once again. I may just go cross-eyed if she asks my opinion on one more piece of ribbon or some such trinket."

"Shall I rescue you? Steal you off to the garden?"

He felt her smile in another rush of warmth. *"I fear that this particular assault is as much your fault as it is mine, Mate. I'd hate to see what she did to me if I interfered or ruined her creation."*

He chuckled softly, earning another of Timmins' frowns.

"Did you really just call on me to say hello?"

There was a pause before she responded, as though she was weighing her words. *"I was just curious if you would still be able to hear me this far away."*

The lie sounded like a discordant note in his mind. *"Are you lying to me, Kiri?"* he teased, curious what she was trying to hide.

"No!" He felt her surprise. *"Okay, so maybe that wasn't the entire truth, although it isn't very gentlemanly of you to call me on it. I was just feeling..."*

Lonely. He had known the answer before she was able to finish her sentence. It seemed their bond came with more than the ability to speak with their minds; it also allowed them to sense one another's emotions and their truthfulness. This revelation was yet another thing for him to consider, especially since it would mean that she could sense his own as well.

Von struggled with his response to her admission. He had never been one to fall for a woman's games, but coming from Helena, the admission was not used to snare, it was simply the truth. That appealed to him.

"You could send for me. I'm sure Alina could use another hand to hold ribbons for her."

"Ha! You really would do anything to escape Timmins. Besides, it's not as if Alina would actually allow someone to see her masterpiece before she was finished anyway. Not even on my orders."

"Really Von, you could at least pretend to pay attention," Timmins snapped.

Feeling like a schoolboy, Von uttered an apology.

"This really is for your benefit you know. You are the one who has to stand up in front of the entire realm this evening."

"I said I was sorry, Timmins," Von's strained voice betraying his irritation.

"Just because she chose you, doesn't mean you deserve her," the older man bit out.

Any vestige of good humor at Helena's mental presence dissipated at those words. Von held himself stiffly, shooting a look of ill-concealed displeasure at Timmins.

"I've killed men for less, Timmins. You may want to choose your words with care."

The man paled but stood his ground. "Even your jaded soul must realize how rare and special a creature she is. She doesn't deserve to be made a fool of in front of her people."

"You think I don't know that? That I would go out of my way to embarrass her? I know the damn words, Timmins." Von stood quickly, his chair crashing to the floor.

"Von?!" Helena's concerned voice rang out in his mind. He ignored her and closed the distance between himself and the older man.

"You think I haven't asked myself what twist of fate made her choose me? Made her soul speak to mine? You think I don't know that I don't deserve her goodness and light after the choices I've made in my life?" His voice a furious whisper. "I will do my part, old man," he finished, stepping away.

"It's not enough to know the words, Von. I had to ensure that you understood them as well. You are binding your soul to hers this evening. More than any other bond, the Mate's vow reunites two pieces of a soul back into one. It is not something that can be done lightly, or without true commitment and intent. You can destroy her if you do not understand the vow that you will make today.

"And I do not merely mean hurt her feelings, or betray her. You can kill her if you do not mean the words you speak tonight. Her destruction is our own. Remember that when you utter those words you know so well, Von."

His temper left as quickly as it came. Von stared at the Advisor, a chill of fear worming its way into him.

The door crashed open, and Helena stood in the doorway, eyes of swirling smoke and chestnut curls flying around her.

"Helena," Timmins said softly.

The Kiri turned her gaze to her Advisor, a growl sounding in her throat. The need to protect her Mate overriding her ability to sense reason.

Von watched Timmins swallow and take a step back.

He understood now what Helena meant when she said that she didn't react well to seeing him with another woman. It was pure instinct that fueled her at this moment.

"Mira," he called to her with his mind. *"He did not truly threaten me. I am fine. Look at me."*

She took a step toward Timmins, lifting her hand as she did.

"Look at me," he ordered.

Eyes of swirling gray met his.

"He hurt what is mine," the multitude of voices snapped.

"You wound my pride if you think the old man could have hurt me, Mira."

She blinked slowly, and her eyebrow furrowed as if confused. Aqua eyes met his.

"But I felt it. I felt your pain."

Timmins watched the silent exchange in surprise but made no move to break the silence.

Von frowned at her comment and spoke aloud for Timmins benefit. "Truly, Kiri, he did nothing more than wound my pride. He was teaching me a lesson, and a valuable one."

Helena met his gaze sheepishly. "I'm sorry for bursting in on you. I'll leave you to your lessons."

"I think, perhaps, we are done now," Timmins murmured ruefully.

"Would you like me to escort you back to your chamber, Kiri?" Von asked neutrally.

As if realizing where she was, and the effect her flight to the chamber must have had on Alina's work, Helena took stock of herself. A few choice profanities rang from her lips.

Von let out a bark of laughter and Timmins raised his eyebrows. Alina chose that moment to round the corner and find her mistress.

"Oh Kiri, what have you done to your hair? We must start all over, and we still have to get you in your gown for the ceremony!"

Pleading aqua eyes met his.

"Come on. I must get to work right away if we're ever going to finish in time."

Shooting him one last look, Helena followed meekly behind her maid.

After a few moments of staring silently at the now empty doorway to the chamber, the two men looked at each other and laughed at the absurdity of the sight.

HELENA STOOD in front of the mirror for what felt like the eightieth time that week. For once, however, she was actually vested in the reflection before her. She stared at the fabric of her gown with something akin to wonder.

"It's perfect, Alina," she said softly, letting the material slip through her fingers.

The gown was stunning in its simplicity. It fit her snugly, molding to her curves from shoulders to hips, and then cascaded like water to the floor. It was a straight line across her neck, baring no skin from the front until she lifted an arm. The sleeves were deceptive, appearing loose and full to the tips of her fingers, and mimicking the fall of material in the skirt of her dress. However, there was a slit from shoulder to wrist, leaving her arms entirely bare.

The material was like liquid smoke, ever-changing and throwing light like a diamond. She twisted to the side, glimpsing the back of the dress, her mouth opening in delight.

All the skin hidden from the front was more than made up for in the deep plunge of the back. She would have felt indecent, had her hair not been a riot of chestnut curls, falling down her back, revealing only glimpses of bare skin as she moved.

Alina had woven a strand of amethysts in her hair, which reflected the light from her dress, and were constantly twinkling in her hair. As a final touch, she fastened the Kiri pendant around her neck, allowing it to rest between her breasts.

The end result was that she appeared to be cloaked in mist, both shrouded behind it and vulnerable to its mercurial nature.

Alina clapped her hands in glee. "You're a vision, Kiri!"

"It's all because of you, Alina, truly."

She shook her head adamantly. "No, Kiri, it takes true beauty to shine through such simplicity."

Helena felt her cheeks warm, her smile shy.

A quick rap on the door had both girls turning toward it.

"I suppose it's time then," Helena murmured.

Alina squeezed her hand in a final display of support and moved to open the door.

Darrin stepped through the doorway. "It's time, Kiri." He stopped, his mouth falling open as he stared at her.

She twirled for him, as she had when they were children. She could see the approval glowing in his eyes as he smiled at her.

"Beautiful," he said simply.

She smiled, pleased, and threaded her arm through his. "I suppose you should walk me down then."

His smile faltered slightly, as though he was only just now realizing he was the one who would be walking her down to present her to the man she would be joining her life with.

He nodded, "I suppose so."

The walk was a short one, only from her room to the chamber where the first of her Circle had sworn their oaths to her. Like with the others of the Circle, the commitment between Mate and Kiri would be done only in front of the Circle. There would be a formal celebration afterwards, but the vows themselves would be spoken with a modicum of privacy, for which Helena was immensely grateful.

Darrin squeezed her arm gently, before leaving her at the door of the Chamber to stand with the rest of the men. Her eyes roamed the room, noting the blazing candles and otherwise barren décor. She smiled at each of her Circle in turn, feeling their pride and approval as they returned her silent greeting. Finally, her eyes fell on Von, who was standing at the window and staring out below, his obsidian hair tied in a queue at the base of his neck.

"Plotting your escape already?" she teased as she admired the fit of his black shirt and leathers.

He tensed at her voice in his mind, but recovered immediately. *"You won't get rid of me that easily, I'm afraid,"* he responded as he turned toward her with a small smile playing about his lips. His eyes widened as he took her in. When they came to meet hers, they were smoky with desire.

Von crossed the distance between them, his hand reaching toward her. Aqua eyes glowed with happiness as she lifted her hand to place it in his. At the display of skin revealed by her false sleeve, Von swallowed quickly. *"You undo me with your beauty, Mira."* Even his mental voice was rough with hunger for her.

Their fingers touched, and she shivered at the wave of warmth it brought. He squeezed her hand to signal he felt it too.

Timmins stepped forward motioning for the two to step into the middle of the room.

She turned to face Von, aqua eyes meeting slate gray. She took a shuddering breath, overwhelmed with the immensity of the moment. It is true, she had bound herself just as tightly to the other four men in her Circle, but this time she was binding her very soul.

She could feel Von's thumbs idly rubbing circles on her hands offering his strength and support.

Timmins spoke, his voice ringing out with authority. "Have you readied and cleansed yourselves for the vows you make to each other today?"

"We have," their voices chorused.

She was pleased at how steady and sure hers sounded, despite the tidal wave of emotion rolling through her.

"Do you understand the importance of the bond you will share?"

"We do."

"And are you prepared to take one another in, to love and safeguard, until the Mother calls you home?"

"We are."

"Then please proceed, and may the Mother watch over and nurture the bond you solidify today." Timmins stepped back, the other men stepping away from the wall and forming a circle around Helena and Von.

Taking her hand, dwarfed by his own, he brought it to his chest to rest over the steady beat of his heart. She felt her own race in response.

Covering her hand with his, he began in his deep growl, "In the name of the Mother, I, Von Holbrooke, bind my life to yours and take you into both my heart and my spirit, to be my Mate. I shall respect and protect you, your beliefs and your people, taking them as my own. I vow to be true to you above all others. I promise to love you wholly and without restraint, in this life and beyond, where we shall meet, remember and love again. From this day forward, my place is at your side, placing your desires and needs before my own, until such a time as the Mother calls us home."

Aqua eyes swirled with smoke as she brought his scarred hand to rest over her heart and pendant. Leaving the hand he had covered on his chest, she covered the hand now resting on hers.

When she spoke, it was with the voice-of-many.

"In the name of the Mother, I, Kiri Helena Solene, accept you as my Mate. I bind my life to yours and take you into both my heart and my spirit. I shall respect you, your beliefs and your people, taking them as my own. I vow to be true to you above all others. I promise to love you wholly and without restraint, in this life and beyond, where we shall meet, remember and love again. From this day forward, you will always have a place by my side. I will hold your life and happiness above all others, including my own, until such a time as the Mother calls us home."

As she finished speaking, the candles flickered and a gentle breeze swirled around them. The wind continued to encircle them, creating an insoluble barrier between them and the Circle. Neither Von nor Helena moved, although their hearts now beat in tandem. She could feel his spirit inside her, much like when he healed her the day before. What had been a whisper of essence was now a firm and solid presence, as familiar to her as her own.

"Mine." Her voice was fierce in his mind.

His lips twitched in amusement. He had never felt stronger or more humbled than he did in that moment surrounded by the full glory of her love for him. He had never understood the emotion before, had not realized that it was what he had been feeling since he first met her. With her spirit infused with his, he knew he would always carry it with him now, like a beacon. She would be his strength and his purpose.

"Always, Mira."

Aqua eyes were bright with tears, as she took a step toward him. Leaning down to meet her, Von sealed their vow with a kiss.

CHAPTER 10

*H*ours had passed since the mating ceremony had concluded, but the revelers had no intention of leaving. Helena found herself stealing glances at her Mate from across the room, the pulse of spirit an unwavering arrow pulling her back to him. It was as simple as a question being formed in her mind, she just had to start wondering where he was and she would know instantly.

She was still unsure of the limitations of this bond between them, in fact, it did not seem that those in her Circle were aware of such a possibility. She had tried to ask Timmins about the bond between a Kiri and her Mate, but he had only murmured a few nonsensical phrases about the two being halves of one whole.

One thing that was becoming clear, even despite any physical distance between them, was that unless she was specifically focused on him, such as when she would speak directly to his mind, his presence would remain a mere imprint. It would be indistinct, like that gentle lapping of waves against the shore or a soft breeze brushing against branches. And while it would give the impression of his general state of mind, it would not provide any detail.

Like now, she could tell without looking at him whether he was actually amused or only pretending to pay attention to his companions (he was pretending) but she did not know what the men were actually saying.

However, this impression of him would sharpen instantly if his own emotions peaked. Flashes of anger or mirth would become currents within her, a wave crashing into her, alerting her to his shifting moods and bringing him to the center of her mind. She was curious if this would become more or less sensitive over time. Would she always feel these subtle shifts in temper, or only be attuned to the sharp blade of anger or jolting tang of fear? Was he just as aware of the same shifts within her?

As if he felt the question, his eyes tangled with hers across the room. And as if in answer he gave her a soft smile, more a slight lifting of his lips at the sides, before turning back to the men in front of him.

Helena felt her own smile in response, and couldn't resist the urge to imagine what it would feel like to walk over to him. Her fingers gently brushing against his when she reached his side. The calluses rough against the tips of her fingers, as she interwove them with his own. She would squeeze gently, just once, as if to say, "I am here."

While her mind wandered, she noticed the slight widening of his eyes and flexing of his fingers, as if he could feel her thoughts being enacted on his body. He turned his head back to her, his eyes narrowing in concentration.

She felt the gentle caress on her palm, almost as if a piece of velvet had brushed against it while simultaneously noting the increasing pressure on her hand. He was squeezing her hand in return!

Helena felt her cheeks warm on their own accord, pleased he had not only been able to actually feel her intentions, but that he wanted to respond in kind. Von's own expression did not shift, except perhaps for the polite smile to warm slightly.

She could now feel a gentle tickling starting in the palm of her hand and working its way down each of her fingers. A phantom finger stroking the length of each one, before starting anew on the next. After all five fingers received a similar ministration, the center of her palm began to tingle. The tingle was constant, like a breath being softly released against it before it was replaced with a very distinct heat.

It took her a moment to place the sensation. It was a kiss! Von was kissing the center of her palm. The tickle returned, but now it was accompanied by a sense of warmth. Wet strokes resuming the exploration along each finger.

Helena felt her cheeks blaze with heat as she realized he was now licking and sucking each of her fingers. There he stood, arms loosely crossed against his wide chest as he leaned against a wall listening to the men continue to joke with one another before him. His head tilted slightly so he could see her clearly. A smirk, proud and male, growing against his will.

"Proud of yourself, Mate?" she asked him, trying to calm the racing beat of her heart.

"Immensely. If that's how you respond to just a thought, imagine what I can do when I'm actually touching you."

She felt his amusement swell within her.

"What?" she questioned warily.

"It will be fun to test what I can do with said thoughts, while I'm touching you as well." With that, he sent her a saucy wink and his smirk became a full-blown grin, complete with wicked promise.

Dazed, Helena blinked a few times, trying to resurface from the sexual fog that now seemed to surround her. The guests around her all begin to shift uncomfortably, the women pulling out fans and the men remarking about whether the temperature seemed to be rising, despite the night sky twinkling above.

As if he could tell her magic had also responded to his seduction, and how those around her were reacting to it, Von threw back his head and let out a bone-deep laugh. The sound rich and warm, wrapped itself around her heart.

Under normal circumstances Von was an imposing figure, towering above most others, all hard lines and arrogance. His sheer size and muscle as much a deterrent to any approach as the ever-present scowl on his face.

But suffused with mirth, Von came alive. The silver eyes which seemed as impenetrable as metal sparkled like molten silver pools. The boyish smile easing the years of hardship and worry from his face.

There was still the coiled strength and promise of violence generating from the muscles that shook with the force of his laughter, but what had once been a wall of stone keeping you out, was now a magnet drawing you in.

Breath catching at the change, all she could do was stare. He was beautiful.

Helena was not a completely naïve farm girl, she had her share of stolen kisses behind the barn with the boys in town, and knew about desire and attraction. But all she thought she knew paled in comparison to the aching throb low in her belly. Nothing she had experienced prepared her for the soul-deep want she was feeling now, as she stared at the laughing man across the room.

VON COULD FEEL the shift in Helena's response to him like a flood of hot water dripping down his body. His laughter slowly subsided, and he brought his eyes back to hers. He started slightly when he noticed the twin aqua pools were now a swirling iridescent storm. Her cheeks were flushed and her chest rose and fell quickly and she struggled to draw in air.

"Mine."

He felt her declaration vibrate within the core of his being. All traces of amusement now completely faded from his face. He took a step toward her before noticing the people around him.

Startled, he looked around, noting the changes in the garden. The dull roar of voices had faded, replaced with the strains of music and the gentle rustle of fabric. Guests were no longer chatting cheerfully in small clusters scattered throughout the room. Instead, they were breaking off into couples focused only on each other. Many were moving deeper into the shadowed areas of the garden, while those closest to Helena didn't seem to concern themselves with the need for privacy. All around, lovers, if only for the night, were paired off, their bodies pressed against each other.

"Mira," his voice rumbled through her.

She was doing this. Her magic, more powerful than anything he had ever encountered, had the ability to influence not just those closest to her, but everyone in attendance.

Poor proper Timmins would be horrified when he was back in possession of his faculties. Currently, his hands were exploring the rather large buttocks of a sharp-tongued healer named Daphne, while his lips trailed kisses along the skin exposed by her dress.

Von allowed himself a chuckle as he made his way to his Mate. That was a memory he would allow himself to dwell on properly later if only as payback for the mind-numbing lectures he had endured over the course of the last week.

"Helena," he whispered as he reached her, his hand brushing back a stray curl that had fallen.

She blinked slowly, aqua eyes searching his. "Von? How did you get over here so quickly? Weren't you just..." she trailed off as she looked around the garden.

"Timmins!" she squeaked in surprise, cheeks flooding with color. It was clear she did not know whether to laugh or hide.

"Von, what did I do?" she questioned, eyes scanning back and forth quickly.

"It would seem your magic responds to the intensity of your emotions. The more intense, the bigger the reaction. Were you thinking about something, darling?" he teased.

Eyes snapped back to his, widening in embarrassment. "How do I uh..." she trailed off.

His hand reached out, fingers gently brushing against her cheek before he leaned over and pressed a soft kiss against her forehead. "I think distance would be a start. A spell of this magnitude is probably best to run its course and wear off on its own."

"But what about"—she gestured helplessly at Timmins—"won't he regret this in the morning?"

Von shrugged. "He might, although he'd be too polite to mention it. Trust me, my love, people are more adept at recovering from a night of unintended loving than you might think. To interrupt them now might cause more embarrassment than letting them wake up in the morning and acknowledge or deny the events of the evening as they will.

"Besides," he continued, "I think to undo what you have set in motion might require a bit more attention than you have at the moment."

Cheeks still tinged with pink, she nodded at him sheepishly. "I think you might be right."

He reached down to take her hand, smiling as he did. "In that case, perhaps it's time we retired for the evening, my love."

An answering smile grew on her face.

THEY STOOD outside the entrance to her room, no visible signs of Von's rage lingering on the door.

She looked up at him shyly, but not without heat, as he opened it and stepped inside, pulling her in after him.

Keeping her close he shut the door behind them and she felt the tingle of magic as he sealed it.

"To ensure our privacy," he said softly, leaning down to brush a soft kiss against her lips. He stepped away from her and walked over to the side of the room to pour them each a glass of wine.

She eyed the door once more, amused that it appeared to be submerged in water. She reached out a finger to brush against the magical barrier, curious if her hand would pass through the substance easily, and surprised to find it was much thicker and less yielding than it appeared.

"Are you sure that's for privacy or is it to prevent my escape?" she mused as she started toward him.

The promise in his heavy-lidded eyes was enough to wipe the teasing smile from her lips.

He offered her the glass goblet full of ruby liquid sparkling like a jewel under the warm glow of the fire. Her hand only trembled slightly as she took it from him and raised it for a quick sip.

He eyed her over the rim of his own glass before taking a longer sip. Her heart was racing under his scrutiny and she quickly set the glass down on the mantle before the trembling in her hands gave her away.

"What were you thinking about before?" he inquired softly.

"Be-before what?" she stammered, the familiar heat flooding her cheeks.

"Before that diverting bit of magic that caused Timmins to behave like a randy stable boy," came the amused response in her mind.

Never good at playing games, Helena responded honestly, "How beautiful you were."

Straightening, Von studied her in surprise. "How beautiful *I* am?"

She nodded. "You looked so at ease, so..." she searched for the word, "alive. It was irresistible."

Setting his own glass down he reached for her. "You that are the beautiful one. Had I known what I would find when I started on this journey, I would have been in much more of a hurry to get to you."

She felt the ring of truth in her heart. *"Truly?"*

"Oh, Helena," he whispered, closing the space between them, "Haven't you realized yet that you were made for me? Had I asked the Mother herself to create a woman to some set specification of perfection in my mind, I could not have come anywhere close to the gift I have found in you. You take my breath away."

She looked down, stunned by the hunger and passion she saw reflected in his molten gray eyes.

Brushing against her softly, his fingers came to rest below her chin and gently lifted until her eyes met his again.

"You are exquisite," he continued in the same soft rumble. "And it's not just your beauty that speaks to me, although when you smile I find it hard not to lean over and kiss you until you forget how to speak." He paused to brush another soft lingering kiss against her mouth.

"And then there's your strength. Your ability to persevere when so many others could never even find the courage to try. But it's your heart that undoes me," he paused again, his voice earnest, "your ability to find compassion for people you have never met, and whom probably do not deserve it. Your unwavering conviction that people are inherently good, even when they've given you no reason to believe in them."

She stopped him then with a kiss, using her lips to convey the nameless emotion that was bursting within her.

He pulled back slightly waiting for her to open her heavy eyes and look at him.

"All that I am, is yours. Regardless of what it is that brought me to you, I am yours. I belong to you, and I will strive to be worthy of you."

"Shh," she whispered soothingly, breathing kisses against his lips. "If I was made for you, then you were made for me. How could you ever see yourself as unworthy? The Mother doesn't make mistakes."

"I-I have not been a good man," came the faltering confession.

Helena merely shrugged. "Do not waste time regretting who you have had to be, Von. You have done what you needed to do, in order to get to me. Now it is my turn to help you carry the burden. You are mine, and I would have no other."

In that moment, he felt a broken piece of his soul fall back into place. "All my life I have been trying to get home, and I have finally found it, in you."

"Von," she whispered brokenly, tears spilling out of aqua eyes.

"Do not cry, my love. I just needed you to know, so that you would have no doubts about me or my intentions."

"I have never had any doubts," the multitude of voices responded. *"I have always known that you were mine."*

"Yes," he breathed before his lips crashed down. No longer gentle, his kisses were brands, each one claiming her as his.

One of his hands wound itself in her curls while the other began to work its way down her back, fingertips teasing the exposed skin.

Helena shivered and pressed herself against him. Impatient, Helena wished that she could feel his skin against hers.

She could feel the change in Von almost immediately, his lips had stopped their assault on hers. "Von?" she asked as she started to kiss along the stubble covered jaw.

She felt the rumbling in his chest before she heard the laughter. "It would seem that you are in a hurry, darling."

Pulling back to look at him, she realized what had him laughing. Her wish had been the only catalyst her magic needed to take action. Their clothes were now piles on the floor below them. Her eyes rounded, she slowly looked up, taking in every glorious inch of him as she did so.

Von's past was etched in every line of his body. Battle-scarred and heavily muscled legs tapered into narrow hips and waist, while his stomach was bricks of muscle stacked atop each other. The deep V between his hips only emphasizing his swelling maleness.

Helena paled at the sight. He was big. Too big. Needing to look away before she panicked, she raised her eyes to his chest, taking in the tattoo that started in its center and wove its way around his right shoulder and arm. The swirling black tattoo was comprised of words, but she was too flustered to make sense of them.

Shaking fingers traced the pattern. He stood still beneath her touch, the rise and fall of his chest the only movement.

"At, at least I didn't completely destroy them," she muttered, daring a glance up at him. His eyes were hooded, but the humor was still on display in the twist of his lips. Blinking she continued, "I really like that dress."

"So do I, I would have greatly enjoyed the opportunity to take my time removing it."

Helena blushed in embarrassment, staring at her toes. "I-I could put it back on," she offered.

"Maybe next time," he responded, before bending to lift her and toss her over his shoulder.

"Von!" she squealed, now face to face with the well-sculpted globes of his buttocks.

He walked toward the bed, each step making her bounce and her hair brush against the back of his thighs.

His warm hand ran up the back of her leg before coming to rest atop the swell of her own backside. He squeezed gently, before giving it a quick swat and tossing her back onto the bed.

The feeling of weightlessness was short-lived before she bounced gently and was splayed beneath him.

Before she could be embarrassed about her own nudity, Von whispered one word.

"Mine," came the low growl.

"Yes," came her heartfelt response.

Placing a knee between her legs on the bed, Von bent down and pressed kisses along the tops of her thighs, before dipping down to run his tongue from the side of her knee up the inside of her thigh.

Helena's legs pressed together on their own volition. Her mind a tumble of thoughts and emotions she was helpless to process.

"Let me taste you," his voice whispered inside her, as he was busy licking and nibbling up her legs.

Swallowing uncertainly, Helena forced her legs to ease back open.

Calloused hands continued the journey his lips had started, touching and spreading her to his liking. Fully kneeling before her on the bed, Von looked up from where his hands were resting on the tops of her hips and straight into her eyes.

"Beautiful," he whispered reverently before he bent down and pressed his lips beneath her belly button. As he continued to kiss back down to the core of her, Helena's hand found its way to his head although she wasn't sure if it was to push him away or hold him in place.

When he finally ran his finger along her seam, she felt the responding tug of their bond inside of her. His fingers began to work her like an instrument, strumming and rubbing as she moved against him. And then his tongue continued what his fingers had started, licking and sucking until she was bucking below him. Gasping for breath, Helena's head tossed on the bed.

"That's it, my love, let go."

That was all it took. One simple command from the deep voice rough with desire and she came undone. There was a loud crash and then the tinkling of falling glass, as all around them the windows and glasses shattered.

Too lost in what had just happened to notice, Helena rode the waves of her orgasm. When she finally came back to herself, Von was sitting back on his heels between her legs staring intently at the floor.

Turning her head to see what he was looking at, Helena finally noticed the broken glass.

"Not again," she moaned, covering her face with her hands.

Von's hand gently circled her wrists before trying to pry her hands from her face. But Helena resisted.

"Look at me," he ordered softly.

Helena shook her head in embarrassment.

"Now, Mate."

She splayed her fingers and looked up at him with bemused eyes.

"Perhaps I should have sealed the entire room?" he murmured.

At that, her shoulders shook with laughter, and she leaned up to wrap her arms around him.

Bringing his mouth to hers, he kissed her gently once, twice. "You are perfect, Helena."

"But I have no control," she pouted.

"I have every intention of ensuring you lose control as often as possible."

"We're going to go through a lot of windows."

"It's a good thing you can use magic to put them back together."

Seeing the gears shift in her mind as she sat up to attempt it, his arm snaked around her and pulled her back to him. "Oh no, you don't. We are in the middle of something or did you already forget?"

Looking over her shoulder she couldn't help but appreciate the sight of Von spread out on her bed.

"I didn't forget," came the soft reply.

"Are you nervous?" he asked gently, fingers running up and down her back soothingly.

Helena shook her head quickly, causing her curls to dance down her back, but he felt the flickers of her nerves as though they were his own.

"What are you afraid of?" he asked, sitting up to better cradle her body against his.

"You're just so large," came the mortified whisper as her eyes dropped to his lap before averting quickly.

He tried not to, he really did, but he laughed.

Twisting in his arms to look at him, her jaw dropped. "That's funny to you?"

"Helena," he gasped, as she scooted, trying to put distance between them. His arms tightened in response, keeping her against him. "Helena, I'm sorry, I didn't mean to laugh. It's just, you have nothing to fear. I promise. By the time we're done you're going to be thankful I'm built exactly as I am."

She raised a brow in disbelief.

"Aren't you the one that said the Mother doesn't make mistakes?"

"I think she may have gotten a little too ambitious when she was working on you," Helena muttered sullenly.

Chuckling Von pressed a kiss to her shoulder. Relenting, Helena laid back down beside him, allowing her own hands to explore the ridges of his body.

"Will you tell me what this means one day," she asked as her fingers explored the whirls of his tattoo.

"Yes, but not now," with that, his lips descended on hers again. It took only moments for the fire to rekindle within her.

Shifting, Von moved so that he was between her legs again. As he felt her stiffen, he whispered, "Look at me."

As she did, he ran his length down her center, twisting his hips to circle her opening. Helena's eyes widened before closing.

"Look at me," he rasped, continuing to tease her entrance.

Helena struggled to keep her eyes open and on him as he began to slowly press into her.

There was no pain, only pleasure, as he filled her. Helena could feel their hearts beating in time, each breath a ragged gasp until he filled her completely. He stayed there, allowing her to get used to the feeling of him within her. Once she began squirming below him, he allowed himself to flex against her.

"Oh," she gasped, eyes rolling back in her head.

She felt his hand run down her chest, pausing to pluck at the hard bud of her nipple, before moving back down to rest on her hip.

"Are you still nervous, Mira?" the deep growl asked.

She could feel that he was at the edge of his control, desperate to make sure she was comfortable before going further.

"More," she purred, arching up into him.

She heard his own answering moan before he pulled back and slid back in.

"Yes," she cried, hands reaching for his as his thrusts picked up speed.

"Helena," he growled.

Iridescent eyes met molten gray, hearts beating in time with each thrust.

Mine. Neither was sure who had uttered the declaration, but with those words, Von buried himself inside her, body shaking with the force of his release, while she wrapped herself around him as she came apart.

He shifted to lay beside her, and she whimpered in protest at the loss. He brushed a soft kiss against her forehead and pulled her close so that her head was resting on his chest.

The soft thundering of his heart became a lullaby that lured her to sleep, but before she drifted off, she felt him stir beneath her.

"What's the matter?" she asked sleepily.

"I was just thinking it was probably a good thing we didn't fix the windows."

CHAPTER 11

*G*illian paced restlessly across the floor of her opulent suite; her fingers tapping nervously against her lips as her mind raced. Now that the pair were mated it was time for her to put her plans into motion. It would have been a fool's errand to try to do anything to stop what fate had already decreed to be, so there were no moves she could have made prior to now. Well, other than preparing the ground for the trap she would spring through her friendship with the new Kiri.

Gillian sighed, still lost to the thoughts that tumbled about her mind. It was a shame she actually liked the girl, naïve though she was. Too bad she would stop—could stop—at nothing to destroy her and that blood traitor she was mated to.

As she continued to walk back and forth in front of the massive fireplace, she no longer heard the crackling of the flames. In fact, she was not aware of anything until the mirror hanging on the wall began to fog.

She stopped suddenly, head spinning to look at the swirling mist replacing the glass. Fear and shock at war for dominance within her. The mirror was ancient, its frame a combination of twisting metal and magic. The words of power carved into the metal hidden in the flowing vines and flowers that the metal was shaped into.

Gillian's heart stuttered in her chest, before she dropped to her knees in front of the mirror, eyes cast to the floor in front of her.

"Mistress," she said hoarsely.

"It is time," came the disembodied voice through the mirror.

"Yes, Mistress."

"You know what will happen if you fail me. The impostor cannot be allowed to remain on my throne." The voice wrapped itself around her in an icy caress, each word scraping against her skin like talons; a sharp and deadly tease. Gillian felt her skin break out into gooseflesh as the waves of power rippled around her.

"Of course, Mistress. It will be done."

"You have until the new moon rises," with that the flood of power that had encircled her ebbed. Gillian risked a glance up at the mirror to see that the swirling mist was fading back into her reflection.

Seeing herself again in the mirror she took in her appearance: pupils so wide they almost swallowed the green of her irises, skin bleached of all color, teeth biting down into her colorless lip. Her heart continued to race as she tried to recover from the unexpected visit.

Gillian took a shuddering breath before whispering, "Yes, Mother."

HELENA TILTED her face up to the sky, letting the warm rays of light kiss her skin. Smiling she knelt in the grass, surrounded by the roses and jasmine in bloom beside her. After days, nay weeks, of endless preparation she finally found herself with nothing to claim her time.

Von had left their bed that morning with a whispered brush of his lips against hers and a promise to see her soon. She could still feel the throb of their bond within her, diminished slightly due to their distance, but strong nonetheless. Her own pool of magic seemed to ripple in answer to its steady thrum.

She flushed in pleasure remembering how he had roused her in the middle of the night, his phantom hands exploring her body while his lips worked their way over the peaks of her breasts. He had grinned up at her wolfishly in the moonlight before using his body to keep the promise his magic had made upon her sleep-slackened limbs. She had lost track of the number of times his name broke from her lips as she shattered and clenched around him.

She shook her head quickly before those kinds of thoughts could get her in any more awkward situations. It was bad enough dealing with Alina's knowing grin when she had finally eased herself out of the bed late that morning noting that the shattered glass had all been repaired; and she had yet to run into any of her Circle, sparing her the need to answer for her loss of control at the celebration the night before.

Cringing slightly, she made herself take in the peaceful beauty of the garden. That reckoning would come soon enough, no need to borrow trouble imagining it now. Instead, she wanted to take the time to explore the garden with her heightened senses. She had been careful to keep herself in the magic dampened state ever since her trial, especially when wandering throughout the Palace. No one else seemed to glow with the force of a thousand candles when using their gifts and she was tired of being the cause of stares and whispers.

Glancing around quickly to make sure she was alone, she called to her magic. It came to her like a sigh, the internal well gradually emptying as it was released.

Standing slowly, Helena drank in the changes. Each enhanced sense was in perfect harmony as the garden came to life around her. It was as if time had paused so that she was able to view each moment as it occurred. Each blade of emerald grass shifting in the jasmine-scented breeze, each rustle of the leaves dancing above her and each beat of wings a gentle strum as the bees floated from petal to trembling petal.

The colors were overwhelming in their intensity. The reds, pinks, and purples more vivid and real than any she had ever seen, almost as if she had been viewing the world from muted lenses, never truly understanding what depth and variations existed.

The scents were intoxicating. Closing her eyes, Helena breathed in deeply. She was able to taste the sun and dew-covered petals in the air, while the aroma of wet earth was vying with the fragrant roses for

MEG ANNE

attention. It was all so alive, so much more than her mortal senses had ever been able to comprehend before.

Iridescent eyes caught a slight movement to her right. Spinning to face it, Helena's hand thrust out to the nearby tree to hold her steady. The force of impact caught her off-guard and the tree pulsed once as it came into contact with the full potency of her magic. Between one breath and the next, the tree groaned as it began to expand and grow; its roots snaking deeper into the damp earth while its flowers exploded to life in its branches.

"There you are!" Darrin called in surprise as a bevy of leaves rained down upon him. Noting the riotous curls and swirling depths of her eyes, his hands moved to the sword at his side and he stepped toward her carefully, each snap of grass causing her to flinch.

Realizing that he was reacting to her appearance as if it were a threat, she willed her magic back into the recesses of the pool. Blinking once, twice, she looked up at him with aqua eyes and smiled sheepishly.

"Good morning, Darrin."

Shoulders easing, he moved his hands from his sword and offered her a lopsided smile.

"Timmins sent me to fetch you. Actually, he said, 'Now that the Circle is formed the time is ripe for making plans.'" Darrin mimicked Timmins voice before smiling conspiratorially.

Helena laughed despite herself, Timmins certainly had a tendency to adopt the lilting tone when he was in full lecture mode, and she could only wonder how much more Timmins had actually said before sending Darrin on his way to find her.

"Not even a day to rest before putting us to work, how very like him," she murmured as she stepped away from the tree to stand beside him.

He gestured to the path ahead indicating that he would follow.

As she stepped toward the path she stole a final glance at the now massive tree in full bloom about three months too early. Worrying her lip between her teeth, she turned back to Darrin.

Matching his steps to hers he asked, "Are you still planning to venture outside of the Capital?"

Helena nodded as she said, "I think it is time to soothe the hurts of the past, don't you?"

Darrin shrugged uncomfortably and spoke slowly, choosing his words with care, "I think that it seems rather soon for you to leave the safety of Elysia, especially since you are still testing the limits of your magic."

"Isn't that what you are for?" she teased.

Wary green eyes met hers. "You know that I would lay down my life to protect yours, Helena. I just know that once we leave these borders, we are welcoming all sorts of new threats that we might be ill-prepared to face. At least without proper planning."

"We're taking a trip to visit my Mate's family and lands, not going on some warring expedition, but your caution is noted Shield. We will make sure that when we leave for the journey we are prepared for all possibilities."

Helena could appreciate his concerns, even as she felt they were unnecessary. While she may be Kiri, she was very much still learning what that meant while he was the one who had been training with the Rasmiri for half his life. More than that, as the Shield it was in his nature to search for potential dangers lurking in every shadow.

The pair continued their way into the Palace. As with many of the common spaces between wings, the floors were polished to a high shine, the wood a glossy mahogany, while the walls were a soft buttery gold. Paintings of all shapes and sizes lined the walls. Helena was unsure who the artists were, but each one told the story of her people. She wished she had more time to stop and study them, but they continued moving swiftly up the spiraling staircase.

As they climbed, Helena noted the lights twinkling above them, not ensconced in any way, but rather floating and moving around freely beneath the massive beams visible in the high ceiling. It was so picturesque here, each window chosen to best reveal Elysia's beauty. She caught glimpses of towering mountains in the distance and shivered with anticipation. Soon she would be traveling through them.

Her life to this point had been sheltered, and she had not traveled much farther than the small town closest to her and Miriam's cottage. A part of her had always hungered for adventure, and now she was in a position to seek it at will. Who knew what waited for her out beyond the snow-capped peaks in the distance? A different kind of chill worked its way down her spine at the thought, and she spared a glance at Darrin. Perhaps she should better heed his warnings.

A small flutter of concern tugged at her through the bond. Helena worked to shake off the lingering sense of disquiet as they reached the threshold of the meeting room. The rest of the Circle were already waiting for them inside; each man standing behind their usual seats around the table. This was Von's first time officially sitting in with them, and she couldn't help the smile that bloomed across her face when she saw him leaning against the mantle.

As usual, his legs were wrapped in his tight leathers; his shirt black and loose, the sleeves rolled up to showcase strong forearms lightly dusted with hair. She admired him, and the way the leather showcased his assets, discreetly for a moment before taking the final step into the room.

His eyes caught her as soon as she appeared in the doorway, a brow raised in silent question.

"All is well," she assured him with a soft smile.

He nodded, returning her smile, and moved to sit beside her as she lowered herself into the seat Kragen pulled out for her. She beamed up at him in thanks before looking expectantly at Timmins.

His voice was warm as he greeted her, "You are glowing this afternoon, Kiri."

She felt rather than saw the smug smile spread across Von's face at Timmins' declaration.

"I'll have you know this glow is the result of me playing with my magic in the gardens," she informed him haughtily.

"Is that what you're telling yourself?" he purred seductively in reply.

Helena stole a glance at him from the corner of her eye, noting that he was staring at Timmins, a small smile playing about his lips.

"That's kind of you to say, I hope you enjoyed the evening's festivities as well."

A slight blush stained Timmins cheeks, as both Kragen and Joquil hid their smiles behind gloved hands. Darrin's sudden coughing sounded suspiciously like laughter, yet no one made any comment.

"Yes, well..." Timmins looked around the table without making eye contact with any of them.

"It was certainly unforgettable," Joquil inserted smoothly.

"Yes," Timmins agreed with relief, "unforgettable."

Helena bit back her own smile. "How wonderful to hear."

Poor, proper Timmins would never hear the end of this, but at least she had turned the topic away from herself.

He fumbled with some papers in front of him before beginning again. "Now, as I see it, with all of the ceremonies and the trial behind us, it is time to shift our attention to the matters of the realm. There have been many --"

Helena cut in, "While I agree that the time for history and politics can no longer be avoided, I prefer to take a more direct path. We will be journeying to Daejara. It is time for us to look to the future and rebuild our alliance with the people we have so grossly neglected."

She felt Von stiffen beside her as the other men traded glances around the table.

"Don't you think it would be more prudent, Kiri, to send someone else on your behalf to start such negotiation?" Timmins murmured carefully.

"Obviously not or that's what I would have suggested," she said mildly.

Von's approval stroked along the length of their bond, yet he remained silent.

"Five hundred years is a long time to go without any sort of communication and simply appear on their doorstep," Darrin attempted.

"Who said anything about simply appearing?" she asked sparing him a glance. "We will notify Daejara's emissaries of our intentions and await our formal invitation from its court. I cannot imagine it will be long in coming, seeing as how their eldest son is now my Mate."

Von let out a humorless bark of laughter. "You flatter me by thinking that my parents are that concerned with my well-being, Kiri. They have all but disowned me due to my years 'running around bloodying my blade for the highest paying arsehole'."

Beneath the mocking words, Helena could feel the pain that admission still caused him; a wound that had never fully healed.

"Then perhaps it is time for them to become reacquainted with their son and his new Mate," snapped the voice-of-many, eyes flashing like diamonds with her ire.

Von studied her carefully from his sprawling position in the chair. His lips raised in wry amusement.

"Perhaps so, Kiri."

She turned her attention back to the other four men. "This is not open for negotiation. The people of Daejara have been left to suffer and fend for themselves for the last five hundred years. There has been no news, no trade, no celebration of the Mother or her gifts in all that time. These people, who have done nothing but have the misfortune to be born on the wrong side of an invisible line, are paying for the mistakes of rulers long since dead. That is unacceptable, and it ends now.

"I do not care how we make it happen," she continued, "but know that this *will* happen. So, let us make the plans that we need to make in order to best prepare ourselves for what we will find when we cross the border. While I am stubborn enough to insist on this meeting, I am not so ignorant as to believe we will be welcomed with open arms by all that we come across."

Kragen was openly smiling at her from his spot at the table. Gone was the girl who had apologized for each question she raised or felt she must ask permission before speaking. In her place sat a woman who was willing to make a stand for what she believed in. Here was a woman he was proud to serve.

Over the years the Mother's power had started to diminish within the ruling families. As the years passed it became more and more diluted in the women who ruled. Few had even passed the trial of the Damaskiri to become crowned true Kiris. Of those, the vast majority had focused on their own comforts rather than on the task of caring for their people. The selfishness and corruption had begun to spread through the courts and their people; a faceless enemy that could not be slain.

Joquil's golden eyes sparkled curiously and he cleared his throat before speaking. "As you wish, Kiri. Perhaps it would be advantageous for Von's men to train the Rasmiri that will come with us? They are familiar with the lands, and opponents, we might find there."

Von shifted in his seat, angling forward as he said, "They are already preparing to do so."

Kragen murmured his approval.

"We will need to plan for more than just ourselves and our guards. I would like to bring some goods we can offer both as gifts and for trade. Perhaps we can see if any merchants or tradesmen would like to accompany us?"

Darrin spoke first. "It is a good idea, but we will need to make sure they are aware of the risks. Let's limit the number we bring with us on this first visit, at least until we can be better assured of our reception."

"Agreed," Helena said with a smile. With that matter of business concluded, at least in her mind, she looked back to her Advisor.

"I will write the formal request and send it this afternoon, Kiri. Once we hear back, we can begin preparations to leave as soon as possible."

"Very well, is that all for now Timmins?" she asked hopefully.

He smiled back indulgently. "We have many nights of travel ahead of us, I suppose my stories can wait for the campfire."

Helena beamed at him.

Chuckling, the men rose to their feet and made their way for the door.

Von reached for her hand as she stood, pulling her toward him.

"I've missed you this morning, Mate."

"Already?" she inquired blandly, trying to hide the way her heart sped up at his declaration.

She felt his amusement at her teasing, but he was solemn as he replied, "Running drills with a bunch of men pales greatly in comparison to waking up next to you."

"Waking up without you did make last night feel a bit like a dream," she admitted shyly.

"I'm sorry I had to leave you," he murmured as he pressed a soft kiss to her waiting lips.

She stepped back with a groan, knowing they didn't have time to finish anything that they started right now.

He chuckled at the distance between them and wove his fingers through hers instead.

"Thank you, for what you are doing for my brother, and for me," he said softly.

Helena tilted her head inquisitively. "I told you he would have a healer, even if it meant I had to go myself."

"Yes, I know, but oftentimes people make promises they have no intentions of keeping."

Helena raised an affronted brow. "Do I strike you as one of those people?"

Von shook his head. "No, you mistake me. I simply meant that I have not had someone I could rely on, outside of my men, in a very long time."

Helena shrugged, trying to find something in the room to focus on instead of the uncomfortable weight settling in her chest at the confession. It was easy to forget that his past was not filled with gentle memories.

He brushed a lingering kiss against her knuckles. "I'm sorry, *Mira*, I did not intend to distress you, merely thank you for your kindness."

She shrugged again, struggling to find her words.

His hand squeezed hers offering silent comfort.

After a moment, she looked back up at him. "Well don't thank me just yet, we don't even know if I'll be able to help your brother, and we have no idea what other events this will set in motion."

"The bravery is not in knowing the outcome, but in being unafraid to try anyway."

To be called brave by this man, this warrior, who had fought so hard and for so long to try to save his people... the emotions overwhelmed her. Instead of trying to reply, she raised trembling fingers to caress his cheek.

Twisting his head, he pressed a tender kiss into the palm of her hand.

Eyes closing at the contact, she savored the feel of his lips against her skin. As her hand lowered, her fingers curled into a loose fist.

"I think I'll save that for later."

His lips quirked in amusement. *"And why's that?"*

"Just to remember what it feels like to have you eating out of the palm of my hand."

Von let out a sharp yelp of laughter: the deep rumbling doing much to ease the ache she had felt at his earlier words. Laughter was the least she could offer to the man who had already brought her such joy. His past may not have many sweet memories, but she would ensure that their future together would be full of them.

CHAPTER 12

*A*s promised Timmins sent the letter to Daejara's court that afternoon. The reply was slow in coming and the Circle was getting restless. In an effort to keep their minds off of the response, Von had suggested that it was time for Helena to get to know his men, especially since they would be traveling together soon.

That was why, two days later, Helena found herself walking out to their training yard, Kragen and Darrin trailing a little ways behind her.

Von had left their room early again this morning to train with his band of mercenaries. Watching the way the men trained together, it was clear that this was more than a group of men that were together for convenience or coin. These were men that had been tested before; that knew how to fight as a single unit. There was brotherhood here, among those others labeled as a bunch of selfish bastards.

Her eyes scanned the yard, quickly dismissing the faces until she pinpointed Von in the center of a ring. Awareness rippled through her at the sight of his shirtless body quietly prowling around his opponent. Sweat was beading and running down his chest and back, creating a path her fingers itched to follow. His dark hair was tied back in a knot, but strands had fallen from it and were sticking to his forehead and neck.

The circling men had no weapons, save the fists that were raised in front of them. Helena eyed his opponent warily. She had seen the man before, oftentimes chatting animatedly with Von, but she did not know his name.

His skin was sun-kissed and his hair a fiery red. It was cut close along the sides but ran in a long braid from his forehead to mid-back. She could not get a good look at his face from her vantage point behind the other men that were loosely surrounding them as they cried out encouragements or curses—depending on who landed a blow.

The red-headed warrior was as massive as Kragen, a mountain of a man with muscles rippling beneath sweat-soaked skin and a tattoo identical to Von's twisting around his chest and arm.

Swallowing nervously, Helena continued making her way toward her mate. She could feel him through the pulsing of their bond but did not reach out with those mental tendrils to offer her own support, afraid to distract him with her presence. She chose instead to stand toward the back of the group of men and watch while she willed her nerves to calm.

The men continued to stalk around each other, every now and then throwing a punch, but they were merely a distraction. The real battle was waging in their eyes, neither man looking away from the other as they scanned for any opening or sign of weakness.

Helena noted the moment that it happened, Von's expression did not change, but his eyes seemed to clear and then sharpen as he flew with inhuman speed at the man in front of him. He landed a series of swift blows and kicks to his sides and neck before swooping low with his leg to knock the giant man to the ground.

The man landed with a resounding thud and laid on his back in the dirt gasping for air.

"You little shit," he growled once he had caught his breath.

Von simply stared down at him with his cocky smirk, legs splayed and hands on his hips.

The men that had gathered to watch them jeered and scattered, but not before many passed coin and insults to each other.

"What are you waiting for? Help me up, fucker," the man growled again.

Laughing, Von reached down offering him a hand. Grasping him by the forearm, Von lifted him easily back to a standing position.

Helena's own lips twitched with amusement as she watched the man grumble and wipe at the dust now coating his back and legs.

Von saw her then, his eyes softening and his smile growing. A gentle breeze rustled the curls hanging down her back and his phantom fingers caressed down her cheek by way of greeting.

Turning his head to see what had caught Von's attention, Helena felt the full force of his gaze before she turned her eyes to meet Von's rival. There was a wicked gleam in his eyes as he sauntered his way over to where she was standing.

The weight of the icy blue gaze kept Helena pinned in place. She felt Kragen and Darrin shift behind her.

Starting at his temple and slashing down to his cheekbone there was a jagged and puckering scar. The scar itself was a pale pink, but the skin around it still an angry red. His sharp nose was crooked from being broken multiple times and his jaw covered by a thick beard, a few shades darker than his hair.

He would have been frightening if it wasn't for the wide grin spread across his face.

"Was there not a healer available to help him with his injuries either?"

She could hear laughter in his amused reply, *"The healers have all offered to help reset and minimize the injuries, but Ronan won't allow it. He feels they are a testament to his foes' inability to kill him."*

"Not his own prowess?"

Von smirked. *"Oh, I'm sure that's the largest part of it."*

"Kiri," Ronan said with a warm smile as he reached for her hand, "I've heard that you have lifted the ban on Daejara."

Helena's hand was lost in his much larger one, the pads of his fingers rough with callouses. She felt her own smile grow. "You've heard correctly."

"I guess that means we'll let Timmins keep his post," Darrin muttered softly enough for only her and Kragen to hear. Kragen's answering laughter was a quiet rumble.

"I could serve you for that alone, but for the happiness that you have brought my brother, I will love you for the rest of my life." He tipped his head and pressed a rough kiss to the back of her hand.

Helena blushed and Von let out a low snarl. "Step away from my mate you silver-tongued sack of shit, or I'll have to knock you on your ass again."

Ronan winked at Helena, but stepped back and turned to address Von, "So territorial, Brother. You must not be assured of your performance in the bedroom if you're worried about something as innocent as a kiss."

Von's eyes flashed and Helena could have sworn she recognized the iridescent shimmer of her own power reflected in his gray eyes. Before she could be certain, it was gone.

Von huffed out a breath. "You have a habit of taking things that aren't yours."

Helena chuckled at the aggrieved tone of his voice. Stepping beside him she placed a sweet kiss on his dirty cheek. "Lucky for you I am not so easily swayed, Mate."

His eyes smoldered as he looked down at her. "That I am."

Cheeks pink now for another reason, Helena changed the subject and asked in a slightly breathy voice, "Brothers?"

"Brothers of the Blade," Ronan offered, at the same time Von said, "Brother of my soul."

"In that case, I must insist you call me Helena."

Something in those ice blue eyes shifted; warmed. "You do me a great honor, Kiri."

She raised a sculpted brow.

"Helena," he amended with a laugh.

She shrugged. "My Mate's family is my family, and I don't believe in such formality amongst friends anyway." Leaning closer, she lowered her voice to a conspiratorial whisper, "Unless, of course, I want to put a certain smart-assed Rasmirin in his place."

"I heard that," Darrin called dryly.

"I meant for you to," Helena replied in a voice dripping with sugary sweetness.

"Does that also apply to certain heartless black-haired bastards?" Kragen asked, eyes crinkled in delight.

Helena nodded. "Most definitely."

"If you want to talk about titles, Mate, we can start with the ones you've given me when you're moaning in our bed," he purred down the bond.

Helena's eyes widened and her blush bloomed a fierce red across her cheeks.

Looking between Von and Helena, Ronan let out a booming laugh that was more of a roar. "Oh, this is going to be fun."

THE GROUP WAS SEATED in the shade of a nearby tree, the morning giving way to the heat of the afternoon. Kragen and Ronan had each spent a few moments assessing each other before they launched into a verbal contest to determine which of them was the bigger badass.

Helena felt like she could easily declare a winner, but had a feeling neither would be willing to accept her choice.

"I appreciate the vote of confidence," Von's voice rumbled.

Helena offered him a small smile. *"I saw how easily you bested him this morning."*

"Neither of us were using weapons or our magic—"

Her mental voice interrupted his. *"Exactly."*

She felt the eye-roll in her mind. *"Ronan is my second in command for a reason, love."*

"Exactly," she repeated for emphasis. *"A commander would never have the respect or loyalty of such a strong warrior unless his own skills were equal or above his men."*

Von shook his head in exasperation, but she could feel the pride her words of belief had caused to radiate out of him.

"Ronan?" Helena asked suddenly.

Four sets of male eyes all turned to look at her. It was a conscious effort not to let herself shrink under the intensity of their combined gaze.

"Yes Kir-Helena?" he asked with a raise of his brow.

"Do you think you could train me?"

The other three men bristled.

"You want *me* to train you?" he asked softly.

Helena nodded. "If it wouldn't be too much trouble."

"Do you mind if I ask why, my lady?"

"Why you instead of one of these lot?" Helena gestured to the disgruntled males around her.

Ronan dipped his head in acknowledgment.

"I don't trust them to—" she stopped as the men sputtered in affronted male pride. Holding up a hand she rolled her eyes, "Let me finish, you bunch of babies. I don't trust the three of them to push me as hard as I would need to be pushed to really learn. I think all three of them would struggle with the idea of putting me in a situation where I might get hurt."

"And I think I would be too hesitant to do anything that might hurt you," she added for Von alone.

He squeezed her hand in answer.

"Hellion," Darrin admonished. "That is what I am for. I am here to protect you, there is no reason you would need to learn to fight."

"But what if something happens to you? What if I am ever in a situation where I am cut off from all of you, would you really want me so handicapped that I could not defend myself?"

"You have your magic," he protested.

"Magic that I can barely control, who knows what would happen?" Her words came faster and were more clearly laced with her growing panic as she continued her list, "Would I be able to even access it in a moment of fear? Or what if I get spent; use too much too fast and cannot withstand a prolonged assault? Or what if—"

It was her turn to be cut-off. "She is right," Von said quietly at her side.

"She should have every possible tool at her disposal, even if we never anticipate a need for her to use it," Kragen agreed.

"It would be my honor to help train you, Helena," Ronan said seriously. "But I think that you should take turns training with all of us.

We have different fighting styles, different strengths. If you really want to have every available tool, then you would benefit from learning all styles. As you said, you never know when a certain maneuver will come in handy."

"I promise not to take it easy on you," Darrin muttered bitterly.

Helena stuck her tongue out in response.

"We will start in the morning. You will come down before the other men begin their drills."

"At least that means I will be waking up with you, instead of to an empty bed."

"Darling, you have no idea what you've just gotten yourself into."

Von at least had the decency to laugh only in her mind.

CHAPTER 13

*T*raining the next morning was a misery. She had known that it would be since the heaviest weapon she'd ever held was a garden rake. Even so, she had thought she was mentally prepared for what to expect, but she had not anticipated the bone-deep weariness that she now felt. Helena's muscles were protesting even as she sat in the steaming hot water.

Ronan had been relentless, he warned her when they began that morning that he was not going to speak to her as his friend or ruler; she was just another recruit and he was now her commander.

He slid his right foot back into the crouching stance he and Von had used in the sparring ring the day before. Motioning for her to imitate him, he had taken one look at her stance and sent her to run laps around the field. After that he had her carry his armor across the field, all the while lifting it up over her head before setting it down to pick it up and do it again.

Through it all, she hadn't complained, just panted and asked if she might stop for a moment to drink some water. She felt Ronan's approval even though he never said anything kind to her. Just continued to push her and complain about her overall lack of strength.

When she'd mistakenly asked when she might train with a weapon or learn some of the movements she had seen the others work through he had laughed at her.

"Little girl, when you are strong enough to hold a weapon correctly, without shaking or dropping it, I will let you train with one. Until then, build up your strength and stamina, now run!"

Even now, hours later soaking in the tub with the oils Tanya had promised would help ease the ache of her muscles, Helena wasn't sure where the certainty had come from that she needed to train.

Seeing the men yesterday, it was as if something that had been at the edge of her vision finally came into focus. Instinct had driven her to ask Ronan to train her, but she knew that it was her magic that had put the idea in her mind. If only she understood why.

"How are you feeling, my love," Von asked softly as he leaned against the doorway, arms folded across his chest.

She gave him a dirty look and slid deeper into the water.

"That well, huh?" he asked kindly, before walking over to her.

He dropped to his knees slowly, grabbing a cloth and some soap before turning that gray gaze upon her.

Helena just watched him above the rim of the water, heart beginning to race at the sight of him fully clothed and on his knees beside her, while she was laying there completely exposed under the water.

As if he could sense her reaction—which of course, he could, she realized—Von smiled softly and shook his head.

"I'm not here for that, not right now anyway." His teeth flashed as he gave her a feral grin. "I don't want to push your muscles any further than they already have been."

He motioned for her to sit forward, and moaning in protest she shifted until her back was facing him. She could feel the tingle of his magic as he ran the now soapy cloth in gentle circles along her back. With each swipe, she could feel some of the pain ease away.

She groaned her thanks and moved to provide him with more access.

Once he was done with the cloth, he swept the wet strands of hair over her shoulder and began to gently rub and press into the muscles of her back and shoulders. His fingers working to help release the tension.

Helena winced as he reached a particularly tight knot between her shoulders, and then whimpered in relief as his skilled hands worked it out.

"How are you feeling now, *Mira*?" he asked softly.

She shifted again in the tub, surprised and relieved to note that the movement barely caused any ache.

Her aqua eyes were thankful when they met his.

Reaching down he scooped her into his arms, disregarding the water that was sloshing onto his clothes, and carried her into their bedroom.

The curtains were closed cutting off the morning sun, and the few candles that were lit guttered out softly as they walked past.

Laying her against the pillows, he crawled in beside her and pulled her back to his chest, curling himself around her.

He pressed a gentle kiss to her forehead. "Rest, *Mira*. I will stay here with you."

"But it's the middle of the morning," she started before a large yawn took over.

Chuckling he snuggled her closer. "Rest now, so that I can reenact all those wonderful things that had your cheeks so pink when I knelt beside you."

Smiling to herself, Helena closed her eyes and wondered how anyone could think Von was heartless.

"Because I was until I found you," he replied down their bond, only to realize she was already asleep.

VON PROPPED himself up on an elbow and watched her sleep. As deep breaths caused her chest to rise and fall softly, he let his fingers trace lazy patterns down her arm, enjoying the feel of her soft skin.

There was no doubt that knowing her had already changed him in numerous and inexplicable ways. He had felt it instantly that first night during the ceremony when their eyes met. There was a moment when everything in him had gone silent and dim before bursting back into sharp focus. As though his soul had recognized itself in hers and came out of hiding to say: *I've been waiting for you. I am here.*

Ever since then, every interaction had only sharpened that awareness. It had disturbed him at first, that connection. It countered every instinct the years of strategy and battle had drilled into him; pulled him toward her light and out of the darkness he'd resided in these past years. He had been helpless to resist it. So, he'd surrendered, to her. To his mate.

He shook his head ruefully, still awed that the Mother saw fit to bless his tarnished soul with such a rare gift. He had been driven for so long with only one goal in mind: punish the self-righteous nobles who saw fit to let thousands of innocents suffer and die. Let their bowels turn to water and their hearts race in fear when they were called to answer for their cruel disregard.

He had been single-minded in that pursuit, willing to sacrifice anything, including himself if it meant that he could save the people he loved. It was that setting aside of pride that brought him to her, he realized. His willingness to beg, if need be, to open the border and get a healer to his brother.

He felt a thousand years old as he brought his eyes back to her beautiful face; the weight of all that death sitting heavy inside him, even while her presence within him continued to soothe the jagged and broken edges he had lived with for so long.

She looked so innocent, so gentle, in her sleep, but he had felt her in those moments when her magic took over. The way that her wrath had been a twin to his own. She was a warrior, every bit as much as he was, although she hadn't realized it yet, or at least not consciously.

A knock sounded gently on the door, startling Von from his thoughts and giving him just enough time to hastily wrap a blanket around his mate before it opened a crack; the warm light of the hallway spilling in behind it.

Alina kept her eyes down as she poked her head in.

"What is it?" Von asked, trying to keep his voice low so as not to wake the woman in his arms.

"There has been news, my lord, from Daejara. The Circle is meeting in the Chambers," she replied, equally as soft.

Von looked to Helena, noting her mouth which had fallen open as she sank deeper into sleep.

"You are going to have to tell them to wait. While I cannot dispute the importance of the conversation they would like to have, their Kiri needs to rest. I do not want to wake her unless I have to."

He noted the small smile playing on Alina's lips as she nodded her head. "Very well, sir. I will inform them that she will be down once she has woken."

With that, she stepped back and closed the door with a whisper of a click. The golden light went with her, leaving the two of them wrapped in shadows.

HELENA WOKE WITH A SIGH, her body feeling heavy and warm. She stretched and rolled toward the center of the bed, meeting little resistance from the limbs that had been quaking with exhaustion before her bath.

Von's scent still lingered on the pillows and she buried her face to drink it in.

As she became more coherent, she sensed a delicate fluttering within the boundaries of her mind. As she focused on the sensation of that flickering presence it came closer, as though it had been politely waiting for her attention before disturbing her.

She reached out a mental hand toward it, beckoning it closer. As it floated to the center of her mind, she felt it expand until it finally released the warm sensual voice she knew so well. The voice resonating in her mind was a mere echo, a diluted version of the deep growl she was used to hearing speak in her mind.

"I hope that you slept well, my love, and that you are feeling better. Word has arrived from Daejara; we will be waiting for you in the

Chamber. There is no need to rush, we will be ready whenever you are."

Surprise warred with delight over the discovery. Yet another facet of the bond had been uncovered. She was curious how he thought to try that bit of magic and how he had achieved that little thought bubble that waited for her so patiently. She sent a gentle tug on the bond to let him know that she was awake.

In response, he sent her what felt like a smile, its warmth causing little ripples of pleasure along their mating bond.

The combination of his voice and presence in her mind, along with his scent surrounding her, gave her a sweet ache low in her belly.

"Missing me already, darling?" came the purr.

She sent him an image of her stretching on the bed.

"Wicked girl," he growled. *"Teasing me so shamelessly when you know I'm surrounded by a bunch of men. What will they say if they notice my reaction to those lovely curves?"*

She giggled at the thought of Timmins or Joquil noticing the evidence of his arousal and took pity on him.

"Thank you for letting me sleep," she replied sweetly.

"Of course, Mira. You needed the rest."

"Will you let the others know that I am on my way and will be there shortly?"

"Already done."

She stood with a small grin, feeling more content than she had since her mother passed away. Her life had become so small before coming to the capital. There was no surprise and very little excitement; just the simple pleasure found in the quiet moments in her garden or sitting before the fire, curled up with a book she had read countless times before.

There had been happiness in that, certainly, but not this sense of completion and purpose. She hadn't realized how lonely she had been, living on her own. She had laughter again, now that she had found her new family, for that's what the Circle had become to her.

Kragen and Darrin were like older brothers, as likely to tease her as to protect her. Timmins the father, providing both caution and comfort for all of them as needed, while Joquil was an uncle that was often away on grand adventures and who would come visit to share stories of the wonders he had witnessed. At least, that's what she assumed they were like, she had never had any of those things before.

And then there was Von...

I'll never be alone again, she thought. Heart full to bursting, Helena dressed quickly, throwing on a simple dress of light purple and braiding her hair.

Her smile was radiant as she stepped swiftly out of the room and toward the men that had become so dear to her.

CHAPTER 14

*R*ounding the corner, Helena saw Gillian standing close to Darrin. Their voices were hushed, so she could not hear what they were saying, but Gillian had her hand resting on his chest and they were both laughing as she stepped closer.

Smiling tentatively, as she did not want to intrude, she offered a small wave before stepping around them.

"Oh, Helena," Gillian called behind her.

Turning toward the pair, Helena raised a quizzical brow.

"We were just discussing the court's impending trip to Daejara. How exciting! You must let me come with you so that you're not bored to death by all those dreary men."

"Being surrounded by a bunch of men sounds exactly like your dream scenario, Gillian dear," Helena replied mildly.

Gillian beamed. "Exactly, so it would be absolutely cold-hearted of you to deny me such a glorious opportunity. Just imagine the potential for wandering off and coming across some delightful male while he's bathing in a stream..." she trailed off and let her eyes wander up and down Darrian as though sizing him up.

"Easy, girl, that one's off limits," Helena replied with a laugh.

Gillian shrugged. "Doesn't mean I can't appreciate the display."

Helena's lips pursed, trying to contain her laughter.

"So, it's settled. I will accompany you as an emissary for Elysia. During our travels, I can keep you company and provide you with much more stimulating conversation than you'd receive otherwise, and once we reach Daejara, I can help rebuild our relationship with their court. You will be glad for the female company. Women are much better at soothing wounded egos than men are."

"She's not wrong on that front, at least" Darrin mumbled.

Helena was still smiling as she said, "Emissary? Promoting yourself again?"

Gillian shrugged. "It makes sense."

Helena shook her head. "If you insist, I won't mind the company."

Gillian clapped her hands in excitement. "Wonderful! I am going to go start packing!"

Standing on her tiptoes, Gillian rested her hands on Darrin's shoulders and kissed him lightly on the cheek before whispering something in his ear.

Darrin's eyes glazed and he stood in place as Gillian rushed off the way Helena had just come.

"Darrin?" Helena called, waving her hand in front of his eyes.

There was no response.

"Darrin," she said more sharply.

Blinking, Darrin straightened and looked at her, the tips of his cheeks and ears turning pink. "Yes, Kiri?"

Shaking her head and rolling her eyes, Helena merely walked into the Chamber muttering as she did, "Men."

The fire crackled merrily in the hearth as a breeze floated through the window; the promise of a storm on the wind.

Helena closed her eyes to take a deeper breath of the rain-scented air. It would be a soaking rain, she decided, heavy but gentle and seeping deep into the earth. Smiling in satisfaction she turned toward the others.

"When do we leave?" she asked no one in particular.

"The Daejarans were humbled by your request, Kiri, but have expressed concern about being able to entertain or house our retinue in the manner we are accustomed."

Helena tried to suppress the roll of her eyes. "*I* am hardly accustomed to the manner in which I am currently housed. Assure our hosts that we shall require no special treatment, save a roof over our heads, if possible. We will make do with whatever they can provide and be thankful for that much."

"There are some, Kiri, who will not be pleased they will have to settle for less than they feel entitled to," Joquil cautioned.

"Then they are not invited. Only those we trust to be respectful shall travel with us."

The men nodded their understanding.

"So, the question stands, when do we leave?"

Timmins was quiet as he made calculations in his mind. He nodded once to himself as if coming to a conclusion and then addressed the room, "We shall need time to pack and extend the offer to accompany us to the merchants we trust; so that would be three days from now at the earliest, Kiri."

"Make it so, Advisor."

Darrin added quickly, "We will also need to ready the Rasmiri, as your guards they will need to prepare to travel with us as well."

"Doesn't it send the wrong message to our friends in Daejara if we arrive with hundreds of armed soldiers?" Helena asked skeptically.

"You cannot intend to travel without them, Kiri," Darrin replied in exasperation.

Helena shifted to face Von, asking as she did, "How many of your men will travel home with us?"

She noted the warmth that flared in his gray eyes when she said home. "All thirty-six will travel with us."

"If we match that number with Rasmiri, surely seventy-two, plus the Circle and the various merchants will be a safe enough number?"

Darrin scowled at her, "Do you value your own safety so little?"

Helena turned aqua eyes shimmering with flecks of iridescence to him and snapped, "Do you think it wise to overwhelm our host with hundreds of mouths they will be responsible for feeding and housing when it is clear that they already struggle to care for their own? We will bring only those we need and no more."

Darrin stiffened in his chair. "And who gets to decide how many are necessary? Our opinions on the matter are clearly divided."

"I will," Kragen rumbled.

Darrin turned surprised green eyes toward the Sword. "What gives you that right?"

"You are not the only one concerned about her safety, Shield," Kragen replied, the usual humor smoothed from his face. "As her Sword, I will ensure the Kiri's wishes are kept in mind while also being practical about our safety measures. I will consider the Circle's opinions, but I will make the final choice."

"As the Shield, it is my sworn duty to protect her, it is my decision to make!" Darrin snapped, hands pressed on the table as he leaned toward Kragen.

"Enough," snarled Von. "You are a child, Darrin, throwing a tantrum because you have not gotten your way. Your Kiri's wishes are clear, it is not your job to question, but to follow orders."

Darrin stood quickly, chair scraping loudly against the floor before coming to rest a few feet behind him. "Of course, *you* don't see the issue," Darrin sneered. "These are your people; you cannot see past your own bias to acknowledge the potential danger."

Von's voice was laced with barely controlled fury as he replied, "I, better than anyone, can speak to what we will face across the border. Perhaps, if you could set aside your own jealousy you would think to ask for my advice rather than sling insults. Do not question my loyalty or concern for my mate's well-being, you spoiled—"

Helena looked between the two men quickly, determining her mate was the bigger threat.

"Von," Helena cautioned gently through their bond while placing her hand softly over his.

She could feel the muscles clench and unclench beneath hers as he tried to get a hold on his anger.

"Child," he finished with a snarl. Despite the warning of violence laced in his voice, Von had not moved.

Helena was certain that if Darrin had come at him, he would have the man on his back on the floor before anyone could blink. Turning back toward Darrin she watched his nostrils flare and his teeth grind as he tried to rein back his temper.

He couldn't meet her eyes as he said, "Excuse me, Kiri," and strode from the room.

Helena looked around at the other men. "None of you thought to step in?"

Kragen shrugged. "Darrin is hotheaded and quick to speak. It was your Mate's right to defend himself, and you. Besides, it would have been fun to watch him learn his lesson."

Joquil and Timmins shared a knowing look but stayed silent.

Helena shook her head in disbelief. "You are *all* a bunch of children," she muttered, clearly unimpressed with their male logic.

Standing she walked toward the door. "It was only his concern for me that caused this outburst in the first place. Concern you all share, I might add. But I will find him, and I will make it right."

She felt a flicker of temper in her mind. *"Let him lick his own wounds."*

Helena frowned at Von. *"You don't always have to be so quick to goad him."*

Von's eyes widened in surprise. *"Are you taking his side?"*

"No, you buffoon, of course not. He was in the wrong and said things he should not have said, but you pushing his buttons only escalated the situation."

Von's eyes narrowed and he looked away from her and back toward the fire.

Without another word, Helena walked from the room in search of her oldest friend.

SHE FOUND him a while later seated next to a fountain in one of the Water halls. It came as no surprise that he would seek out a place meant to soothe after the heated words in the Chambers.

She followed the blue and green mosaic path toward him, the soft lights flickering against the twinkling tiles like sunlight. She enjoyed the way it made the depiction of the stream seem to move beneath her as she walked.

Darrin was running his fingers through the crystal surface of the water and watching the colorful fish scurry away from the ripples; he did not acknowledge her as she approached.

She sat and studied him before speaking. He was frowning into the water, his shoulders curved into himself as though making himself as small as possible.

"I'm sorry."

"You do not need to apologize for your desire to keep me safe."

He looked up at her hopefully.

"Besides, it is not I that requires an apology; you owe one to him," she added in the same soft voice.

He grimaced and she noted the shame that crossed his face. Reaching out a hand, she gently placed it on his shoulder.

"Helena," he began, her name coming out as a tormented whisper.

Stiffening at the tone, she sat back and waited in silence for him to continue.

His gaze met hers, something she did not recognize shining in the green depths.

"Don't you understand what it does to me? Seeing you with him. That unworthy bastard's hands all over what is mine."

Surprise at his words held her in place.

"It should have been me. We were meant to be together," the words fell out of his mouth in a rush.

"Darrin..." she started, eyes widening in confusion.

He dropped to his knees before her, hands grabbing hers.

"I love you. I have loved you since we were children. My future was always you."

As he stared up at her, she could not find her friend anywhere in those glowing green eyes.

Mute, Helena just stared at him and shook her head in denial.

Taking her silence for agreement, Darrin pushed himself up and pressed his lips against hers.

Wrong, this is wrong, she shouted in her mind, panic clawing through her. As she struggled to break away, he wrapped himself around her; trapping her in the prison of his arms.

He continued to kiss and nip at her lips, as she struggled to break free of his grasp.

"Helena?" her name a question in her mind.

Calloused fingers were trying to work their way down the front of her dress, nails scraping along the delicate skin as she squirmed.

"Helena!"

NO! She screamed in her mind, retreating into herself until she was staring down at the shimmering depths within her.

As if in answer, the magic rose and built until it broke through like a wave.

Darrin was flung from her like a rag doll, flying through the air until he crashed against the wall with a sickening thud.

Then Von was there. Helena had never seen anything like it. If her magic was a wave, Von was a storm. Each blow came faster and with more force than its predecessor; the snap and crack of Darrin's bones a grim harmony.

Von grabbed Darrin by his shirt and lifted him off the ground, holding him pressed against the wall.

"You dare to touch what is mine?" he roared, deadly violence in every word.

Darrin hung limply from his hands, blood dripping from a face that was no longer recognizable.

Von slammed Darrin back into the wall, a small groan coming from swollen lips.

"Enough," Kragen said softly from behind Von.

Von growled in warning, turning to glare at the man over his shoulder.

Helena saw his eyes and pressed her fingers to her lips. Slate gray was now a swirling molten gold.

Her legs shook as she stood and made her way toward him, studiously avoiding looking at the man pressed against the wall.

"Mate," she called to him.

The molten eyes looked toward her but did not see her.

"I am fine."

His lips curled back as he snarled, *"He hurt you. You were afraid. I could feel your fear as if it were my own."*

From a distance, she could hear voices shouting orders to get help, but did not look away. *"Do I look injured to you, Mate?"*

Molten eyes swept down the length of her. Confusion was working its way onto his face, replacing the rage. *"But I felt..."*

"I was scared, but I am safe and unharmed. Let him go now and come to me, my love."

Blinking Von released Darrin, who slid down into a bloody heap at his feet. Gray eyes peered up at her in shock.

Assessing the damage, Von stepped away from Darrin. Remorse and guilt flooded those gray eyes.

With shaking fingers, she reached for him and pulled him to her.

"What have I done?" he whispered hoarsely.

Holding him tightly, she shushed him and pressed herself into his body.

He trembled against her but held tight. *"I—I thought he was hurting you. All I could think was to protect you. I did not mean..."*

Her warrior was afraid of her reaction to what he had done to her friend. Helena was too confused by what Darrin had done to be able to process anything else as they stood there by the fountain.

Tanya rushed into the room, firmly ordering Kragen and Timmins to step back. She ran her hands along Darrin's body and closed her eyes and she began murmuring under her breath.

Helena watched as twisted limbs began to right themselves and as the swelling in his face went down. He was still covered in blood, but he looked like the boy she recognized.

With a groan, Darrin struggled to open his eyes.

Looking around at everyone standing above him, and then at the healer, his brows lowered in confusion, "What happened?"

His voice was a rasp from Von's fingers being wrapped so tightly around his throat.

His green eyes sought hers. "Helena?"

There was something in his expression that stayed the harsh words she wanted to launch at him.

"What is the last thing you remember?" she asked softly instead.

His brow furrowed. "The meeting... yelling at Von... walking out." He lifted scared green eyes back to hers. "How did I get here? What happened?" he repeated, trying to push himself up off of the floor.

Helena felt ice wrap its way down her spine.

Joquil stepped forward quickly and went to his knees beside Darrin. Gesturing for Tanya to move aside, he placed his hands on either side of Darrin's head and closed his eyes.

Darrin's own eyes rolled back in his head, and after a few moments of tense silence, both men opened them at the same time.

Joquil was breathing heavily when he turned to address the group.

"It was a spell."

"What?" Helena breathed in shock.

"It was too finely worked for me to be able to trace it, but imagine a snare, Kiri. A certain set of conditions needed to be met in order for the trap to spring. Once it did, whatever happened next was the result of the spell."

"H-How?" she asked, fear and anger at war within her.

Joquil shook his head. "I would have to know what happened in order to hazard a guess."

Helena blushed fiercely and shook her head in protest. It was one thing to have to live through the confusion of that last few minutes, but to risk further damage to any of them by repeating it... it wasn't a chance she wanted to take.

"Perhaps we should speak privately, Kiri," Joquil offered, sensing her concern.

Helena looked up at Von, who appeared as if he wanted to argue.

Helena nodded and stepped away from him.

As they stepped away from the others, Joquil created a soundproof barrier around them. Instantly the noises surrounding them became muffled. She could no longer hear the gentle lapping of water or the hushed voices of the men across the room.

"What happened, Kiri?" Joquil asked, not unkindly.

"He… he…" Closing her eyes and taking a shuddering breath, Helena started again, "He apologized, and I tried to comfort him. I told him he owed Von an apology, and then when he looked at me it was like he was someone else, I didn't know him anymore." Helena shook her head in frustration. "He told me that he should have been my Mate, that I belonged to him, and then he, then he…" she trailed off.

Joquil nodded in understanding. "Would you say that he was not acting like himself?"

Helena thought back, before nodding. "I couldn't say whether the words or feelings he was proclaiming were really him, but never, in all the years I've known him, have I ever seen him act that aggressively. The man I know would never force himself on me like that."

Joquil's expression was grim as he processed her words. He let out a long sigh.

"It was a sloppy spell, but strong. Whoever cast it effectively seized Darrin's mind, so that once it went into effect he would do and say what they had requested, like a puppet. Fortunately, they are not well-versed in the mating bond and did not understand that Von would respond to your fear."

"Or maybe they did," Helena whispered, eyes widening in horror. "Do you think whoever did this meant for Darrin to go further? Or for Von to kill him for it?"

Joquil merely shrugged, but his lips were pressed into a flat line as he considered her questions. "I could not say, Kiri."

Helena's eyes shot back to where Darrin was still sitting on the floor.

"Does he really not remember?"

"No, it is as he said, Kiri. His last thought before coming to consciousness on the floor was about leaving the Chambers."

"I do not think we should tell him. The shame and humiliation… it would break him," Helena murmured, aqua eyes pleading with his.

"Are you sure, Kiri? It could help us better understand what happened to prevent it in the future."

Helena's hand gripped his. "Please, Master Joquil. Isn't there another way?"

"I will see what I can do without us having to give Darrin back that particular memory."

She squeezed his hand in gratitude. "Thank you."

His eyes shifted away from hers to look about the once peaceful room. Lowering his voice even further he uttered, "One thing is clear: there are enemies in the Palace."

Helena felt the color leach from her skin, aqua eyes scanning every shadow as if they would reveal their secrets.

HOURS LATER, Von and Helena were curled up on their bed listening to the rain fall outside. Her head rested on his chest, his heart's steady beat, combined with the pattering of rain, a peaceful lullaby.

His fingers were brushing through her hair and down her back in quiet apology.

"It was not like going into a battle," he began, his deep voice quiet in its contemplation. "I could see what I was doing, but only as if viewing from very far away. I had no control. Even when I knew it had gone too far, I could not stop myself."

Helena was still against him, afraid to say or do anything to stop the words.

"When I felt your fear through our bond and you could not speak to me, I went insane, *Mira*. My only thought was to get to you and make whomever was hurting you pay with their life. I would have killed him, if you hadn't have stopped me."

"I know," she whispered softly, pressing a kiss to the skin above his heart.

She felt the shudder roll through him.

"I wanted to kill him," he admitted.

Helena sat up and looked down at his face. He was staring at the fire across the room, afraid to meet her gaze.

"Von, look at me," she pleaded softly.

She saw his jaw clench as he turned his eyes up to her, as though afraid of what he would see there.

MEG ANNE

"I am not afraid of you," she promised as her fingers caressed his cheek.

His eyes closed and he swallowed.

"I think it was my fault," she continued aloud, and his eyes snapped back open.

"Helena—" he began.

She pressed her fingers to his lips. "No, listen, please. I think my magic sent something down the bond. When he was touching me," she paused apologetically as his eyes shuttered at her words, "I turned inward, and it was my magic that responded to my fear. I think through the connection some of that went into you. It would explain why you felt like you were out of control. My magic was fueling your response when I felt like I couldn't protect myself."

Her voice had gotten small as she confessed.

He brushed back the hair from her face. "Helena, I would do it again. I would have done the same thing to any man that touched you. You cannot place this burden on yourself."

Wet eyes looked up at his.

"You are mine. Mine to protect. Mine to touch. Mine to love." With each declaration, he pressed a kiss to her cheek, her forehead and then her lips.

"But your eyes... they were like mine."

He raised a brow in question.

"Not iridescent specifically, but they were swirling and gold."

His other brow lifted in surprise.

He shook his head dismissively. "Perhaps I was enhanced because of the bond like you suggest, but it was my instinct that drove my actions. You are not responsible for what I did today."

Helena frowned but did not speak.

"We are figuring this out together, *Mira*, but perhaps we should speak to Timmins and Joquil about it to see if they can help us better understand."

The worry faded from her eyes at the suggestion and she nodded.

Wanting to leave the fear from this afternoon behind them, she tentatively touched the swirling words on his chest.

"Will you tell me what this means now?"

His mouth tilted up in a grin at her change of subject.

"It's called a Jaka; a Daejaran blessing. Most soldiers get this tattoo once they complete their training and before they go into their first battle. It is given as part of a rite performed by their commander." His hand took hers and pointed out certain words along his chest and arm as he continued, "It asks for the Mother's protection on any field of battle, and for her to take away our fear so that we may only feel the honor of fighting in her name. In a more practical sense, it also helps enhance and hone our power."

Helena's fingers traced the words of the prayer. "So it acts both as a focus and as a shield?"

Von nodded, fingers absentmindedly playing with the ends of her hair as it fell down her back.

"Maybe I should get it as well."

Von's smile was warm as he replied, "You have one session with Ronan and already assume you're done? Or are you simply anticipating walking onto a battlefield sometime soon?"

Helena's answering smile didn't quite reach her eyes.

Von's own eyes softened as he studied her. "Do you sense something coming, *Mira*?"

Helena shrugged. "I don't know."

He pulled her back down to lay on him. "Do not borrow worry until you have to, my love. Whatever comes, we will face it together."

Helena could not fight the shiver that ran through her body at his words. Staring at the rain splattered window, she wasn't certain this storm was the one she was waiting for.

CHAPTER 15

The next few days moved quickly. The Palace was a study in controlled chaos; everywhere she turned, people rushed down corridors, their arms filled with the supplies that would be traveling with the group going to the Daejaran border.

The lingering sense of unease she had felt ever since Darrin's attack was slowly starting to fade, but she still struggled with the idea of being alone with him. She had, in fact, avoided doing so at all.

While he did not remember exactly what had happened, he also seemed to be keeping his distance from her.

She sighed, knowing that she would have to face him sooner, rather than later.

Taking a final glance in the mirror, she admired Alina's handiwork. She was definitely going to miss the girl while she was away, there was no way she'd be able to replicate the intricate braids that encircled her head.

Helena had decided to forego her usual dresses in favor of more practical traveling attire. Her legs were encased in soft gray leather, her dark boots wrapping up to her knees. Her tunic was a creamy white, held in place by a black leather harness. The tunic was open across the top of her chest, revealing the sparkling pendant hanging just above her breasts.

As a final touch, she wrapped a soft blue cloak around her shoulders. The deep hood hanging down her back would do much to protect against both the sun and any other weather in the days to come.

Helena's hands ran over the curves so prominently displayed by the snugness of the leather. Her lips rose in amusement as she imagined Von's reaction.

As if the thought summoned him, Von chose that moment to walk back into the room.

He stopped short, eyes hungrily raking over her.

"You expect me to be able to ride, while you're wearing that?" he groaned.

"Perhaps not comfortably," she teased.

"You don't play fair, Mate."

Stepping toward him, she placed a swift kiss against his cheek and wove her arm through his. "Will all the Daejarans be riding on wolves?"

Von nodded as they made their way toward the stables. "Yes, the pack trains with the riders so that their instincts meld until they are seamless. A Daejaran never feels truly comfortable riding unless they are on their wolf."

"Will I have a wolf?"

Von quirked a brow at her. "Would you like one?"

"They certainly seem much cuddlier than a horse. Perfect to snuggle into if I want to take a nap, for instance."

Von stopped in place, sputtering, "Helena, you cannot call a Daejaran wolf cuddly! These are beasts renowned for striking fear in the hearts of our enemies before tearing their throats out. They aren't pets! You don't snuggle them for naps!"

Helena's laughter rang through the hallway. "Maybe you don't."

"Helena!" Von protested as she continued without him. "Helena, don't you dare!"

By the time he caught back up with her, she was already in the yard holding out a hand for his wolf to sniff.

"Traitor," Von growled at the smoke-colored animal, the white eyes focusing on Von seemed to laugh.

"Does this beautiful boy have a name?" Helena cooed, still looking at the animal sitting before her.

"Karma," Von muttered dryly, narrowing his eyes at the wolf who was acting more pup than pack leader.

"Hi, Karma. Hi, my sweet boy," Helena continued in her sing-song voice as she gently ran her fingers up Karma's snout, before giving him a few brisk scratches behind his ears.

Von's wolf closed his eyes in pleasure.

Von crossed his arms, annoyed with his wolf and with himself that he was jealous he wasn't the one she was petting.

"Oh hush, Mate, I promise to rub you later."

Von's cock twitched in response.

Helena was laughing when a couple of stable hands approached them.

"Kiri," one with straw-colored hair said nervously, the hands holding his cap twisting it unconsciously.

Helena gave Karma one last scratch before turning her attention to the young men standing a bit away from her.

"Yes?"

"There's something you ought to come see."

Without another word, the boys spun on their heels and ran off back in the direction of a wooden fence.

Helena and Von shared a look before following close behind them.

As they rounded the fence they noticed a group gathered, all murmuring excitedly as they pointed and stared at the small clearing in front of them.

"What is it?" Helena murmured, looking up at Von who had a better view due to his height advantage.

His gray eyes had widened in wonder as his mouth fell open.

Curiosity eating at her, she stepped toward the crowd. Noticing her, they parted to make room for her to pass by.

She stopped in stunned silence when she noticed the creature the others had all been staring at. It was a massive feline. Its fur a glittering white, but what had captured her attention were the impressive black wings that were currently unfurling as it arched its back to stretch its front legs. The wings were capped with glossy black talons that seemed sharp enough to disembowel a man in one fell swipe.

"What is it?" she whispered, in awe.

Hearing her voice, the cat focused glowing turquoise eyes on her.

Her breath caught in her throat; it was beautiful.

Tentatively she stepped closer, offering it her hand as she had done with Von's wolf only moments before. It stalked quietly toward her, twin curls of smoke flaring from its nostrils.

"It's called a Talyrian, Kiri," Joquil said in a low voice behind her.

"They've been thought to be extinct, no one has seen one in thousands of years," Timmins added, his voice trembling slightly.

"They are magical beasts, the sacred mounts of the ancient ones," Joquil continued as if Timmins hadn't spoken.

Helena shot them both a wide-eyed glance over her shoulder. "Where did she come from?"

Timmins shrugged while Joquil shook his head.

"It just showed up this morning, Kiri, and has been snarling at anyone who tries to get too close," Kragen stated in his deep rumble.

The cat nudged her hand with its head, demanding that she pay attention to it.

"Hello, beauty," she murmured, rubbing her hand along its velvety fur.

"It is said that many hunted the Talyrian. Their fur is impenetrable, making their pelts ideal for armor or cloaks."

Helena grimaced at the thought of such beautiful animals being slaughtered.

Those glowing eyes met hers knowingly before dipping in a low bow before her.

Gasps of shock rang out behind her, but she could not look away. Uncertain what the beast was asking, she remained still.

It stood and stamped a front paw into the ground, the earth shaking in response. All around people stumbled to maintain their balance, many eyeing the Talyrian warily and stepping further away.

"I don't understand," Helena said apologetically, as the cat folded down in front of her again.

"I-I think it is asking you to climb onto its back, Kiri," Timmins sputtered, the shock of the moment causing his voice to rise.

"Is that right, beauty? You want to take me for a ride?" she asked as she took a tentative step closer.

The beast snorted and nodded its massive head, smoke again flaring out.

Helena stepped to its side, trying to determine how she was supposed to climb on. The beast dipped lower so that she could easily lift and slide her leg up and over its neck.

Once she was settled it rose swiftly and flapped its leathery wings.

"Helena!" Von called, moving as if to grab her.

The cat snarled at Von, a small stream of fire shooting from its mouth in warning.

Ronan was close enough to wrap his arm around his friend's chest and hold him back.

The cat flexed its wings twice more before its muscles bunched below her and they were launched into the air.

Helena screamed as her stomach flew to her throat, hands digging deep into the silky fur to hold on.

With a few more flaps they were soaring in the air, the people below them tiny indistinguishable specks. The flight was smooth and the Talyrian covered distance very quickly. She stroked the soft neck and leaned forward to speak in its ear, "This is amazing!"

She felt as though she could observe the entire span of Elysia from this vantage point. The sprawling Palace a mere dot among the gardens and forests which glittered like jewels around it. The mountains that had seemed so far just days ago looked as though she could reach out and touch them.

They flew through a cloud, its dew gently coating her skin and bringing her back to awareness.

"We should probably get back before they worry about me," she shouted, her delight at flying through the air at war with her sense of duty.

The Talyrian huffed, those smoking jets curling around her, but it began its decent, flying low over a small stream, its wings brushing along the surface of the water.

Helena glanced at her reflection, noting the flush on her cheeks and wild joy alight in her eyes. She and the Talyrian were similarly colored, the soft grays and crisp whites blending together as if they were one.

Just as quickly as they had taken off, they were back, the Talyrian landing smoothly, shaking out its wings before bringing them back into the sleek body.

Helena slid down its side, turning to stroke its fur in thanks. The cat moved its head, nudging her just hard enough to make her take a few steps to the side to regain balance.

Looking up, she noticed the men running toward her, and the dark gray and black shapes of the wolves. Surrounded by the darkness, the Talyrian shone like starlight.

"May I call you Starshine?" she asked softly, looking directly into the glowing eye.

The Talyrian huffed again, pressing its face into her hand, as it nodded.

"Are you, are you mine?" she asked.

The Talyrian shook out its wings and mane, but huffed once more, as if to say it didn't belong to her, but she belonged to it.

Chuckling, Helena pat it again. "Thank you for the ride, Starshine. I look forward to next time."

The glowing turquoise eyes rolled to look past her at the men now panting behind her.

It swept its wing up and pushed her back, as though to shield her from them.

"These are my friends, Starshine," Helena said cautiously, instinct urging her to distinguish friend from foe.

Von reached for her, needing to touch her and ensure she was really safe.

Starshine's lips curled back revealing her impressive fangs, but Helena spoke quickly, "This is my mate, Von."

At that, the Talyrian twisted its head back to her. Standing beside it, it easily dwarfed her, the tops of its arms well above her head. After studying her for a moment, Starshine lowered her head in a small nod toward Von and then settled herself onto the ground, as if dismissing the group.

Helena could feel the tremble in Von's hand as he pulled her toward him.

"Please never do that again," he whispered fiercely as he folded her in his arms.

"I'm sorry I scared you," she responded, hugging him tightly.

Ronan's arms were crossed, as he grinned at them in amusement. "Haven't seen him almost piss his pants like that since the first time I swung an ax at him."

Von leveled a steely gaze on him, his jaw set.

"What, eighteen years is still too soon?" the red-headed man taunted.

"Shut up, you good for nothing asshole," a sultry female voice said.

Helena turned in Von's arms to better see the tall blonde with spiky hair that had just stepped up to Ronan.

"I should whip you for that," Ronan growled without heat.

She smiled up at him wickedly. "Oh, promises, promises!"

Ronan's smile grew and he leaned down to plant a hot kiss on her lips.

Stepping away from each other, the couple looked back at them smiling smugly.

"I'm Serena," the woman said, stepping toward Helena while offering her hand. "Von's third in command, and this one's" —she tilted her head toward Ronan—"better half."

Helena felt her own smile warm in response, liking this woman already. "Helena," she responded, shaking her hand.

Serena's violet eyes sparkled with mischief. "It's a pleasure to meet you, Kiri."

"Likewise, I didn't know Ronan had a partner."

"He doesn't like to admit to that particular weakness," Serena said mildly, rolling her eyes.

"Never my weakness, always my strength," the large man said affectionately.

Helena was shocked to hear such tenderness out of his mouth until she recalled Von's own confessions.

"You'll have to let me know if the rumors are true," Serena said mischievously.

"Rumors?" Helena asked in confusion.

"If Von's performance in the bedroom really matches his prowess on a battlefield."

Helena blushed fiercely. "I couldn't say."

Serena's light eyebrows rose in surprise. "Oh?"

"I've never seen him on a battlefield, and I'm usually too tired from the night before to see him practice with the others."

Ronan and Von roared with laughter.

"Oh, I like you. We're going to be very good friends," Serena murmured with approval.

As the group gathered, Helena couldn't help but wonder what would happen to Starshine, or why the Talyrian had chosen that moment to reintroduce itself to the world.

She had hoped she would be able to ride the cat while the others mounted on their wolves or horses, but as Kragen had pointed out, the Talyrian was made to fly and there was no way they were going to let her fly in the air while they were hours, if not days, behind her on the ground.

Helena just hoped that she would have an opportunity for another ride among the clouds soon.

Helena heard Gillian's soft drawl and turned toward her. As always, Gillian was the epitome of genteel femininity. Whereas both Serena and Helena had opted for pants and tunics, Gillian was wearing a bright pink gown adorned with small rosebuds along the low scooping neck that showcased her delicate gold necklace its purple stone shining in the sunlight. Her copper curls were swept up in an elegant twist, topped with a wide-brimmed hat that tied off under her chin. The hat was angled to shield both her eyes and bared skin from the sun.

Gillian wasn't quite able to school her face in time, and Helena noted the distaste at her own appearance. Though short-lived, that moment was enough to make her question her own decision to wear the leathers.

Feeling her unease, Von ran his hand along her back, pausing to cup and squeeze her backside and whisper into that space in her mind that had become his, *"You are beautiful, Helena. No wrapping could ever diminish what the Mother has given so freely."*

Pleasure and embarrassment swept through her, but when he kissed her, all she could think of was him.

Serena let out a low whistle causing the couple to break apart.

Chagrinned, Helena turned toward Serena; the tell-tale flush staining her cheeks.

"You shouldn't have let me stop you, Kiri, newly mated to a male like that..." She whistled again. "I'm surprised you two have left your rooms at all."

Before Helena could respond, Timmins called for the group indicating it was time to go.

Von winked and used phantom hands to gently caress her lips, a promise for later, as he started toward Karma.

Helena watched him walk away, struggling to bring her eyes back toward her companion when she asked, "Shall you ride with us, Kiri, or are you going to hole up in that box with the other one?"

Blinking she considered, frowning at the thought of being stuck in a carriage with Gillian rather than out in the fresh air.

"I'd like to ride."

Serena didn't quite contain her look of approval. "Very well, Kiri, let's get you sorted."

The women headed for the pack of wolves that were waiting for riders. The wolves were still, allowing the girls to walk through them as they made their way toward Serena's mount: a light brown she-wolf named Arrow.

Gesturing to a smaller black wolf, Serena said, "That's Shepa. She's a sweet girl, fast and fierce. She will see you safe, Kiri."

Serena checked both mounts before helping Helena mount up.

As soon as Helena was seated there was a bellow back where they had come from.

Startled, Helena looked over her shoulder and saw the Talyrian just as she was stamping her front foot. The ground shook, nearby horses whinnying in fear. The Chosen struggled to remain standing and let out shouts of warning as Starshine reared up to drop down with both front legs.

Oh please. Please don't. Helena prayed as she stared, wide-eyed at the Talyrian.

As if understanding Helena's wish, it leapt into the air instead but shot a quick burst of fire into the air as it roared.

"Mother's tits!" Serena swore. "If I didn't know better, I'd say that cat was jealous you mounted someone else."

Helena's heart clenched, watching the Talyrian fly away. "You heard Kragen, they weren't going to allow me—"

Tilting her head, Serena interrupted, "When are you going to realize that people don't get to tell you what to do anymore?"

Helena's mouth closed as she pondered the question.

Eyes still on the sky, Helena didn't take another easy breath until she saw Starshine circle back. The Talyrian wasn't leaving then, just keeping guard from above; while she was grounded.

Helena was trying, and failing, not to sulk.

"It's not your fault, Shepa," Helena murmured to the wolf as it trotted off behind the rest of the riders.

"I wonder what she'll do the next time you take Von for a ride," Serena mused aloud after a few moments of silence.

Helena's laughter was choked as the image came to life in her mind. Serena gave her a saucy wink and urged Arrow to go faster.

CHAPTER 16

*J*ust before dark, Von's men called a halt for the night, after finding a large forest clearing to set up camp.

Helena tried not to moan as she dismounted, her legs quaking after the exertion of the day.

Joquil had decided that now would be a perfect time for another lesson. Since her trial, he had been urging her to try testing her limits to see what she was capable of when she focused, and not just what her magic was prone to do in response to her emotions.

He was whistling cheerfully as she limped over to him, it was all she could do not to punch him straight in the teeth.

Her lips twitched in amusement as she imagined Ronan's approval at that style of greeting.

"I'm glad to see you are still in good spirits after such a hard day of riding."

Helena narrowed her eyes, shooting imaginary darts at his face.

Joquil chuckled, "Easy, Kiri, I do not have anything extreme in mind tonight. I simply thought it might help you tap into your own powers if you could start to identify others'." His eyes scanned the scattered people, eventually coming to rest on Kragen.

Kragen was making quick work of some tree stumps for the evening's fire.

"Earth," Helena responded automatically.

Joquil rose an eyebrow as a prompt to continue.

"Strength," Helena added, lowering herself to the ground as her legs protested the movement.

"And?"

"Air?" Helena guessed.

"Yes, the speed with which he wields his ax certainly confirms it. What of Von?" Joquil asked.

Helena's eyes scanned the crowd for a glimpse of her obsidian haired Mate, but she had not seen much of him since he left her side that morning.

She thought back as she answered Joquil's question. "He utilizes Air to create shields, he has minor healing abilities from Water, and obviously strength from Earth."

"And what of the Fire branch, Kiri?"

Helena's eyebrows wrinkled in confusion, "I-I'm not sure, Master Joquil. I have not seen..." she trailed off, remembering the feel of his hands, warm against her skin. "He can manipulate his body's temperature."

"Well done, Kiri. The subtleties of the five branches are not always easy to recognize. It's those details, however, that set apart those who have mastered their branch, and those that are simply gifted with one or two skills."

"Furthermore, the ability to combine two branches together..."

Helena's mind wandered as the Master continued his lecture. She hadn't known that Von was using both Fire and Water magic when he was gently working the knots out of her back after Ronan's ruthless practices. She had just assumed the magic of Von's hands was all him, but her Mate had used the soothing heat of Fire combined with the healing properties of Water to completely eliminate the aches in her body. That effortless and subtle use of magic was the trademark of a real master.

Is there anything he isn't skilled at? Helena wondered idly.

"I'm an abysmal cook," came the amused reply.

Helena's eyes were heavy as she rested her head against a tree, Joquil's voice a soft buzz beside her.

"I'm starting to believe that our definitions of abysmal might differ."

"On my honor, Mate, I've only had to prepare meals over a campfire. I rarely have the foresight to pull something off the fire before it blackens on one side, and I have no mind for plants. One shrubbery looks very much the same as any other, which means I'm as likely to poison my meal as season it; much to the dismay of my potions master growing up."

Helena's lips lifted in a sleepy smile as she thought of a young Von at his studies.

"When we get to your home, Mate, I will cook for you. My mother always said I could make a feast with scraps."

"You are my home, Helena. There is no building in any realm that will bring me as much peace at the end of the day, as the feel of you in my arms. I could call a patch of dirt underneath a sea of stars home, so long as I am with you," Von's deep voice was a seductive purr, wrapping her in its warmth.

Helena wasn't aware she had fallen asleep until she felt Von's strong arms lifting her and carrying her to their tent set aside from the rest of the group.

Her eyes opened only briefly, seeing the strong line of his jaw gently shadowed with the day's beard. She pressed her lips against his neck, snuggling closer into him, her last semi-conscious thought sent down their bond, *"You came home."*

"I will always come home, to you," he responded softly, his kiss a whisper against her forehead.

GILLIAN MOVED QUICKLY along the outskirts of the camp, holding her skirt up to avoid brushing against the plants. She didn't have much time to find what she was looking for, that nosy bitch Serena had been

165

keeping an eye on her all night. At least until she wandered off with one of the men from Helena's Circle; the big broody one whose name she could never remember.

Although the sky glittered with stars, very little light was making its way through the treetops. Gillian blinked and reopened her eyes, which now retained the abilities of her hawk form. Few of the Chosen knew of the ability to shift into another form, and Gillian had worked hard to keep that particular talent of hers a secret.

Her eyes scanning the ground could see much more clearly as she worked her way over to the plant she had noticed earlier that evening.

Gillian had thought Helena would be riding with her in the carriage, giving her time to put her plan into action. She had been dismayed this morning to realize her error, once she saw Helena had dressed for riding. Luckily, Gillian was anything if not adaptable, she would simply have to take matters into her own hands.

Reaching the plant, she squatted down quickly. Fingers carefully plucking the heart-shaped leaves, so dark they were almost black. Known as *Bella Morte,* it was a beautiful, but deadly, plant. Used in small amounts by skilled healers it could induce long-term sleep in patients that required excessive treatments. In larger doses, it caused powerful hallucinations that could trap somebody in the prison of their mind. When in bloom, *Bella Morte* had luscious purple blossoms, but many did not attempt growing it in any garden. Just a small scratch from one of the sharp sides of the leaves would be enough to knock out a small child for many hours.

Gillian gathered as many leaves as she could stuff in the small satchel tied around her wrist.

Hearing a branch snap behind her, she spun and stood quickly, hand pressed against her chest as if to contain the heart beating wildly inside it.

"It's not safe out here for a woman alone," a low female voice said.

Serena stepped around the large trunk of a tree, her blonde hair seeming to glow in the darkness.

"Oh, it's you," Gillian said flatly.

"One would think you were trying to sneak off. What with the way you are out here deep in the forest and far away from the safety of the guards. Are you taking a late-night stroll? Meeting someone?" Serena asked mildly. While the words were idle, it was clear from the predatory gaze in those violet eyes that Serena assumed she was up to something.

"Just relieving myself in peace, lady," Gillian lied smoothly.

Serena lifted her brow. "Of course, you were."

"I would appreciate your company on the way back to camp," Gillian said, attempting to win the woman over, "We are, as you said, far from the safety of the group."

"Why did you stray so far, if you were worried about being alone," Serena asked instead, her arms resting on her hips, fingers within easy reach of the weapons strapped there.

"Privacy, lady. It's hardly in my interest to stop somewhere I could be come upon. Not exactly the position I like men to find me in."

Serena snorted in amused disbelief, although she wasn't sure if it was because of the frank admission or if Serena simply found her to be a foolish female.

"After you." Serena gestured back toward the camp.

Gillian nodded stiffly and walked beside her back into the warm light of the campfire.

HELENA WOKE up to the sound of songbirds; it was still early, the sunlight barely peeking through the cracks of the tent.

She assessed her body as she stretched her limbs, pleasantly surprised that all the aches were gone. *Von,* she realized with a smile, twisting to curl into her Mate's warm body.

He was still asleep, chest rising and falling with his deep breaths. Propping herself up on her elbow, Helena rested her head in one hand, while lightly trailing her other over the expanse of skin revealed by the blanket riding low on his waist.

It was rare that she woke before he did, and she reveled in the opportunity to study him at her leisure. He really was beautiful, all those hard angles exuding power even in his sleep. Her eyes flickered up to his face, noting the way his long lashes created crescent-shaped shadows on his cheeks and how those full lips were slightly parted, almost as if they were begging to be kissed.

Helpless to resist the silent request Helena leaned forward. Her hair fell like a curtain around them as she pressed her lips softly against his, her hand continuing its journey down Von's rippling stomach.

She felt him stir against her hand, her fingers meeting velvety smoothness as she continued the caress.

He pressed into her hand, eyes fluttering open to find her smiling knowingly down at him. "This might be my new favorite way to wake up," he declared, his voice rough with sleep.

"If I recall correctly, I promised you a rub," she murmured closing the distance between their lips with another soft kiss; her hand stroking his swelling length.

He let out a low moan of pleasure against her lips as his hips thrust into her hand. His own hand fisting in her hair, holding her mouth pressed to his.

There was a rustling at the flap of their tent followed by a loud cough.

Von's head dropped back to the blanket as he closed his eyes with a groan. "This better be important you bastard!" he growled, the threat of violence in every word.

Ronan's cheerful voice replied, "Indeed it is! The two of you are joining me for a short training session before we head out today. No reason to skip our sessions just because we're traveling."

He opened one gray eye to peer at her. "You don't suppose—"

"That means now, Brother! You have one minute or I'm coming in and carrying your ass out," Ronan shouted.

"The Mother hates me," Von muttered morosely.

Helena couldn't help chuckling, although she felt his disappointment every bit as keenly.

"There's always tonight, Mate," she offered, her voice warm with desire.

He stole a final kiss, his tongue caressing hers before he pulled back with a frustrated growl. He stood, shaking his head and letting out a stream of curses as he began gathering his clothes.

Dressing quickly, they exited the tent before Ronan could make good on his threat. Helena was still braiding her hair as they made their way to a small clearing beside the camp.

Serena offered her a sleepy smile, lifting a small tin cup in salute before taking a deep swallow.

"Tea?" Helena asked hopefully.

Serena nodded and offered the cup to her. Helena took it gratefully. Lifting the steaming cup to her lips, she took a small sip. She closed her eyes in pleasure before taking another deeper gulp and letting out a low moan of approval.

"I thought you only made that sound for me, Mate," Von teased, his voice a sensual purr in her mind.

Helena sputtered, tea flying as she coughed. She spun toward him with wide eyes, her cheeks flaming in embarrassment.

Von threw his head back and laughed. Before she could respond, Serena and Ronan joined in, guessing at what had her looking as though she were ready to throw the cup at her Mate's face.

"Easy now, Kiri. Don't go wasting good tea on a stupid male," Serena's laughter-tinged voice called from behind.

Helena thrust the cup back at Serena and gave Von a narrow-eyed stare that had him attempting to school his grin into a chastised expression.

"See if I let you do any of the things that cause those sounds you like so much now, Mate," Helena growled back through the bond as she stomped to Ronan's side.

"Hey now," Von protested.

Helena looked back at him over her shoulder and smirked.

Von's brow lowered over heated gray eyes. *"You promised."*

"A woman, especially a Kiri, has every right to change her mind."

"I was teasing!"

"Maybe you should have saved your teasing until after I had my tea, Mate," came the haughty reply.

"Technically I did—"

Helena scowled at Von from across the training circle Ronan had corded off.

More laughter was threatening to spill from his lips as he studied the aggrieved woman standing before him. Her face was flushed with color, her aqua eyes sparkling beneath her sooty lashes. She was breathtaking.

"Truce, my love," he said soothingly. *"It seems we are both feeling on edge this morning."*

Helena crossed her arms and pointedly looked away.

"I'm sorry for teasing you, Mira, I promise to make it up to you later."

"How?" she asked, narrowed aqua eyes meeting his.

Von sent her an image of exactly what he planned to do, chuckling to himself when her gaze became unfocused and her scowl slackened.

"All right, you two, enough of that." Ronan grunted, a flush stealing up his own cheeks as he adjusted his pants.

Serena shifted beside him uncomfortably, pulling at her shirt as if seeking a breeze.

Blinking, Helena refocused on her friends. Noticing their reaction, she threw her hands up in the air. "Oh for the love of the Mother!"

Von's shoulders shook with mirth.

She pointed an accusing finger at him. "Don't you start! This is your fault."

"My fault?" he asked with faux innocence.

"You know exactly what you did."

"It would seem to me that Ronan got exactly what he deserved for his wake-up call this morning." Von smiled seeming pleased with himself.

"Apparently, we all have extra energy to burn off this morning," Ronan replied dryly.

"I'm sorry," Helena offered softly, embarrassed that once again her feelings were not only transparent but could so easily manipulate her friends.

Serena grinned. "Don't be, Kiri."

"That's easy for you to say."

Serena wrapped an arm around her shoulder and squeezed, whispering in her ear. "I will teach you some things you can try when you are alone together that will wipe that smug smile right off his face."

"What's all that scheming going on over there?" Von called.

Helena responded with her own smug smile causing Von's brows to lift in surprise.

"If we're all done wasting time," Ronan started, his voice no longer the teasing voice of her friend but the annoyed snap of her commander, "perhaps we can begin our lesson?"

Helena turned her gaze back to Ronan, her body falling into the stance he had taught her during their first session. Legs shoulder width apart, shoulders back, chin up, eyes straight ahead and arms behind her back, each hand grasping the opposite elbow. It was the position all Daejaran trainees assumed when they were at attention. Not only was it a position of respect, it was also one of submission. With their arms in that position they were unable to draw a weapon or defend themselves, or at least in the case of the recruits. Any fully trained warrior would be able to cause massive damage even without their weapons, but it was a symbolic position as much as anything.

"Very good, Kiri," Ronan murmured before continuing, "today we will practice shielding. Are you familiar with how to cast a shield?"

Helena shook her head.

"Shielding most commonly comes from the branch of Air. Most warriors create an impenetrable barrier that they wrap around themselves for protection. However, those that are not gifted in that branch have learned how to use their other talents in a similar fashion. Those with Earth may reinforce their skin with its strength, making it all but impossible for a weapon to penetrate. Those with Fire may make their skin so hot it can melt any weapon or burn any who touch it."

Helena listened, fascinated.

"It is one thing to be able to form a shield and another to be able to fight while maintaining one. Serena, help me demonstrate."

Serena stepped in front of him, violet eyes shining as she called her power to the surface.

There was not a visible shift in the air, but Helena could feel the shift in the air as it thickened and reformed around Serena. It was not a bubble as Helena had assumed, but a skin-tight layer that moved as she did.

"May I?" Helena asked, lifting a hand.

Serena nodded while Ronan and Von watched in silence.

Moving toward her, Helena pressed her hand against her friend's arm, feeling a slight resistance before her hand settled on warm skin.

"How can I still touch you?" Helena asked curiously.

"My magic recognized you as a friend."

"Shields can work in a variety of ways, Kiri, it depends on the talents of the Chosen that has called it. Serena is gifted with Air and Fire. Her shield is both barrier and transformative. It will keep magic and weapon from breaking through, at least so long as her magic can sustain the shield, but it will also adapt to the threat."

"How is that possible?"

"Fire is known for its transformative properties. It not only burns, it makes the elements shift between their various forms. When I weave it into my shield, it adds an additional layer of protection. Here, it will be easier to show you than explain. Try summoning a ball of Water and throwing it at me."

Helena raised a dubious brow but called her magic to her. She felt the cooling rush of Water as it rose to the surface. Concentrating, she willed the Water to begin filling the palm of her hand. She let it go when the Water was the size of a melon swirling and spinning in her hand.

Lifting iridescent eyes, she drew back her arm and willed the ball of Water toward Serena's chest.

The Water sizzled turning to steam as soon as it made contact with the shield. Serena grunted and took a startled step back, her hand lifted to rub at her chest.

Ronan placed a concerned hand on her shoulder.

Shaking her head in surprise, Serena looked up at them with wide eyes. "Usually I do not feel much of an impact through my shield, but your magic felt like a full-grown Talyrian running straight into me. I was not expecting it."

Helena grimaced. "I'm sorry, I hope I didn't hurt you."

"Nonsense, Kiri. It is I who was unprepared. You have reminded me that even in practice I cannot lower my guard."

Serena bowed her head in thanks before offering her usual sassy smirk. "Perhaps you should help the men learn that lesson as well."

Seeing the playful light in her friend's eye, Helena's own smile grew in response.

"What?" Ronan asked as Von shouted, "Wait!"

It was too late, calling twin balls of Water to each hand, she flung the magic out to both men, aiming for their heads.

The unexpected assault had both men sputtering and dripping. Ronan shook off, his long braid causing droplets to fly and shimmer in the morning sun.

Von stalked toward her, a low snarl lifting his upper lip.

Helena's laughter froze as she shifted her body bracing for his attack.

One moment he was across the clearing, the next he was standing directly before her. Helena hadn't even blinked, but Von had cleared the distance in an instant.

Before she could ask how he managed it, his arms were wrapped around her pressing his drenched clothing into her.

She squirmed in his arms, but his hands moved faster than she could track them to begin tickling her sides.

"No fair!" she cried between bursts of laughter.

"Keep squirming against me like that and I'm throwing you over my shoulder and carrying you back to our tent, no matter what Ronan threatens," he whispered hotly in her ear.

Helena felt the stirring low in her belly at the words. Still, his hands continued their assault.

"Shield," his voice commanded in her head.

Trying to focus, Helena called her power to her once more. She tried to weave Fire and air to make a shield like Serena's, but it felt unwieldy and she could not make it take shape.

"Focus," Ronan called.

"I am!" Helena panted, still twisting in Von's arms.

"It should feel natural, Kiri. You should not have to force it into being, merely call it to you," Serena offered.

"If he would just. Be. STILL!" Helena emphasized each word before shouting the last, Von freezing in place around her.

She watched his eyes move comically side to side before looking up at her in approval.

"Well, that's one way to do it," he drawled.

Serena had her hand clasped over her mouth to hide her smile. Ronan shook his head smirking at the pair.

"Release me, darling?" Von's sweet words in sharp contrast to the molten heat in his eyes. Helena's heart fluttered in her chest.

Be free, she thought, pulling her magic back toward her. Von's limbs lowered until he was standing relaxed before her again.

"And again!" Ronan shouted, giving her no time to prepare.

Von dipped low, aiming for her knees.

Twirling, Helena sidestepped him and called her magic to her. Instead of trying to force it she merely shouted into the swirling depths of her power: *shield!* As Von reached her, she felt her magic snapping into place, Von making contact only briefly before flying away from her and landing on his back in the dirt.

She felt the impact through their bond, her own breathing a bit strained as a result.

Gasping, Helena rushed over to him and knelt at his side. "I'm so sorry! Are you okay?"

Von struggled to sit, bemused eyes meeting hers. "Next time, Mate, Ronan gets to be your target."

The group exchanged amused glances before laughing.

"I think that's enough for today. With the day's ride still ahead of us, I'm not sure we can withstand too much more of your abuse, Kiri," Ronan said with the laughter still sparkling in his blue eyes.

The teasing tone of his voice removed the sting of his words. She still had much to learn about controlling her magic, and even more still about its limits, but each day she could feel that simmering pool inside her becoming more responsive to her will. She just hoped that she would be ready when it mattered.

CHAPTER 17

The group was scattered around the campfire, it had been another long day of travel and many had already sought out their tents to get some rest. The Circle, along with Helena and some of Von's men remained.

Von's arm was snaked around Helena's waist as her head rested on his shoulder. She stared into the center of the fire, watching it dance in the gentle breeze. Next to her, Kragen sat, his legs stretched out in front of him as he leaned back against a tree. Darrin was beside him, arms crossed over his chest. Serena and Ronan were seated to his right both sharpening their blades in companionable silence. Across from Helena, Joquil and Timmins were chatting softly, voices indecipherable over the flicker of the flames.

The scenery had started to change that afternoon, shifting from the gently sloping hills into the harsher jagged peaks of the mountains. The air was already feeling cooler and smelled more of pine than the heady scent of flowers that had been following them from the Capital. It was peaceful there, around the fire, but Helena could not escape the feeling that something was waiting for them.

A shiver raced down her spine causing Von's arm to flex and pull her closer.

She felt the ripple of a question within her mind and offered him a small smile in response.

A rustle caused the group to shift as they sought out the source. From the back of the camp, Gillian stepped out from her tent and walked over to the group, pulling the sides of her dark cloak tighter around her.

"I'm exhausted but I can't sleep." She pouted as she stepped over Kragen's legs and folded herself into the space next to Darrin.

Darrin shifted over to accommodate her, but she scooted closer, her body following his.

"It's cold out tonight," she murmured, pressing against him.

Darrin eyed her warily but wrapped his arm around her shoulder to offer her his body heat.

"What are you all doing out here?" she asked, her voice loud after the silence.

"Just enjoying the evening," Helena responded in a more subdued tone.

"Are you just sitting here in silence?" she asked almost accusingly as she looked around at them.

"Would you like a story?" Timmins offered before anyone else could speak.

It wasn't clear how Gillian felt about the suggestion, her face obscured by the shadows.

"You did promise me some stories, Timmins," Helena offered when Gillian didn't respond.

"In the tradition of the campfire, I suppose I shall make it a good one," Timmins said with a laugh.

"If by good, you mean bloody, by all means," Ronan chimed in with his deep growl, setting his ax down and resting his elbows on his knees.

Timmins offered a dark smile and took a moment to settle himself, eyeing each of them before clearing his throat and beginning.

"Many generations ago, long after the Mother had found her Mate and given birth to the Chosen, a prophet arose foretelling the fall of the Chosen. As the Mother's children, the Chosen ignored the warnings of the prophet and as the years passed the warnings were forgotten."

"Time went on and the Mother's gifts began to weaken, fewer of the Chosen were able to access more than one of her branches. Of those, few, if any, ever learned to Master their branch. And still, the Chosen flourished—"

"So much for the prophecy," Gillian snorted as she interrupted Timmins' recounting.

Timmins raised a brow, waiting for her silence before he continued. "And so it was, years turning to centuries. There were some that had not forgotten the words uttered by the prophet, those that had continued to pass the warning through the generations, knowing the day would come when it could no longer remain unheeded.

"Finally, the day had come when the first of the prophets' signs came to be: a Daughter of Spirit would be born on the longest day of the year. This girl would be marked by the Mother, bearing her sign on her flesh."

Helena's spine stiffened, the hand that was interwoven with Von's going slick with sweat.

"It can't be me they're speaking of," Helena sent the worried thought to Von, *"They got the prophecy wrong. I wasn't born in the summer, and I don't bear any mark of the Mother."*

Phantom hands brushed the hair off of her face while his warm hand squeezed hers reassuringly.

Unaware of the silent exchange, Timmins spoke on, "This Damaskiri's Circle would never be complete as she would not find her Mate. Feeling betrayed by the Mother she would seek to grow her power. Eventually, she would learn how to twist the Mother's most sacred branch of magic, and thereby corrupt it completely."

"How—" Helena began, but Timmins silenced her by holding up his hand.

"The Chosen were unaware of this corruption and continued to serve their Lady faithfully. By that time, the second of the prophecy's signs came to be: A Mother of Spirit would be born, and she would grow to be more powerful than any in living memory, her power more akin to the First Born, the original Chosen. She would be born to an Ungifted, identified again by the Mother's mark upon her flesh. She would rise once the ultimate corruption had occurred."

Despite her attempts to tell herself it was just a silly story, panic rose in Helena's chest, her hand clamping down and squeezing Von's as she fought to breathe.

"Once this Kiri came into her power, she would become the ultimate vessel of the Mother. Her purpose to seek out the corruption that continued to spread across the land. She would use her gifts, like calling to like, so that she may identify the unworthy and destroy them."

Timmins paused and Helena felt herself shaking in Von's embrace.

Gillian yawned loudly. "A tale that has been told to every Chosen child so they would jump at shadows. Everyone knows no Kiri has ever been born of an Ungifted."

The family that she had never met... was is possible it was because they had never existed? Had Miriam really been her birth mother, never realizing who her daughter was destined to be? The questions whirled in Helena's mind, her heart continuing to race as she struggled to make sense of the story.

"I had heard," Helena stopped to lick her lips, mouth suddenly dry, "that it was possible for this Kiri herself to be corrupted, that she could give rise to the Shadow Years?" The last word a question.

Timmins tilted his head quizzically, studying Helena across the fire. The flames casting eerie shadows across his usually kind face.

"And what have you heard of the Shadow Years, Kiri?" Timmins asked.

"Only that it would be a dark time when the Chosen were tested, and that if the Kiri was corrupted, she would destroy those that had remained true to the Mother's gifts."

"I suppose that is one way of looking at it," Timmins murmured.

The men shifted around her, the rustling of clothes blending into the crackling of the flames.

"The Shadow Years refer to the rise of the Shadows, although no one has seen a Shadow for thousands of years," Joquil offered.

"I've only ever heard whispers about the Shadows," Ronan said, his voice somber.

"What's a Shadow?" Von asked, Helena's thoughts echoing his question.

"A Shadow is the remnant of a Chosen."

"A remnant?" Helena asked, still confused.

"When a Mother or Daughter of Spirit is corrupted, they use their ties to the Spirit branch to enslave the Chosen. Over time the souls of the Chosen are consumed by the one controlling them, burning out all that they are until they are mere shadows of themselves. Even after their souls have been expended, a Damaskiri can continue to control the Shadow, creating a mindless husk that thinks or feels nothing other than what it is told to."

Ice ran through Helena's veins. This was what they feared she would do? Create an army of soulless warriors? Why put her in power at all if that was what she was capable of?

Helena's thoughts continued to churn as she retreated into herself, no longer listening to the voices that continued to speak around her. Nothing was making sense. How was she supposed to be the girl they spoke of in the prophecy? Was the prophecy even real, or was it just a story told to scare children as Gillian had suggested?

"Hush, Mira, *your thoughts are so loud I can hear them as if you were shouting them into my ear. It is just a story, you and I both know in your heart you could never misuse your power so completely."*

"But—"

"Hush. I know your heart better than my own, and it is pure. You are filled with light, Helena. I am the half of you that was created in darkness. You never need to doubt yourself in that regard."

He stopped her protest with a gentle kiss. "Come," he said aloud, his deep voice warm and comforting, "let's get away from the others and spend some time under the stars."

Appreciating the attempt at a distraction, Helena willingly stood, waving a half-hearted goodnight at the others as she followed quietly behind Von.

"Do you think that Talyrian of yours would allow a second rider?"

Helena stopped, considering. "I'm not sure. She's certainly big enough to carry another."

"Call for her and let us see if she will take us for a ride amongst the stars."

Helena let out the low warbling whistle that had become her call to Starshine. Within moments the burst of brightness in the dark sky streaked down, landing nimbly before them. With a great huff, she shook out her mane and gently pressed her face into her mistress.

Helena stroked the velvety fur lovingly. "Would you take us for a ride Starshine?"

The great beast turned its glowing eyes toward her Mate, snorting loudly.

"Please, Starshine. For me?" Helena begged sweetly.

The Talyrian studied her for a long time, Helena certain that she would take off and deny the request. Finally, she folded her front legs, bowing low.

"Thank you," Helena whispered, as she wrapped her arms around the wide neck and hugged her affectionately. "I promise to spend extra time brushing you tomorrow!"

Small jets of smoke shot out as if to reiterate her annoyance at the request.

"Okay." Helena chuckled "And give you a special treat."

The Talyrian flapped its wings, suddenly impatient to be off.

"All right my beautiful girl, let's go."

With that Helena quickly mounted, pulling Von up behind her. Wrapping his arms around her waist he pressed against her, his lips leaving a trail of fire along her neck as he placed gentle kisses against the bared skin. Suddenly, the Talyrian flapped its massive wings twice more before launching them into the air.

Von let out a startled cry, unprepared for the takeoff. Helena laughed as his arms squeezed her tightly, the sound a joyful tinkling that followed them into the night.

THEY FLEW AMONGST THE STARS, the weightlessness of flight doing much to alleviate the anxiety she had been feeling these last few days. Feeling Von pressed against her back didn't hurt either. They hadn't been properly alone since leaving the Palace, and she had missed those quiet moments with him.

"I can feel you thinking. What could possibly be distracting you from such a view, *Mira*?" Von asked in his soft rumble.

"I was just thinking about how this is our first time away from everyone in days."

"I would say that's a reasonable distraction," he murmured before biting down gently on the back of her neck.

She shivered in his arms, the heat of his mouth more noticeable with the cool breeze washing over them.

"Perhaps we should take advantage of it," he whispered in her mind as he continued to nibble and lick the skin he could reach.

"I think you might be right," she responded, her voice breathless even through the bond.

Helena nudged Starshine and the Talyrian started her descent.

Soon they were landing in a small clearing in the forest. The ground was dappled with moonlight and there was the soft burbling of a stream in the distance. The night was cool, but Helena felt nothing but heat as Von pulled her against him.

Starshine's eyes glowed in the darkness, and she let out a soft huff before padding away from the couple.

"It's like she knows what we intend," Von murmured with a chuckle.

"She's smart. I have no doubt she does," Helena agreed before adding, "She won't stray far though."

Looking at her, he brushed his fingers gently down the side of her face. She pressed into the caress, her eyes closing as she did.

"You look beautiful bathed in moonlight, Mate. I think it should be all you ever wear, at least when we're alone."

His voice was a harsh rasp that moved along her skin, phantom hands plucking at the bindings of her gear as they undressed her.

"Which one of us is in a hurry now," she teased, remembering their first night when her magic had done the work for her.

"Don't mistake me, Helena. I have every intention of taking my time enjoying you tonight. I'm just ready to get started."

No longer in a mood for teasing, Helena's eyes opened to meet his, the hunger shining in their depths a twin to his own.

They stayed there, holding each other under the watchful gaze of the stars for a heartbeat before his lips were on hers.

The kiss started gently, but it wasn't long until he was groaning low in his throat and deepening it. Helena responded in kind, her mouth parting under his as his tongue slid in to taste her. As they kissed, Von's hands, both real and phantom, continued their exploration of her body. She could feel garments slacken before falling to the ground, and then the gentle breeze swept against pleasure-heated skin.

His hands were gentle as they traced a path along her back, although the skin was rough from his time wielding his sword. She felt them settle at her hips before following her curves back up and resting just below her breasts.

"Please," she begged, her lips still tangled with his own.

His fingers teased the soft globes, gently running back and forth on the undersides before splaying beneath them and lifting her breasts a bit higher. She could feel them grow heavy in response, aching for the feel of him.

He pulled back from her, studying her body, now bared, before him. His thumbs lifted to brush against the tips of her breasts, turning her nipples into tight buds before lowering and taking one into his mouth. His fingers continued to pluck and tease at the other as he pulled back to blow softly on the wet tip.

Helena let out a low moan, her head falling back. She could feel her braid brush against her skin, the sensation an additional tease that had her gripping Von's shoulders.

Von's answering growl was pure male satisfaction as he dropped to his knees before her, his mouth continuing to kiss and lick down her belly.

Helena licked her swollen lips before biting down on the bottom one. Her hands stroking Von's hair as she watched him lick up the skin between her hip and thigh. Her heart was racing, and she was struggling to catch her breath.

Von's hands slid around her hips and grabbed her ass, pulling her into him as he licked up the center of her. Helena gasped, pleasure shooting through her as he lapped at the small bundle of nerves. She felt Von's hand slide down the back of her leg, coaxing it to bend so that he could lift it to rest on his shoulder. She teetered, but he steadied her without stopping his assault.

Watching his head work between her legs was quickly pushing her over the edge. She could feel those phantom hands playing with her breasts while his real one teased and circled her entrance. Helena's hips were rocking into him, begging him to fill her. Her cries becoming wild as he finally relented and slid two fingers inside her.

Around them, wind began to whip through the tree, its intensity growing with hers.

"Von!" she cried, his name a plea.

"Yes," he ordered, *"come for me."*

Helena shattered, her muscles clenching around his fingers while he greedily sucked on her bud.

The wind died down as quickly as it had appeared, but all around them leaves began to fall from the trees.

Von looked up at Helena, his gray eyes molten as he gave her one last lazy lick. He chuckled, lips still against her when she struggled to keep her eyes open.

"Oh no, you don't. I'm nowhere near done with you yet," he said in her mind, her limbs going liquid at the promise.

Still kneeling before her, he pulled her down to him. Without releasing her, he quickly laid out her clothes to create a makeshift bed and then laid her down while getting rid of his.

She lifted a hand to his face, pulling his lips to hers.

"I love you," she whispered before their lips touched.

"And I you," he replied as he slid into her fully.

Helena moaned and arched into him, her body stretching to accommodate his length.

"Now let me show you how much," he purred as he began to thrust.

"We're going to be here awhile," she finally said, her voice panting in his mind.

"Oh, Mate. You have no idea." His laugh was wicked as her nails scraped down his back.

Their cries were lost among the trees as he proved how much he loved her there beneath the stars. Again, and again. And again.

CHAPTER 18

*H*elena fought to keep her eyes open as Shepa moved beneath her; the steady rhythm of the wolf's easy lope lulling her to sleep. She had barely slept last night due to Von and her not making it back to camp much before dawn, not that she was complaining.

Blinking rapidly, she struggled to focus on the scenery around her, before she embarrassed herself by falling sideways off her mount. While they were not quite at the Daejaran border, they were only a handful of days away and were finally starting to move into the more inhabited parts of the borderlands.

Around them the effects of the ban were evident. The people were poor, their small houses in disrepair and their children running around in scraps of cloth that looked as though they'd barely make it through another washing.

Her heart tugged in her chest as the little ones stared at the procession with acute distrust in their eyes. That they were so young and still had that kind of reaction spoke volumes to the quality of the interactions to which they were accustomed.

Ahead of her Von let out a sharp yell, holding up his fist in the air. As one the group slowed to a full stop. She let her concern flow through the bond.

He twisted in his saddle to meet her eyes, ordering as he did, *"Find Kragen or Darrin. Do not leave their side."*

Before she could respond with how she felt about that particular order, he was off, Ronan and Serena following close behind.

She let out a low growl, annoyed at being left out. Sighing she looked around at the grim-faced men encircling her; eyes scanning for the familiar faces of her Circle. They were not far, only a couple men away in fact.

She motioned for them to come join her and watched as they wove their way over to her on their horses. Kragen's bulk would be much better suited to the fierceness of a Daejaran wolf, she thought errantly.

"Kiri?" he asked, his voice low.

She shrugged as she responded, "I'm not sure what's going on, Von told me to stay with you."

His jovial face became serious, brows lowering over vigilant eyes.

Darrin moved so that he was in front of her, his shoulders stiff and his lips set in a harsh line.

The horses and wolves were snorting impatiently, but otherwise, it was quiet. The clear blue sky had filled with dark gray clouds as they had progressed throughout the day, the dark sky now adding to the ominous undercurrent surrounding them.

They waited for what felt like an hour, but it could not have been more than half that before Von, and his small party returned to the group. None were smiling.

"What is it?" she asked, while she attempted to decipher the emotions she felt flickering through their bond.

He looked at her, uncertainty shining in his gray eyes before he finally said, *"A warning."*

She sat up straighter on her mount, eyes widening in disbelief.

"A warning for us?" she asked aloud for the benefit of the men around her. "Who would want to leave us a warning, and how would they even know we would be coming through here?"

The soldiers began murmuring and shifting around her, their unease palpable. There was a soft click, and Gillian descended from the carriage.

"What's going on?" she demanded, her eyes narrowed as she took in the scene.

"The town has been leveled, the buildings burnt and the bodies ..." Von's face seemed to pale, and he swallowed thickly before continuing, "what remains of the bodies has been left for us to find."

Helena felt her stomach twist; it must be terribly gruesome for her Mate to be so affected by the sight of a few dead bodies. She felt his gratitude as she sent a wave of her strength to him.

"What did the bodies look like?" Timmins asked sharply.

Serena opened her mouth to respond before quickly closing it again, her face tinged with green. Quickly she dismounted and rushed away from the group before heaving into a nearby bush.

Concern gave way to outright fear as she watched her friend continue to be sick at what she had seen. From the corner of her eye, she saw Gillian play with the small gem hanging from her necklace, her own face worried as she stared at Serena.

"They were shriveled as if they had been sucked dry. Their skin was bleached of color, except for the eyes which were pure black. All had their mouths gaping open, stuck in a scream that will never end," Ronan finally said, shuddering at the recollection.

The murmurings grew in strength at the news.

"How do we know it was a warning?" Helena asked, her voice strained.

"The bodies were lined up beside the road. If they weren't a warning for us, they were certainly a message to someone."

"What could do something like that?" Helena asked. At the silence she turned toward Timmins and Joquil, "What could do that?" she demanded again, her voice blending into the harmony of many.

Timmins' eyes were troubled, but he shook his head mutely.

"I do not know, Kiri, but I will send a message to the Capital and have our scholars search through the records to see what they uncover."

"Do it at once."

With a clipped nod Joquil set off back toward the cart that carried his supplies.

189

Helena's unease and fear were reflected in the lightning flashing in the sky.

"We will stop here for the day," she ordered.

"Helena," Darrin protested.

Unleashing the full force of her swirling gaze at him, she snapped, "That was not a request."

He flinched at the harsh edge of fury in her voice and nodded meekly, "Yes, Kiri."

Turning back toward Von and Ronan she added, "Gather as many men who are willing, we will ride back to the bodies and give them a proper burial. They have suffered enough; it is time to return them to the Mother."

Ronan opened his mouth, but Von stopped him with a shake of his head. He could feel her determination and anger vibrating through him. She would not be denied.

Swiftly dismounting from her wolf, she let out that low warbling whistle.

Starshine circled the group once before landing a bit away. Helena made her way over to the Talyrian, comforted by the thought of such a beast in the face of potential danger.

"Mate?" Von asked, concern laced in the word.

"This is something I need to do," she responded without looking at him.

"Let me do this for you. Spare yourself this burden, Mira."

"No. These are my people; I was unable to protect them once. I will not hide from my duties to them now."

"Helena," he said once more, the voice in her mind a gentle plea.

In response she mounted Starshine, using the pressure of her thighs to convey her readiness to move.

They were in the air between one heartbeat and the next, flying over the procession and straight toward the devastation that awaited them.

BILE ROSE in her throat as she noted the seemingly endless row of bodies. Each had been placed with precision, by height. The smallest of the bodies so offensive she could not bear to look at them.

Over the rise, she could make out the Rasmirin soldiers coming to assist with the burial, but she could not wait.

Starshine landed softly, smoke curling up from her nostrils as the glowing eye studied her mistress. Helena placed a palm on the velvety neck, before stepping away.

I need to dig a grave, she thought; debating her options. Each one of these people deserved their own grave, but as there were none left to tell the stories of their lives or remember them, she would settle for one mass grave. The thought of any of these people not being with their loved ones was unbearable. At least this way any that had been family or lovers could at least go to their final rest together.

Helena eyed the scorched earth dispassionately, looking only for the best place to dig. Her eyes finally settled on a patch of land at the base of a mountain. There was a small stream burbling to its side, the weak sunlight glittering off of it prettily.

Taking a deep breath, Helena dove into the depth of her magic, calling it to her. She felt the comforting strength of Earth and the gentle play of Air before her magic went to work. The ground before her shuddered, she heard the startled cries in the distance and felt Von's own shout within the recesses of her mind. She ignored them all, continuing to focus.

Dirt rose before her, rising in a funnel that spun and twisted as it gathered speed. She looked to her left, and the twisting earth followed, moving up out of the ground. She let out a soft breath, and the dust settled into a giant mound of dark earth leaving a chasm where it had once been.

That much done, she stepped toward the tiniest body, her eyes blurred as she saw the streaks of dirt and tears that remained on the hollowed-out face. While the body was practically weightless, still she trembled as she carried it over to the hole. She lowered herself carefully down and leaned forward calling her magic toward her once more.

"Rest now, little one. The Mother will keep you safe," she whispered as she pressed her lips to the cool forehead.

The little girl was gently lowered into the grave on a cloud of Helena's magic. Once her body was settled, Helena rose and went back to the row of remaining bodies to continue.

Seeing her resolve, the men started at the other end, each picking up one of the fallen and carrying them to the side of the grave. When Helena would reach them with another of the children in her arms, she would call the wind that would carry the bodies down to the bottom.

"Why doesn't she just move them all that way?" a wary voice asked.

"Because this shouldn't be easy," she spat, her voice strained with the effort such continued use of magic cost her. The reservoir of strength was there, but it was still an untrained muscle, shaking with exertion.

"These people did not die easy, and it is not for us to do what is merely convenient because we do not want to be faced with such a reality. This is the least we can do."

The men straightened, her words humbling them.

Von placed a warm hand on her shoulder offering comfort and support. "Rest now, my love. Give us the opportunity to pay our respects as you have yours. We have the need for this as much as you do."

She blinked at him, iridescent eyes shifting to aqua as she did.

Nodding, she stepped back, allowing the men to finish moving the bodies into their final resting place. Once they were done, they turned to her.

Calling back the wind, the mound of dirt swirled and danced in the air, falling as gently as rain until it filled the hole completely.

Ignoring their stares, she moved to kneel again. She pulled the small dagger out of its sheath and cut the base of her finger.

The Circle all let out surprised shouts, but Helena pushed her now bleeding hand into the earth, her heart speaking the words she could not utter.

Mother, protect this place. Make it a testimony of your love for your children. Let no one disturb the rest of those that were so violently taken from this land. Please, let them rest gently.

This was no time for harsh words, although the need for vengeance was also loud in her heart. There had been enough anger and violence here; now it was time for peace.

When she finally rose, the clouds had cleared, and the sun was setting behind the peaks of the mountain. When she looked down, she was startled to see a burst of color. What had been a dark patch of earth was now a riot of flowers all in full bloom, each seeming to glow with a gentle light.

There were awed gasps as she stepped away, her knees shaking so badly that she stumbled. Von was there, his strong arms catching her and pulling her to him.

She blinked up at him, dark purple smudges looking like bruises under sunken eyes. The magic had cost her. The queen had handled the assault of her people, but now the woman needed to make sense of the tragedy. Her eyes were filled with tears, and her shoulders shook when he pulled her head into his neck.

"It's okay my love. I'm so proud of you for being so strong. Cry as long as you need. I've got you. I will be your strength now."

With that, he lifted her in his arms and carried his crying mate away from the equally wet eyes of her soldiers.

THE NEXT FEW days were more of the same. Each new town had more bodies awaiting them by the side of the road. Every time, the procession would halt, waiting while Helena buried them. With each corpse that she carried, her cheeks became gaunter and her eyes more haunted. The physical toll her magic demanded finally became too much for her to continue. That was when Starshine took over. The Talyrian flew low over the row of bodies, spouting her flames until the dead would turn to ash and drift away on the gentle breeze.

The Circle was beyond concerned. Helena had retreated into herself, becoming more silent and withdrawn as the days passed. Von could feel the strain Helena had put on herself and tried to reinforce it with his own power just to keep her standing, but even he was at the point where he felt drained.

"We need to rest," he declared to the Circle.

The men nodded their agreement, but Helena opened her mouth in protest.

"Enough, Kiri. Your people are exhausted, let them rest for awhile and regain their strength." He knew that she would not consider her own need for rest, which was why he guilted her into considering the fate of the others.

She closed her mouth and eyed the group, her eyes filling with concern as she saw how haggard they had become. "Fine."

The Circle let out a collective sigh.

"She needs to eat," Darrin said in a voice only Von could hear. "She is wasting away before us."

Von's lips were a flat line as he nodded. "She is punishing herself."

"Punishing herself?" Darrin sputtered, "But why?"

"She feels guilty that so many have died and she was helpless to stop it," Serena said softly as she joined them.

"What could she have possibly done?" Darrin asked, his voice rising with the question.

"It does not need to make logical sense, Shield. She is reacting with her heart which rarely follows such rules," Serena stated, her blond brow rising as if daring him to challenge her assessment.

"She's not doing anyone any good by not taking care of herself," he finally muttered.

"On that, we agree," Von said darkly.

He could feel his Mate's pain, each day it gnawed at him through their bond; a dull ache he could not ease. Despite understanding the cause of her distress, he had no idea how to help relieve it. Back at home, when he would get twisted up in his own feelings of guilt over his brother, he would resort to training to try to sweat it out of his system. It did not necessarily solve the cause of his guilt, but it helped dull the edge enough that he could focus on other things. Perhaps that could work for Helena as well, not that she was in any shape to wield a weapon.

He studied her snuggled into the side of her Talyrian whose wing was protectively curled around her. For now, he would let her sleep, but while she slept, he would speak with Ronan about his plan. Once she woke he would bully her into eating, certain her annoyance at his pestering would at least do something to put some color back in her cheeks.

SHE WOKE WITH A START, struggling to rise, her heart pounding in her chest. As she sat the top of her head smacked the underside of Starshine's membranous wing. The Talyrian huffed in annoyance, twisting its head to glare at her.

"Sorry," she murmured, scooting out from under its protection.

Starshine continued to stare at her until Helena began running her fingers through the silky fur of her mane.

Letting out a deep rumble that was more like the scattering of rocks down a mountain than a purr, the giant cat finally closed its eyes.

She felt his presence before she saw him. She closed her own eyes, breathing in his scent as he drew near.

His hand caressed the length of her back, and she felt herself arching into it.

"How are you feeling, my love?" he asked in his deep growl.

She looked up at him, the weight of the last few days still in her eyes. "Better."

He lifted a dubious brow.

"I can feel them"—she rubbed at her chest—"all those lives taken before their time. They're a weight in my heart. I can't just forget about it."

"No one is telling you to forget about them, Helena," Von chided sternly, as he wrapped her in his strong arms. "But you have to take care of yourself. You won't do them any good pushing yourself so far that you are too weak to care for them, or avenge them."

His words stirred something in her, and some of that weight shifted allowing her to take her first deep breath in days. It was still there, that weight in her chest, still pressing her to *do* something, but it was less insistent. She knew he was right; she was no good to anybody in her current state.

Her stomach growled loudly, and she covered it with her hands, cheeks flaming as she looked at Von.

He threw back his head and laughed. "Ronan will be so disappointed to know I won't need his help anymore."

Confused, she furrowed her brows and asked, "What?"

He shook his head, his laughter enveloping her with its warmth through their bond. "Nevermind, Mate," he said, kissing her forehead. "Let's find something for you to eat."

They rejoined the group around the fire, Helena thankfully accepting a bowl of some sort of vegetable soup.

The men gently teased her as she ate, relaxing when she would snap at them and return their taunts with her own. It was a far cry from the easy banter they usually shared, but it was a start, and for now, that was enough.

Gillian watched the group from a distance, fingers still mindlessly stroking her necklace before she stepped back into the forest and blended into the darkness.

CHAPTER 19

They started again early the next morning. Von would have preferred that they rest for another full day, but Helena refused. She had to admit the evening of rest and a good meal had done much to ease the bruised look from her eyes. Feeling his attention on her, she met his gaze, sending him a warm smile.

It began with a sound, or rather, a lack of sound. Birds had been chirping animatedly as they hopped from tree to tree alongside the caravan but were now strangely absent.

Disoriented, Helena glanced around, noting the unease that rippled through the procession. Both Darrin and Kragen maneuvered their animals in closer to Helena's, creating a barricade around her.

Next was the smell. The air, still heavy with morning dew was quickly being overcome with the overpowering and acrid scent of smoke. The wolves began growling low in their throats, their eyes swiveling wildly as they attempted to locate the source of the fire.

Then came the screams. There was a moment of stillness, a deep breath waiting to be exhaled before everything came alive with motion. It would have been pure chaos, if not for the utter precision with which it was executed.

Von's chin lifted toward the sky as his mouth fell open, his war cry filled with promise. Her heart was in her throat as she watched her

Mate prepare for battle. There was no time to do anything more than send a plea down the bond for him to stay safe before she offered a quick prayer to the Mother asking for the same.

Von's men, all mounted on their wolves, led the charge over the hill. Helena's Circle stayed close to her, faces set in harsh lines as they followed close behind. A few of the Rasmirin stayed back to protect the merchants and their carts, but the rest were closing in on the Circle.

The sky was black with smoke, the small houses all alight. Everywhere people were screaming and trying to flee the burning buildings.

Who's attacking? Helena wondered, eyes scanning the scene below her, desperate to try to make sense of the situation. Were these the men that had been leaving the brutalized bodies as a warning for them? Would they be too late again?

Then she saw them. They were creatures of one's darkest nightmares; things from a tale children would spread to horrify and torment each other. They had been human, once. Their limbs skeletal, the gray flesh stretched taut over bone. The awkward jerking movements of the bodies reminiscent of a marionette attempting to dance.

The creatures were hairless, faces gaunt, but it was their eyes that had her screaming. Where life had once shone, there were now milky white pits run through with shimmering black lines. Their mouths were almost as bad. The lips were flaking and peeled back to reveal teeth blackened with rot. They didn't close their mouths, the jaws hanging open to emit an endless wet gurgle.

Helena felt her stomach twist with revulsion, everything about these bodies grated against her with their sense of wrongness. It was then she noticed, one of the things reaching elongated fingers toward a child too terrified to do more than hold onto its stuffed toy while it sobbed for its mother.

I cannot lose another one, she thought, not even aware she was already moving.

"Kiri!" the men shouted behind her, but it was too late, she was flying down the hill in a race to save the child.

She grabbed the girl, pulling her up onto Shepa and using her body as a shield, leaving the bony fingers clutching air.

The little body trembled in her arms as Helena's eyes frantically searched for a safe place to hide her so that she could get back to her men and help save the rest of the villagers. There were some villagers loading up carts with people and fleeing. Helena gave the child to one of the women, their wide eyes showing white as they took in the scene around them.

"Keep her safe!" Helena shouted, spurring the wolf back to the burning buildings.

There was a scream of rage, and Helena saw Starshine shoot from the sky straight toward a group of the creatures. Fire poured from the Talyrian's mouth while her claws tore at their bodies. Still, the creatures moved, immune to the pain.

Mother's teeth, what unholy creatures are these?

All around her, wolves tore into creatures who continued to fight with one or more missing limbs. They didn't bleed so much as drip a thick oily substance that shimmered slightly before evaporating. In a blur of fur and fang, Karma lunged at one of the monstrosities. The wolf's teeth shining wetly before closing around its throat and tearing head from jerking body. Karma let out a savage snarl as it dropped the head from his teeth, letting it bounce and roll before turning back into the fray.

Helena's initial reaction was concern that Von had been separated from his wolf, before the realization that Karma had discovered how to stop the creatures had her shouting wildly, "Their heads! You've got to remove their heads!"

She continued screaming at the top of her lungs, also using her magic to enhance her voice and carry the message across the battlefield. She felt the fresh surge of adrenaline throughout the crowd as her people attacked with renewed vigor.

The Circle were still working their way back toward her, Joquil's lips moving frantically as he called down shields of protection while also blasting the monsters back to give the men time to work through them. Timmins fought beside Kragen, the latter towering over everyone and smiling maniacally as he made quick work of the skeletal bodies in front of him. His massive swords were glowing with the molten heat of Fire. When they made contact with one of the creatures they would cut through their limbs like soft butter. It was clear, Kragen was in his element, his laughter when another body fell causing Helena to shudder, but her eyes continued their scan.

Darrin's teeth bared as he used his sword to hack and cleave at the bodies before him. His green eyes met hers, and she could feel his frustration with her. His sole duty was to protect her, and she had taken that from him when she ran thoughtlessly straight into the battle to save the child. She shrugged apologetically, his head dipping in acknowledgment as he focused back on the creatures coming toward him. The entire interaction took less than a second. The rest of her men accounted for, Helena turned her attention toward the pull of her bond to lead her toward her Mate.

As she moved forward, she saw Ronan and Serena fighting as one. Their backs were toward each other, their gift of Air making their axes swing faster than her eye could follow. Their blades had grown slick with the creature's black substance, but they were relentless as they continued to behead them. Helena's eyes narrowed as one of the creatures reached its hand toward Serena's arm, but her shield sizzled at the contact. The creature jerked back, giving Ronan enough time to swing his ax down and sever the head from the body.

A sudden searing pain knocked Helena from her mount. She stood and looked down trying to identify the source of her injury, but found none. She looked back up, her braid whipping through the air with the speed of the movement when she realized it had been Von who took the blow. That the pain had been strong enough for her to feel through their bond had her gaze hazing with red. She stumbled slightly as it continued to throb within her, but she used their connection to pull the pain to her so that it could not distract or weaken her Mate.

Helena tried to control her flare of panic when she saw four more of the beings close in on him. She gripped Shepa's fur, using it to help pull her back astride the wolf's back. Angling herself toward Von, she pushed with her power to reach him. Spurred by her will, Shepa leapt into the air and flew into the chest of one of the creatures, knocking it down before ripping its throat out. There was no screech of pain, just a wet gurgle while its limbs continued to flail.

Molten gold eyes met hers. There was no time for words, Helena dismounted and dove into the swirling pool of her magic; a controlled plunge straight to the bottom before pulling up and unleashing the power around her. The sky came alive. Bolts of lightning were bright scars among the black clouds, while thunder roared so loudly the few remaining trees shook from its intensity.

Von let out an approving growl, turning his focus back to the other three still moving toward him. He stood still letting them come closer with each jerking step. Once they were within range, he blinked away. That was the only word Helena could think of for the move she had first noticed when they were practicing her shielding with Ronan.

One moment Von was standing beside her, the creatures an arm's length away, the next he was facing them his teeth bared in a feral grin from over fifty paces away. The creatures twisted in confusion, searching for their prey. Von struck. Instead of his sword, a rope of Fire was snaking in his hand. He pulled back an arm before lashing it forward and wrapping the flame around one of the beings and pulling it to the ground. Once on the ground, Karma dove forward and finished it.

Helena was tired of being an observer. It was time to end this. *Now* she urged.

Fire rained from the storm her magic had created in the sky. The glowing red embers turning to ash if they touched anything but the creatures. When an ember would hit one of those skeletal bodies, it would erupt into a pillar of Fire before consuming them completely.

Just like that, it was over.

Helena could feel the heat of her Fire still pulsing under her skin. Rage caused her body to shake, and she snarled when she felt a hand touch her shoulder.

Darrin stepped back, his face leached of color.

"Kiri," a voice called softly. She turned to the voice, her teeth still bared and her eyes swirling with iridescent fire.

Von stood before her; eyes gray once more.

Her heart continued to race, fueled by the rage she could not seem to contain.

"She pulled too much power too quickly if she releases it she could kill us all," Joquil murmured to the others, his voice laced with fear.

"If you don't have anything helpful to say, get the fuck away from her," Von growled without looking away from Helena.

"Helena," Von called to her through their bond.

She was still staring at him unblinkingly.

"Mira," the deep voice begged.

She shuddered, trying to focus on the images that flickered through her mind: Von holding her close as they danced; Von kissing her after her trial; Von's eyes devouring her in her mating dress.

With a gasp she came back to herself, knees shaking so hard she started to fall.

Von's arm shot out to grab her, cradling her as she dropped to the ground.

His warm hands brushed the hair that had fallen out of her braid back from her face as she began emptying the contents of her stomach on the smoking remains of a creature.

Von's hand gently ran along her back, her stomach continuing to heave even after it was empty.

"You don't have to all stand around watching me humiliate myself," she rasped.

"They need to see that you are okay, Kiri," Serena said from behind her.

Her arms shook as she tried to push herself back into a sitting position.

Von eased her back until she was sitting beside him.

The Circle along with Ronan and Serena surrounded them, each looking grimmer and more battle-worn than the last. All were coated in ash, their sweat leaving dark smears along their skin. None appeared injured, save a few tears in their clothes, which could have been scratches that have already healed.

The rest of the Rasmirin were helping the villagers put out the remaining fires while the Daejarans tended to their wolves.

"Starshine?" Helena asked, eyes scanning the sky for the streak of white.

The Talyrian prowled over to its mistress, dropping down to lay beside her. Helena rested her head against its side, brushing trembling fingers over the soft fur.

"What were those things?" she asked wearily.

"Those, Kiri, were Shadows," Joquil said, his voice graver than she had ever heard.

She looked from face to face, trying to gauge how bad this news was.

All shifted uncomfortably, seeming troubled.

Helena recalled their conversation from the campfire and gasped, horrified. "You mean those things were Chosen?"

Timmins and Joquil nodded grimly.

"That's awful," Helena whispered. Another piece of the story clicked into place and had her asking, "But who was controlling them? I thought only one who was gifted with spirit was able to create a Shadow."

Von picked up the question for her, "I thought with Rowena's death that no other damaskiris remained."

"Could there be another out there?" Helena asked.

Timmins shrugged; worry making him look years older.

The group eyed each other, all with more questions than answers.

Around them what was left of the blackened bodies smoked, while ash flew through the red and black sky. Had she been paying attention, Helena would have recognized this scene from her trial. Instead, her brows were frowning in concern as the question tumbled through her mind, *was there another like her out there?*

CHAPTER 20

*T*he group had been exhausted after the battle, none wanting to go farther that day. It was not so much that they were too tired to move on, but that they were afraid of what they might find when they got there. That did not mean, however, that there was not work to be done.

After the storm had cleared, and Helena's strength had returned enough for her to move about on her own, Kragen insisted that the Circle have a meeting. At Helena's request, both Ronan and Serena joined in. As Von's next in command they were fast becoming an extension of her own Circle, and she trusted them just as much as she did the others.

They met in Joquil's tent, the space cramped with the excess of people. Helena sat resting between Von's thighs; his arms wrapped tight around her waist. They were waiting for Serena, and for the moment, Helena had her ear pressed against his chest. She was listening to the beat of his heart which was still beating in time with hers.

Despite the gravity of the day, she couldn't help the smile that appeared at the reminder of their connection.

"Mine."

"Yours," he agreed, a hand lifting to caress her cheek before pressing her head a bit closer to his heart.

It still surprised her, how gentle her Mate could be with her. He exuded a raw fierceness and was more likely to scowl than smile when around the others. Despite that outward display, with her, there was an ever-present tenderness. She could feel it lapping at her through their bond, sometimes warm with his love and other times burning white hot with his need for her.

She had just turned in his arms and pressed a gentle kiss above his tattoo when Serena rushed in offering an apology for the delay.

"Sorry everyone, I had to go back and grab what I wanted to show you from where I kept it in our tent."

"Is this what you found on the bodies?" Joquil asked eagerly, sitting forward in his chair.

Serena nodded, holding the object out for his inspection. Within her palm, there were several small gems. They were a dark purple, almost black, and dull. Joquil kept one of the gems and passed the others around.

Helena held one in her hand, holding it up to the light for a better look. No matter how she twisted the gem, it did not shine when it hit the light. Rather it seems to reject it, as though it was pushing the beams away so that it could stay shrouded in shadows.

Laying the gem flat in her palm, she was startled at the feeling of revulsion that spread through her. There was a malevolence within the gem, something that recognized her and was promising nothing but harm.

She quickly shoved it into Von's hand; eyes narrowed as she tried to shake off the feeling of unease holding the gem had caused. Von lifted a brow in question, but she didn't know what to say.

Facing the others, she asked, "Do we know what these are?"

Serena shook her head. "No clue. We didn't notice them when we first checked the bodies, but by the time we found the third one, we figured they must mean something. Each stone was sewn into the hem of a shirt or tied off in a leather cord they wore around their wrists or neck. Most of the leather and fabric had burned away, so the stones came loose, but there were a couple that still had them intact."

"How many of these did you find?" Kragen asked.

"Not many, considering the size of the horde. Only about fifteen."

Joquil's frown was severe as he studied the pearl sized gem.

"Joquil, is something the matter?" she asked softly, the others all turning to study the Master.

"I do not know, Kiri. I feel as though I have seen a stone like this before, but I cannot recall where. Another reason to search through the records it would seem."

"I will help you," Timmins offered.

Joquil offered him an appreciative smile. "More eyes would be helpful, thank you. I feel certain we will find the answer to how the Shadows came to be in that village today if we can find out more about these gems."

"Did you have anything else to report?" Kragen asked Serena and Ronan.

The two shook their heads and stepped back to allow space for Darrin to enter the center of the tent.

"I think we need to discuss the carelessness with which Helena acted today."

"I'm right here, Darrin. There's no need to speak of me as though I'm a child."

"Then perhaps you should stop acting like one," he snapped.

Helena's back went straight as she narrowed her eyes at him. "Excuse me? Would you like to say that again, Shield?"

"I think you heard me the first time, Kiri." He was primed for this fight, his frustration from the battle rising to the surface now that she was safe.

"He is concerned for you, Mate. As your Shield should be. You scared him today riding headfirst into danger without any thought to your safety. You left them behind scrambling to try to reach you."

Helena's tried not to let her face show her surprise at the admonishment. Von always took her side. *"You left me behind,"* she accused instead.

"It is a habit for me as the Daejaran commander to take the lead in battle. I am used to defending those I care for, not fighting beside them."

"You fight with Serena and Ronan," she pointed out.

"That is different, Mira. They have trained as long as I to be warriors. I met them in the training ring when we were all mere babes. With you, Helena..." his voice seemed to sigh and linger on her name, *"you are the purest soul I have ever known. I will do anything in my power to protect that. It's not that I don't believe you can hold your own; I just do not want you to become tainted by the realities of the battlefield. There is no place for you in that sea of death."*

"It would seem you have a lot to learn, Mate. My place is at your side. We are stronger together, did you not feel that today? The way that our power was enhanced when we fought side by side?"

"I did. My power feels different since we were Mated, deeper somehow. Almost as though there is more for me to access than before."

"Like how you can teleport from place to place now?"

She felt his chuckle in her mind. *"Yes, that has been a useful new skill. It surprised me the first time it happened. I merely had to think about where I wanted to be, and I appeared there. I cannot go far distances, only within the range of what my eyes can see."*

"I've been calling it blinking."

"Blinking?"

"Yes, in the time it takes to blink you manage to appear in a new spot."

He let out a surprised laugh at her explanation. The group, having become used to these bouts of silent communication between them, were studying them expectantly.

Only Darrin continued to glower at her. "Are we interrupting?" he asked dryly.

Helena met his glare with one of her own. "You shouldn't be so quick to speak, Darrin. Von was taking your side."

Surprise flashed across his face momentarily before he schooled his features back into a mask of haughty superiority.

"You do realize, Shield, that I'm the one in charge here? You don't get to lecture me for being naughty."

"You seem to be the only one here, Kiri, forgetting what we vowed to you. We are here to protect you, with our lives if need be. How can I do that when you throw yourself in the heart of a battle against an enemy we know almost nothing about?"

Finally chastened, Helena's shoulders drooped, and she sighed heavily. "I did not mean to be thoughtless; I just could not stand the thought of burying one more child. When I saw the Shadow reaching for her, I just…" she trailed off, heart heavy again with the weight of the bodies she had given back to the Mother.

"And how do you think we would feel, Helena, if the next body we place in the ground is yours?" Kragen asked. The rebuke from him came like a slap compared to the ribbing she was used to from Darrin.

The rest of the men were silent, the words filling the tent as silent tears dripped from her cheeks.

"I will be more careful next time," she said weakly.

"That is all that we ask, Hellion," Darrin said, his voice gentle, before turning and leaving the tent.

Von hugged her to his chest. *"Do not cry, my love. It is only their love for you that makes them speak so harshly."*

Helena nodded, too overcome with emotion for words, spoken or otherwise.

After speaking with the Circle, Helena made rounds throughout the camp, stopping to check on the wounded; of which there were blessedly few. She also offered small words of comfort to the villagers that remained. They had all been effusive with their thanks, overwhelming Helena with their gratitude. Most no longer had homes, but many had at least walked away with their lives. They had been lucky.

There was something about the attack that was niggling in the corner of her mind. She couldn't quite put her finger on it just yet, but it was almost as if they had won too easily. Like it had been a test of sorts, to feel out their strength before the real strike came. Helena was the first to admit she was not an experienced warrior, but even to her it had seemed too convenient that they came upon those Shadows at precisely the right moment, when for days they had always been far too late.

Her thoughts had taken over, and she was standing still staring into nothing when Gillian found her.

"How are you feeling, Kiri?" Gillian asked softly.

Helena jumped, the words snapping her out of her reverie.

"Oh, I'm sorry, Kiri!" Gillian apologized profusely, placing a hand on her shoulder to steady her, "I did not mean to startle you."

Helena offered a wan smile that didn't quite meet her eyes. It was hard to participate in idle conversation with the events of the day weighing so heavily on her mind.

"It's not your fault, Gil, I should know better than to let my thoughts wander like that. Did you need something?" she asked as she studied her friend.

As always Gillian was the perfect portrait of a lady, her hair pulled back into a riot of curls and her purple dress pristine, the same color as the stone in her necklace, hugging her curves shamelessly before draping more demurely as it fell toward the ground.

"Not especially, Kiri. I mostly wanted to check and see how you were. You've been so concerned with the others, and it didn't seem like anyone had thought to look in on you."

"That's sweet of you. I'm fine, all things considered. A bit tired, if I'm being honest."

Gillian smiled kindly. "That's to be expected, of course. I've never seen magic like yours, Kiri. When you called that Fire from the sky," Gillian paused as a shiver coursed through her body. "It was terrifying. I'm certainly glad to be on your side."

Helena felt the twin of that shiver in her own limbs. Gillian wasn't the only one who had been frightened by the intensity of her magic. In those final moments of battle, Helena had not been herself, had not even been aware of what she was doing; only that she needed to protect her people.

No, if she was being honest, she hadn't been thinking of her people at all. She had only been thinking of Von. It was her desire to protect him that had her taking that deep dive into the depths of her magic and channeling her rage into the storm that had been its result. She hadn't known Fire would rain from the sky with such deadly abandon. How had it known to only harm the Shadows?

The question had been plaguing her for hours, but she was too afraid to voice it to any of the Circle. Too ashamed to admit that so much of her power was still a reflection of instinct rather than intent.

"Kiri?" Gillian called.

Helena blinked and looked at the girl, smiling apologetically, "Sorry, I don't mean to keep doing that."

Gillian squeezed her shoulder affectionately, "No need to apologize. Let's talk about something a bit more cheerful to get your mind off of things for a while!"

Helena tried not to frown at the suggestion. What she really wanted was to be alone with Von for a while, the warmth of his body against hers blocking out everything but him.

"How are things going with Von?" Gillian asked impishly, as though she had plucked the name straight from Helena's thoughts.

She tried to fight the blush that rose to her cheeks at the question. The truth was things with Von were better than she ever could have imagined they would be. Never had she imagined such a connection was possible with another person. Mates were something only the Chosen were gifted with finding, and having grown up thinking she was Ungifted; it was never an option open for her to consider. Not since she had been a little girl prone to flights of fancy anyway.

Even then, her dreams of finding a Mate were woefully inadequate compared to the truth of the bond. The overwhelming intensity and completeness when he was buried inside her, their bodies as connected as their minds. Being able to feel his response when she touched him, knowing exactly what caused him to lose control and spend himself inside her… the thought trailed off, and she found herself once again staring off into space, Gillian smirking knowingly beside her.

"Ah yes, a much more pleasant thought, I can see."

Helena shrugged. "He is wonderful," she said simply. "He is brave, and so strong, in every sense of the word, but he can also be quite tender when he wants to be. I never imagined there could be so perfect a man, or at least perfect for me."

"I wouldn't say he was perfect, Kiri," Gillian said, doubt coloring her words.

That caught Helena's attention, and her focus zeroed in on the girl beside her. "What do you mean?"

"Well," she started hesitantly before her brows lowered with a frown and she shook her head. "Never mind, Kiri, it doesn't matter. All has ended well."

Gillian had started to walk back toward the camp, but Helena's hand shot out and stopped her, turning her back to face her.

"No, Gillian, tell me what you mean." There was no request in her words, only demand.

The playful teasing from before was gone entirely. "Please, Kiri. It's better if you do not know. It will only hurt you."

"Tell. Me." Helena's teeth were gritted; she could feel her magic waking inside her, responding to the uncertainty and need to protect coiling within. Whatever rumor Gillian had to share, Helena knew it was tied to Von's colorful past. He had more than admitted he was not proud of who he had been before he met her. She couldn't believe they would still be so foolish to whisper such insults after all he had done to protect them. She wanted to hear what others were still saying so that she could put an end to it once and for all.

"Kiri." The word was a whimper.

"Now!" Helena shouted, lightning flashing in the sky as thunder growled in the distance.

"Helena?" the concerned voice asked in her mind, feeling her loss of control.

"It's just, one of the girls at the Palace. She had mentioned…"

Gillian seemed to pale as she watched Helena transform as her magic took over. Those swirling eyes pinning the girl in place.

Helena did not speak, her silence a clear instruction.

"The girl had mentioned how Von singled her out to pleasure him. The night of your ball. She had been bragging about how she had ridden one of the Damaskiri's stallions because she was more of a woman than you, despite all you stood to inherit."

Helena saw red. There was a sharp pain in her hands as her fingers, no not fingers, claws, punctured the flesh of her palm. Where her nails had once been jet black claws, very similar to the Talyrian's, now jutted out of her fingers. Helena let out a low hiss as visions of Von smirking while thrusting into another woman surfaced in her mind. The images from the trial were coming true. The wind howled, and around her a tempest raged, her hurt and anger fueling the storm.

"Helena!" Von shouted, running from their camp to her side. Seconds behind him the rest of the Circle followed.

She turned to face him, her lips curled in a snarl. "I warned you, Mate. I warned you that I would not share." Despite the chaos of the storm, her words were low, guttural.

"Leave us!" she snapped at the Circle as they approached. They paused, considering defying her order, but finally relented, slowly stepping away as they returned to the camp.

"Not you!" she added as Gillian attempted to slink away. "Tell him the story you were so eager to share with me."

"I wouldn't say eager is quite—" Gillian hedged before Helena cut her off.

"No more games, girl."

Von looked between the women, eyes wide. She could feel his confusion snaking through their bond; his desperation to connect with her. She closed him out, not wanting him to feel what Gillian's words had done to her. Not wanting him to feel the doubt that was taking root in her heart; a part of her still trying to protect him.

Gillian repeated her story, frightened green eyes studying Helena's claws before moving to stare at the ground. The rain pelting her had turned her elegant hairstyle into a sopping mess.

Von stiffened, his face losing all of its color.

"Tell me she's lying, Mate, and I will remove this memory from her mind so that she may never repeat such filth again," the Kiri ordered, no hint of Helena in the voice infused with many.

Von hesitated, and in that moment, she felt the flicker of shame.

The emotion was like a whip across her heart; she felt both its lash and the resulting sting.

"Tell me," she begged, her voice, once again her own, thick with emotion.

"Helena, I love you..." he started, his hand reaching out toward her in a pleading motion.

Her eyes swam with tears, and she could no longer make out his face through the blur. That lying traitorous face. The face that had become more beloved to her than any other.

"I warned you," she whimpered, face crumpling as her tears began to fall.

"It was before—" he tried, but she shook her head holding up her clawless hand for him to stop. There was nothing he could say at this moment that would make anything better. That one moment of hesitation costing him more than he may ever realize.

He was clutching at his chest as if he could feel her heart breaking. At least one of them could; she had gone numb. Her falling tears the only visible sign of her pain, inside there was only a lonely howl within a vast emptiness.

"You took another as your lover after you declared yourself to me. You know, as I do that as soon as you uttered the words, our souls recognized each other. You were mine from that moment. How dare you stand there and try to tell me it had happened before we were Mated. How. Dare. You!"

Von stood before her, his head bowed in shame, and his eyes clenched shut in pain. Still, he clutched at his heart while the storm raged around him, drops of water running down his face like tears.

"Leave me," she whispered.

His eyes opened at that, surprise shining in the gray depths. *"Helena..."* echoed within her mind, but it was faint, as though he was shouting it from a distance. Silently she continued to build the wall that would close him off from her mind, not wanting to share that intimacy with him when she was feeling so shattered. Not wanting him to know how much power he held over her by seeing the damage his carelessness had caused.

"I cannot look at you right now. Leave. Take some men and go on without us. We will meet up with you at your parents' home in a few days' time."

He dropped his head once more, shoulders sagging. He did not try to speak again, merely turned and walked away, each step looking heavier than the last.

Despite her words, Helena watched him. Her heart protesting the distance between them, while a small voice within her was begging for her to relent. With her eyes focused on her Mate, Helena didn't notice the small smile of satisfaction curling Gillian's lips.

CHAPTER 21

*V*on sat with his head in his hands, his third cup of Ronan's home brew almost empty. He couldn't get the image of Helena's face out of his mind. How that small flicker of hope was still shining in her eyes when Gillian had repeated her story; and the moment it died.

Shame was too small a word for what he felt right now. Loathing was little better. One stupid moment brought on by a lifetime of bad decisions; all of which were made in response to years of being found unworthy, could be his undoing. Von slammed his fist on the table, causing the wood to crack under the force. The blow wasn't enough to temper his pain, so he let out a roar and flung his arm out causing his cup to fly across the tent.

He stood quickly, his chair falling behind him. He had made one choice that he regretted as soon as he made it, and now he was left on the brink of losing all that he had come to love. There was his brother, and his men, but those relationships were tainted by a sense of duty. Only Helena had ever loved him freely, without ever demanding anything from him in return; besides his faithfulness.

His chest rose and fell with labored breaths; the need to dull his pain a siren's call. He knew he had failed her; knew with a bone-deep certainty she might never forgive him. It didn't matter that they had only just met at the time, she was right, he had felt something shift in him in that moment. It had scared him. He was there to finish a job, period. It should have been no different than any of the other jobs he had taken in the last decade. Granted, this was a task he had given to himself, and for once it didn't involve bloodshed, but regardless of that, he had planned to see it through.

Von's head throbbed, alerting him that he was nowhere near drunk enough for this line of thinking. Moving to where his cup had fallen, the thoughts continued. When he had come to Elysia, he doubted he'd even make it across the border, but years had a way of making people forget the threat that was supposed to exist, and it was easy to bribe a guard to allow his men through the pass. His only goal had been to lift the ban and find help for his brother. He never anticipated he might actually be the Damaskiri's Mate. He had never allowed himself to imagine any sort of future for himself at all, save clearing his family's name.

Von pressed calloused fingers against his eyes. His thoughts were splintering, and it was becoming more difficult to focus; the brew was starting to create a pleasant fog in his mind.

He felt like a coward as he hid in his tent, but he couldn't leave her. No matter what she asked; his heart felt like it was being pulled from his chest at the thought. Instead, he had decided to get completely shit-faced while he waited for her to calm down.

He knew he didn't deserve her forgiveness, but he was not above begging. He had once planned to humble himself just to become one of her suitors, knowing the Chosen would taunt him as soon as they heard his name; but that had been no real hardship to bear. He didn't give a Shadow's shriveled cock about their opinion of him. But for a chance at her forgiveness... for that he would walk, no he'd crawl, naked through the streets of Daejara. Nodding emphatically for good measure, he crouched down before the cup, swaying slightly.

Recovering his balance, he checked the cup for dirt. Blowing on it and shaking it twice for good measure; the silent tirade continued in his mind. His pride, the one thing that had got him through years of neglect and battles, had no place here now. Not when Helena's trust in him was on the line. He would do what he must, even if it required debasing himself completely.

Von had just stood and was reaching to refill his glass when Serena walked through the tent. His eyes were blurry enough that he squinted to try to see her more clearly.

"What are you doing here?" he demanded, the cup slipping through his fingers and rolling back across the floor. His eyes followed its progress across the floor, but he made no move to recover it. Instead, he narrowed his eyes and stared at it as if he could will it back to him.

"Let me get that for you," she said dryly after they stood there in silence for a few moments. Stepping around him, she reached down and picked it up.

Von blinked trying to keep her in focus as her image began to swim in front of him.

Serena turned and crossed the short distance to where Ronan's small cask sat, her back facing Von.

"What are you doing here?" he asked again his voice sounding decidedly petulant.

"We could hear you roaring from across the camp. Everyone is talking about what happened. About how Helena has thrown you out of the camp..." She looked over her shoulder at him briefly as she continued to fill his cup. "I came to check on you." Once she had finished, she faced him again and offered him a cup now brimming with the pale red liquid.

Von snatched it from her hand, the liquid sloshing over the rim as he took a greedy gulp. He scowled as he looked into his cup. "Ronan is losing his touch, each cup's bitt'r than th'last," he slurred.

Von smacked his lips together, surprised to find them feeling numb. "Fuck maybe not," he groaned as his legs gave out and he sat down hard on the floor. "I haven't been this drunk since... since..." he trailed off, staring at Serena in confusion.

"Are there two f'you?" he asked, his words blending together.

Serena laughed, one hand coming up to rest just above her necklace. "You are that indeed, Commander. Are you feeling better at least?"

Von stared at her stupidly. He didn't know if he was feeling better, he couldn't really feel much of anything as he sat there. He felt like there was something important he had been thinking about; something that he needed to do, but he just couldn't make sense of anything with the fog thick in his mind.

"Here now, drink up, you'll feel better after a good rest."

"Now ther'sa good 'dea." Each word was harder to pronounce than the one before, but Von held up his cup, staring at it with one eye to make sure it made it the full way to its destination. Slurping down the last of the bitter liquid, he wiped his mouth with the back of his hand.

Serena peered down at him with amused green eyes.

Wait. There was a single moment of clarity that broke through the fog before Von slumped over; unconscious. Serena didn't have green eyes.

GILLIAN STARED down at Von's motionless body with a sneer.

"Pathetic," she sneered, "letting a woman get you worked up enough to leave yourself so defenseless, and you call yourself a warrior."

She shook her head, not accustomed to the lightness of such short hair. She ran a hand along the back of her head, the silky fine strands sticking up in its wake.

Mother would be so proud if she could see all that she had accomplished in just a few days. Rowena had never believed her daughter would be capable of pulling off such a glorious deception, but it had been easy really. It just required a few well-aimed suggestions, offered when they would be most effective.

For Helena it had been simple, the girl was too naïve to do anything other than take a story or person at face value. Everyone had seen that she had been worn down for days. The constant barrage of death had taken its toll on her physically and mentally. Delivering her message right after the battle, when any possible defense was completely gone, was priceless if she did say so herself.

Gillian set about the room, clearing up any sign of her presence there.

Von had been a little trickier to manage. Luckily the *Bella Morte* in his brew had worked out. She had a plan B, but it was much less elegant. Her fingers caressed the ax hanging from her hips. Less elegant, but just as effective.

For a man with such a notoriously strong will, he had been surprisingly easy to manipulate. Both times. Then again, today it was Helena that had delivered the fatal blow. Gillian had merely set events into motion.

The first time though... Gillian sighed wistfully. It had been fun to ride him, his powerful body leaving its imprint on her for days after. All it took was a few whispered words as she slipped something into his drink and he had taken the bait gratefully. She wondered idly if anyone had ever found the body of the serving girl whose appearance she had borrowed.

It wasn't like she could be certain Von had really gone through with the deed unless she was there to see it through, and it was essential his guilt be real when she presented Helena with his indiscretion. And she certainly couldn't do it as herself! No, stealing that woman's form had been the only option, and it wouldn't have gone well at all if she showed up while Gillian laid her trap. Not at all. Sometimes death really was the only option.

Too bad her mother wanted this one alive. He would have made a fun plaything. Unfortunately, orders were orders, and she didn't dare break one. Not with Micha's life on the line.

Gillian looked around the room, scanning for anything she may have overlooked. She needed to move quickly. She could not risk the Circle, or even the real Serena, finding her. Seeing nothing out of place, she moved back toward the body now sprawled on the ground. She ran her hand through his hair gripping it tight and yanking his head back. She wet her lips as she watched that luscious mouth fall open.

What the hell, Mother will never know if I had a taste before completing my mission.

Gillian licked up the side of his face, his sweat salty and tasting of guilt. *Delicious*, she thought before pressing her mouth to his and biting his lower lip until she drew blood. She lapped it up and smiled, heady with the sense of accomplishment.

"Let's go home, lover. Mother is waiting for you." Her voice was a sensual purr, completely at odds with the pointed nails that raked roughly down his chest. Drops of blood beaded until they pooled into a crimson feast, which she quickly bent to devour. Using some of her power she closed the scratches. No one must know she stopped to take a sip. Mother would be furious.

Gillian's hand lifted to her necklace, the purple stone beginning to glow faintly against her fingers. Her other hand still woven through Von's hair. One moment they were there, and the next they were gone.

CHAPTER 22

*H*elena's heart felt like it was splintering. Not a metaphorical breaking, but a physical tearing apart. It was a tightness in her chest that caused her breaths to come out in shallow gasps. She felt lost; her anchor cut away, leaving her at the mercy of a storm-fueled sea. Even her skin didn't feel as though it fit right. It was clammy, as though a part of her essence was leaking through a casing that could no longer contain her.

Blind to her surroundings, she paced the length of their room. Helena's mind raced as it combed over every moment since the first when his hand had brushed hers, and an unknown part of her came into being. Flipping through the memories, she searched for some sign of his betrayal; any small moment she might have missed because she was too busy falling in love with him to see him clearly.

Even as the thoughts crossed her mind, she dismissed them. It wasn't as simple as falling in love. She had found her Mate. Her soul's other half. The part of her that she hadn't realized was missing until she felt what it was to be whole. As much as one can lie to themselves, one cannot ignore the magnitude of such a moment; the feeling of utter completeness when you are reunited with the person that carries the other piece of you.

It came as no surprise that Von had a history, he had warned her of it often enough. He went so far as to tell her the night they were formally mated that he hadn't been a good man. It wasn't his past that had its claws tearing at her heart right now. Never mind the other lover, she had been fleeting. Someone he had used while trying to deny the bond that had already taken root inside of him. Although a small part of her still itched to test some of the new powers she had discovered, perhaps rake those lovely claws right down the bitch's face. She could feel a flicker of Fire in her, but it was sluggish, calling to her from far away.

Helena squeezed her eyes shut, her head pounding in time with her heartbeat.

No, the part she kept replaying was the feel of his guilt in her mind. The confession of his heart, when his words proclaimed innocence. Even in knowing she would be able to feel the deceit through their bond, his first impulse was still to explain it away. Since knowing him, her every instinct had been to protect him. Could that be what caused his hesitation? Had he been trying to protect her feelings from a mistake that was made in a moment of weakness? Or was he merely trying to protect himself?

She struggled to clear her thoughts, the pulsing in her temples overwhelming her with the pain. Opening her eyes, she winced at the brightness of the room. Her mind was telling her that she had overreacted, telling him to go ahead without her. Her heart told her that she should run after him and throw herself into his arms.

Not even a few hours later and she already felt his absence. Rather, she couldn't feel him at all. It was the first time since waking up after facing her trial that his essence wasn't hovering at the edge of her awareness. She felt its lack pressing against her, wanting her to collapse into its void. Even her soul wanted to chase after its Mate and beg his forgiveness for doubting what it knew to be true. Her trial had warned her this test would come, and she had failed.

Helena sighed. She had been foolish listening to Gillian's story. She had just been so tired from the battle and so heart-sore after days of burials, she wasn't thinking clearly. Not to mention her surprise when Von didn't immediately shut Gillian down with one of his scathing dismissals. Instead, he had hesitated, his face losing some of its healthy glow, and their bond throbbing with his shame.

Noticing a flash of white, Helena turned to face the trunk she had been using as a side table next to their bedding. The Magnolia.

The ghost of a smile flit across her lips. She remembered Von's teasing words when presenting her with the gift. She had made a point to ask Alina to pack it with her things, wanting to keep close the physical reminder of the moment she first met her Mate.

With that thought, a piece of her settled back into place. It was an answer to a question. Even when Von thought he was just playing a part, he had cared enough to give her something personal. Simple compared to some of the other courtship gifts, yes, but so much more memorable for its specific meaning to her. A music box or book spelled to tell stories were lovely trinkets, but they were gifts that could be given to anyone, and therefore meaningless. Von had taken the time to give her something she would find special, proving that even before he met her, when he had no reason to, he had cared about her.

Von regretted his decision to bed the other woman, and though it had happened before they made any promises to one another, he had done so after presenting himself to her. Feeling as he did now, that act still ate at him, a small splinter that he couldn't quite remove. His guilt stemmed from that; it was not a desire to lie to her, but rather his regret that he couldn't deny Gillian's claims.

Helena had no doubt of Von's love for her. She felt it in every look and every phantom caress he sent through their bond. She took a deep breath, finding it a little easier this time as the tightness in her chest had started to ease. She wasn't pleased with what he had done, but she wouldn't punish him for it. Much. Especially when the punishment seemed to hurt her just as much as it did him.

The headache continued to pulse but seemed to be fading. She decided to go find Starshine and see if the Talyrian could catch up to Von's party. They couldn't have gotten too far, even if they had left immediately.

Holding open the flap of the tent, she let out the soft whistle that had become her call for the Talyrian. She waited, eyes scanning the horizon until the ball of white appeared and streaked through the sky toward her.

"Take me to him," she requested softly, projecting an image of Von to Starshine as she did so.

Those turquoise eyes seemed to roll, but she lowered until Helena could mount easily. Between one breath and the next, they were in the air and already too far for Helena to see her Circle calling after her.

THE SKY WAS dark when they made it back to the camp. The first thing she noticed as Starshine landed was Timmins pacing before the campfire, his hands tugging at his hair.

Kragen was leaning against a tree, sharpening his ax. Darrin and Joquil sat around the fire and stared into its flame. At her appearance, all four stood and faced her.

Timmins had opened his mouth to launch into what was sure to be a tirade, but Helena stopped him with a glance.

Her face was tear-streaked, her aqua eyes blinking furiously as they filled again.

"Helena?" Darrin asked softly, hands outstretched as if to catch her.

She took a trembling step toward them, her whole body shaking.

"He's gone," she whispered.

"What?" Ronan asked sharply, just reaching the group, Serena close on his heels.

Helena swallowed before turning to him. "Von is gone. I—I can't feel him anymore. Starshine and I rode for hours, and then circled back to double check, but he's not out there."

Her hand was clutching at her chest, trying to ease the ache.

Ronan snapped out orders, but she couldn't make sense of them. He couldn't have gotten too far; it had only been a few hours since she had sent him away. She knew he would have continued on their path toward his parents' home, it was only another two days ride from here, but even still she and Starshine had searched, the circles increasing with each pass.

When they had gotten closer to the border, and she still couldn't reach him through their bond she had started to worry. As the hours went by and the sun faded from the sky worry had given way to fear. Von was gone, without a trace, or at least too far for her to be able to sense him through their bond. Unless her asking him to leave had done something to their bond.

She was trying to recall if she had felt something in her shift when she had stopped him from coming toward her and telling him she needed time. His face had been frozen in shock, his pain at her words a twin to her own, but that had been it. She would have felt it, wouldn't she, if she had broken their bond?

"Helena?" Darrin called, shaking her slightly.

She blinked up at him. "Yes?"

"How long has he been gone?"

She shook her head. "I don't—I don't know. We had—there was... I told him to leave." Her face crumpled, and she couldn't stop the tears as they flowed from her eyes.

"Shh, *Mira*, we will find him. Tell me what happened." The order was gentle, his hands soothing as they rubbed up and down her arms.

Helena hiccupped as she tried to control the tears. Around her the others were quiet, waiting for her story.

So she began, haltingly, telling them everything that Gillian had said about Von seeking the girl out and sleeping with her after declaring himself at the ceremony. The men exchanged surprised looks but asked her to continue.

She told them how she had sent him on ahead, asking him to give her some time to process what she had heard before she had to speak with him.

"So he could have only been gone for a couple of hours at most, but he wouldn't have left, Kiri. Not even if you had ordered him to, he would have come to one of us and stayed out of your way until you cooled off, knowing you would come for him," Serena stated.

Ronan nodded. "Nor would he have left without Karma." Ronan gestured at the wolf pacing restlessly among the others.

Helena felt foolish, of course Von wouldn't have left Karma. She should have checked immediately once she realized he wasn't within range.

"So if he didn't leave, where is he?" Helena asked, silently adding, *and why can't I feel him anymore?*

Ronan and Serena shared a look.

"What?" Helena snapped, looking between them.

"Where's Gillian?" Serena asked, her violet eyes seeming to glow.

Helena's back stiffened. "Gillian? I don't know; I haven't seen her since this afternoon."

"I caught her out in the forest, our first night out. There was something about the girl that wasn't sitting right, so I wanted to keep an eye on her. I saw her keep stealing glances at me, so I made a show of going off with Ronan and then circled back to watch her. Almost immediately she snuck out of camp and hurried through the forest. I came upon her crouching over something, but couldn't see what it was in the darkness."

"Why are you just telling us this now?" Kragen demanded.

Serena shrugged. "We didn't have proof of anything, just my feelings. I didn't want to come between the Kiri and her friend unless I had good reason."

"Wait a moment," Joquil's voice interrupted, causing the group to look at him. "Didn't Gillian have a necklace with a purple stone?"

She saw Darrin's eyes widen in recognition. "Yes, I don't think she was ever without it. It was very similar to those gems you found on the Shadows."

Joquil's face was grim. "I think I know how Von disappeared, Kiri."

"How?" she asked sharply.

"Gillian had a Kaelpas, as did those Shadows."

"I thought the knowledge of how to make those died centuries ago," Timmins whispered in awe.

"What's a Kaelpas?" Helena asked, her voice strained as she pronounced the unfamiliar word. She could feel her magic, usually a calm pool, bubbling inside of her.

"It's a very rare, very powerful bit of magic. Completely

untraceable unless you carry one of the spelled gems. They work like beacons. Let's say you and I both have one, Kiri," Joquil explained, "I would be able to teleport to you, wherever you were because your Kaelpas would guide me to you. I could also travel to a destination I had been to before, even if there was no one with a Kaelpas in the vicinity. It takes powerful magic to create a Kaelpas; it requires mastery in three of the branches: Earth, Air, and Fire."

"They also take the entire cycle of a moon to charge. The farther you travel or, the more people you try to transport with a single Kaelpas the faster is it extinguished," Timmins added.

"So what you're saying is that Gillian brought those things, those Shadows, to us before. It was how they knew where to strike so that we would find the bodies."

"It certainly supports our theory that their presence was a test of our forces," Ronan murmured.

"And how Von could vanish without a trace," Serena concluded.

Helena could no longer hear them, her blood roaring in her ears. Gone. Her Mate was gone. Not just gone, taken.

She flexed her fingers, the rise of magic causing them to tingle. The tingle quickly turned to a burn as her fury continued to feed on her reservoir of strength.

There was no rational thought, just a word on an endless loop in her mind. Taken.

Her magic continued to build, a tidal wave getting ready to crash. She was losing herself to the swell of magic within her.

When she looked back at her Circle, and Von's most trusted warriors, her eyes were swirling iridescent pools, flashes of lightning in their depths. Thunder filled with the promise of her retribution echoed in the sky.

"Helena?" Darrin asked, eyes wide.

As she leveled her eyes on him, he paled. There was no sign of the woman they knew in those eyes.

"We will find him," the Kiri said, her voice a harsh harmony of many, her words an edict that would not allow disobedience. "And when we find her, we will repay her hospitality. For every new mark on his skin or scar on his heart, she will pay with her blood." The last word came out as a snarl. The wind tore through the trees, growing in intensity as she spoke.

"As you command, Kiri," the Circle said as one.

She knew nothing but endless glittering rage. She had warned them; no one would harm what was hers. She would show them what happens when they disobeyed. One way or another she would find her Mate. Like calls to like—they would not be able to keep him from her indefinitely. And when she found him, his captors and any that tried to stand in her way would pay.

With their lives.

HELENA AND VON'S STORY CONTINUES IN REIGN OF ASH, BOOK 2 IN THE CHOSEN SERIES.

KEEP READING FOR A SNEAK PEEK!

PROLOGUE

*G*illian could feel the weight of her mistress's stare and allowed her eyes to dart up to the woman on the throne. She had many titles, but Gillian knew her best as mother. At least, she had. Once.

There was nothing left of the mother Gillian had once known in the woman sitting above her. In truth, it felt like there was a chasm that separated the once kind, if only mildly affectionate woman who raised her from this aloof and cold-hearted queen. Now instead of mother, she was simply referred to as Mistress by Gillian and Rowena by those too stupid to know what was good for them. Or those that had a death wish.

As the last Damaskiri, she was both Helena's predecessor and a woman believed dead by the people she once ruled. She was a Queen in hiding, biding her time until she could strike against her enemies and reclaim her rightful place amongst the Chosen.

Rowena leaned back slowly, her eyes never drifting from the red-haired girl kneeling before her. Sitting as she was, she was the personification of queenly grace, her posture perfect and unflinching. She was stunning in a cold and frightening way. Her face was currently schooled into an expressionless mask; her ice-blue gaze glacial as she stared. Her colorless blonde hair was pulled up into an elaborate mess of braids and surrounded by the glittering and twisting spikes of metal that comprised her crown. A fitted black satin dress encased her lithe body, the severity of its color only enhancing the luminosity of her skin.

Rowena tilted her head to the side, the movement deliberate and calculating, a predator assessing its prey. The silence lengthened and became uncomfortable until Gillian finally shifted nervously, her skirts rustling as they moved against the ground. There was a metallic tinkling as Rowena's fingers tapped a steady beat on the dark arm of her throne.

Gillian's green eyes widened, noting the sharp-clawed tips of the rings which adorned each of the slender fingers on mother's right hand. She forced herself to look away, shifting her focus back to the stone floor.

After another long moment of strained silence, Gillian bowed her head lower, allowing a waterfall of copper curls to spill over her shoulder and obscure her face. The protection from Rowena's scrutiny was welcomed, even if only imagined. That icy gaze missed nothing.

"The prisoner?" Rowena finally asked, her voice as expressionless as her face and as weighted as her stare.

Gillian felt her shoulders stiffen as she relayed the latest report. "Still under the effects of the *Bella Morte*, Mistress."

"You were careless in your dosage." It was both a statement and judgment, the words leaving absolutely no room for doubt; she would be punished for her transgression.

She swallowed thickly. Her mistress's punishments were unfailingly harsh and varied. One thing Gillian had come to expect was that she would never see it coming.

"I do not believe he is lost to the dreaming, Mistress." Gillian winced, hearing the quavering in her voice.

"You do not *believe*?" The question was a harsh crack.

Gillian found herself grinding her teeth before she could respond.

"He is not showing any side effects besides the hallucinations," she amended.

"Other than remaining in a drugged stupor since his arrival," Rowena contradicted caustically.

"Yes, Mistress. It is as you say," Gillian meekly agreed.

"You had better hope that he wakes, and soon. For your brother's sake, if not your own. Micha's remaining days on this earth are a direct result of your success…" She paused for one endless moment before adding contemptuously, "Or your failure." The words were savage but measured, the threat delivered as matter-of-factly as one might discuss the weather.

Fear scratched down her spine and Gillian could feel her body break into a sweat, despite the chill in the room. Before she could respond further she was dismissed, Rowena standing and exiting from one of the doors in the back of the cavernous room.

Gillian did not move immediately, not trusting her limbs to support her or that her mother would not be back. While she waited, she let her eyes bounce from the arched windows and soaring ceilings back to the throne of twisting metal sitting in the center of the dais.

Once it was clear Rowena would not be returning, Gillian stood and made her way to the door. Her legs trembled as she exited the room but she made it to the safety of the corridor before slumping against the stone wall. Her eyes fluttered closed as her heart raced and a thought tinged with desperation raced through her.

One moment. I just need one moment.

Gillian struggled to calm her heartbeat. Eventually, she peeled herself off of the wall and took a final, shuddering breath as she continued her journey to the prisoner.

He would wake; she would see to it. She would bring his mind back to his body even if it required her to take him to the brink of death to do so. There was no room for failure. Micha's life depended on it. No matter how much she enjoyed her plaything, Micha's life was worth infinitely more to her than stolen moments in a prison cell.

One way or the other, it was time for Von to wake up.

CHAPTER 1

*H*elena sat beside the fountain, a picture of quiet devastation. She could no longer see her reflection rippling in the water's pristine surface. She also couldn't remember the last time she moved, or even hazard a guess as to how long she'd been sitting there. Despite her statue-like stillness, the serenity was only an illusion. Every night since Von's capture she had sought out a place where she could be alone to search for some sense of their bond, some spark that would help guide her to him. And just as it had been every night since she started her search, there was only a vast and endless darkness.

Helena flinched violently as a warm hand brushed against her icy shoulder. She spun around, teeth bared in a feral snarl until she recognized the green eyes studying her with concern.

"You forgot your cloak again," Darrin murmured gently, offering her the deep purple garment lined with sable fur.

"Oh, thank you," she rasped, her voice raw with disuse.

Her stiff fingers tried to take the cloak but could not bend enough to grasp it before Darrin let go. It fell clumsily to the floor. She sat unmoving; her eyes, which tracked its progress to the ground, were the only sign she was aware of what had happened.

"Here, let me," he offered finally when she made no move to pick it up. He lifted and deftly wrapped the warm fabric around her shoulders.

Helena shivered as its warmth seeped into her skin.

"What time is it?" she asked, her words coming slowly as she struggled to come back to the present.

"It's getting late, and you missed the evening meal. Again." His voice held none of the gentle rebuke she was used to hearing. In its absence, there was only worry.

She had not been taking very good care of herself and it showed. Her aqua eyes, usually shining with light, were bruised and dull. She had missed more meals than she ate and had gotten little, if any, sleep. The sleep she had managed to get had been fraught with nightmares, which only added to the haunted look in her eyes. The lack of food and quality sleep, combined with a headache which had only grown in intensity since Von's disappearance, left her looking decidedly haggard.

Von would be so disappointed in her if he saw her walking through the corridors of his home like a ghost of the woman he loved. She could almost hear his deep growl echoing in her mind: *What do you think you're doing, Mate? That body belongs to me; take better care of it.*

The wave of longing that slammed through her at even that paltry imitation of him had tears blurring her eyes. She swallowed the emotion back down and gave herself a mental shake. She could not go on like this for much longer; both her body and her heart would give out on her soon. If not for her own sake, she could at least try to take better care of herself for him. She had vowed to find him and destroy his captors after all. She could hardly make good on the promise to avenge him if she was too weak to do more than sit there and scowl menacingly. The mental image caused a barely discernible smile to flit across her lips before quickly fading.

Helena blinked back the last of the tears and really looked at Darrin for the first time. "Do you think there's something left for me to eat?"

Relief flooded his face at the request. "Yes, Kiri. I believe we can scrounge something up for you."

She nodded once and stood, ready to follow him back into the manor. They had reached the Holbrooke Estate only a day after discovering Gillian's betrayal. Helena winced as she remembered her first meal with Von's family.

THE CIRCLE SAT around a massive oak table that was colored and pitted with age. The room was bright, lit both by the fire roaring beside them, and by soft balls of light which floated above them. Helena had been given a place of honor at the head of the table, although the sneers Von's father, Darius, wore whenever she caught him looking at her did much to undermine the display of hospitality. Margo, Von's mother, was much kinder. She had welcomed the group with warm hugs and wept silently when she had learnt what had become of her eldest son. Von's younger brother Nial had not been feeling well and was unable to come and greet the group, although he had sent his apologies for his absence and promised to meet with them soon.

Helena had moved through the introductions numbly, allowing Timmins to explain what had happened. All of the fury and promises of vengeance had burned out of her, leaving only a fragile shell in its place. Well, that was not strictly true; her wrath continued to simmer along the surface of her magic, but it was leashed by the lack of a target. Without it to fuel her, she was left with little to buffer her against the storm of emotions raging within. Guilt. Fear. Sorrow. All were relentless as they continued to crash against the inner barriers of her mind.

She couldn't recall much of the short tour they were given as Margo led them to their rooms. Despite being at the base of a mountain the manor was warm. It had wide halls and vaulted ceilings that created a sense of openness and flow from room to room. There were also large windows in every room so that the beauty of Daejara was incorporated throughout their home. It often seemed as though they were sitting outside, although the fact that they were sheltered from the biting winds was certainly a welcome reprieve.

The dining hall sat to the east of the home, overlooking the view of the massive cliffs and sparkling blue ocean below. Helena had never seen the sea before, but there was something about the roar of the crashing waves that called to her. Perhaps, if she could get away from the prying eyes of the Circle, she would take Starshine out over the water to get a better look.

Thinking of Starshine had her remembering her last night with Von under the stars. The feeling of his warm hands running along the length of her back. The scrape of his teeth as he ran them over the cords of muscle in her neck before biting down gently, and then licking his way back to her ear to trail sweet kisses down to her lips.

She felt her lower lip quiver at the memory. Her desire for her Mate was quickly overshadowed by her grief at his absence, and at the way things had been left between them. It was her fault he had been taken. If she had not been so stupid and believed Gillian's lies... if she had not trusted the harlot in the first place... if only she could tell Von how sorry she was, and how much she loved him.

The sniffling brought her out of her memories. She looked around the table with wide eyes, shock quickly replaced by mortification as she watched each person sob. Serena had her head buried in Ronan's neck, while the warrior hastily wiped at his eyes. Darrin had his head bowed over his plate, shoulders shaking with tears. Timmins was blowing his nose while Joquil dabbed at his dripping eyes. Margo and Darius clung to each other, their cries echoing loudly in the spacious room.

Kragen's eyes were dry but despondent, anguish cutting deep lines in his usually smiling face. "I much prefer the days you would have us seeking out dark corners to fumble beneath a maid's skirts to this, Kiri," he muttered.

Helena blinked and let out a startled bark of laughter. That was all it took to break the spell; the men and women parroted Kragen's sentiment as their tears were swiftly replaced with watery laughter.

"You and I both, Sword." While her smile didn't quite reach her eyes, the gentle teasing had worked. She was no longer drowning in her misery and was able to get through the evening without further incident.

"PERHAPS I WILL ACTUALLY MAKE it through a meal without embarrassing myself," she murmured, heartened by the fact she would be eating in relative solitude.

Darrin chuckled beside her. "No one blames you, Helena."

She sighed. "No, I know that... it would just be nice to have my feelings be a little less," she paused searching for the right word, "contagious."

He placed his hand lightly on her shoulder. "One would only have to look at your eyes to know what you were feeling."

She blinked up at him before smiling sadly. "I haven't been doing a very good job of being a leader these past weeks, have I? I've been too busy wallowing."

Darrin made a dismissive sound, not bothering to answer.

Helena squared her shoulders and said with forced determination, "Well, no more of that. It's time I got back to my training. Will you let Ronan know I would like to work with him in the morning? And tell Joquil I'd like to continue with our lessons as well."

Darrin's eyes widened in surprise before he nodded quickly. "Of course."

I really must be pathetic these days if that was enough to shock him, she thought dejectedly.

"Oh," she added aloud, "and I would like to set aside some time to see Nial. He was the entire reason for this trip, at least originally. I would like to see what I can do to help him."

"Are you sure you're strong enough for something like that?" Darrin's question mirrored her own concerns.

Helena shrugged as they rounded the corner and walked into the kitchen. "Honestly, I have no idea, but until I see what I'm dealing with, it's too hard to say one way or the other."

Helena had met Nial only briefly. She had taken one look at his dark hair and those familiar gray eyes and practically put down roots in the floor. The similarity between him and his brother had been enough to have her heart lodge in her throat. She had stood there like a slack-jawed fool, staring at him with hopeful longing. It had taken a few moments for her to recover enough to stumble through an apology, her cheeks a blazing pink. Nial had kindly waved it off, smiling as he adjusted the soft blue blanket in his lap.

Once her heartbeat had returned to its normal pace, she realized there were a number of subtle differences between the brothers. To start, Nial's voice lacked Von's deep growl and his gray eyes were more a stormy gray-blue than silver. Helena had also noticed that his wavy dark hair was much shorter than Von's. Even so, it hurt to look at him, the visual reminder of what she had lost was more than she could bear, and she had limited her interactions with him. Yet another reason she had avoided so many meals. *Coward. No more hiding, Helena*, she chided herself. *Von deserves better than this.*

Darrin moved across the room, opening a chilled cabinet to gather the leftovers from the evening meal. She watched him open up various containers before selecting one that appeared to be full of a vegetable stew and another full of a fluffy white substance.

"Potatoes," Darrin said in answer to her lifted brow.

Helena's stomach growled as the smell of the food hit her nose.

Darrin laughed loudly, his eyes crinkling with mirth as he said, "Well, I guess I don't need to ask if that sounds good to you."

She stuck out her tongue in response as he quickly dished out large portions of each.

"Can you manage reheating these?" He gestured toward her hands. "I'm not certain where anything is in here or I would offer to do it myself."

Helena nodded and stepped over to him, her fingers running over the smooth surface of the large wooden counter as she did. Grasping the dish, she closed her eyes and called the smallest tendril of magic to her. She felt the heat of Fire quickly rush to the surface, and found herself making soothing noises to gentle the rush. She released her magic entirely once the spicy steam was wafting up to her face.

Darrin let out a low whistle. "Such a convenient talent."

Helena nodded in agreement, accepting the spoon he was holding out to her. She dug in greedily and immediately let out a startled yelp as her eyes began to water. Her hand was pressed over her mouth while she blinked back tears.

Darrin howled with laughter beside her. "All right, perhaps it's not as convenient as I thought if you make it too hot to eat."

She glared at him. "You're lucky I'm too hungry to dump this on you."

He held up two hands and stepped back. "Merely an observation, Kiri."

She rolled her eyes. "Standing on formality will not protect you, Shield."

He lifted a shoulder while his smile grew. "You can't blame me for trying, Hellion."

She winked at him, before taking another spoonful of the stew and making a show of blowing on it. His laughter died down and he stood across from her, watching her silently.

She lifted her brow. "What?" she asked, her mouth full of stew and the word coming out garbled.

He just shook his head, a small smile playing about his lip. "It's just nice to see you looking happy, Helena."

She swallowed and looked down into her bowl before speaking. "I miss him, Darrin."

"I know," he said gravely.

She shook her head slowly. "No, I don't think you do." Her aqua eyes blazed brightly as they met his before continuing, "I feel as though a piece of me is missing. It's not something as obvious as a limb, but I feel just as crippled. Nothing feels right without him here. I'm so lost..." She trailed off, averting her gaze as she did, her voice thick with emotion.

"We will find him, Helena. Do not lose hope."

He watched a small tremor work its way through her body, her fingers gripping the spoon in her hand more tightly. When she looked back up, there were hints of the swirling iridescence in her eyes and her voice resonated as though spoken in harmony. "I haven't and I won't."

Darrin nodded, his shoulders relaxing at the small appearance of her power. "Good. Now eat up."

Helena made a face but continued to work her way through the meal until it was mostly gone. Taking the bowl from her, he made quick work of rinsing it out and setting it to dry with the others.

"Feeling better?" he asked, his voice too inquisitive to be casual.

She nodded, smiling ruefully. "Yes, mother."

Darrin laughed, and pulled her into him, hugging her tightly. "We are going to get through this; you'll see." The words were soft as he rested his cheek atop her head.

"I know," she said just as softly, her words muffled by his chest. She clung to him as they stood in silence, willing his promises to come true.

FROM THE AUTHOR

If you enjoyed this book, please consider writing a short review
and posting it on Amazon, Bookbub, Goodreads and/or
anywhere else you share your love of books.

Reviews are very helpful to other readers and are greatly
appreciated by authors
(especially this one!)

When you post a review, send me an email and let me know! I
might feature part, or all, of it on social media.

XOXO

♡ Meg Anne

meg@megannewrites.com

ACKNOWLEDGMENTS

First, let me start off with the most important one: To anyone reading this, you are literally making my dream come true. Thank you so much for taking the time to read my words, I'll never be able to adequately express how much it means to me.

Ser: If not for your insistence on reading a silly little word doc entitled "ReMastered" this story would never be finished. Your belief in me is overwhelming. Thank you for the countless late nights staying up with me to discuss things like practical limitations of magic and flying cat dragons. There are really no words to convey what you mean to me other than: What's brown and sticky? Well, perhaps these: Sweet dreams my prince; good night my love; I love you all of the muches.

To my tribe: Maggie, Paula, Stacy, Marie. They say it takes a village. You women have been role models since before I can remember. Thank you for the hugs, tissues, huge glasses of wine, and every single bad habit (the good ones are all right too) – they make me a better person. Your support is everything and I would not be where I am today without you.

J. Mill: You are my hero. More than that, you are my friend. Thank you for the love and support, and all the words of encouragement. There is forever a place with your name on it in my heart. This book would not exist without you.

Fran: You know what you did, and I love you for it. Please don't ever cut me off, I need your smart-mouth in my life.

For my girls at AFWB: Heather and Hanleigh, your messages & massive amounts of !!!!! as you read my draft brought tears to my eyes. I have them copied and pasted into a folder so that I can pull them out and read them over and over. Thank you for helping me create the best version of this book, and for helping me believe in myself. I am so proud of what we created.

For my original beta readers: Steph, Sarah, LeAnn, Gabby. Some of you have been reading my stories since I wrote them inside notebooks alternating colored pens between lines, others are newer to the worlds that come to life in my mind. In either case, you are freaking awesome. Your support and excitement about this adventure give me hope that it may not be completely foolish. Love you!

ALSO BY MEG ANNE

FANTASY ROMANCE

THE CHOSEN UNIVERSE

THE CHOSEN

MOTHER OF SHADOWS

REIGN OF ASH

CROWN OF EMBERS

QUEEN OF LIGHT

THE KEEPERS

THE DREAMER – A KEEPERS STORY

THE KEEPER'S LEGACY

THE KEEPER'S RETRIBUTION

THE KEEPER'S VOW

PARANORMAL & URBAN FANTASY ROMANCE

THE GYPSY'S CURSE

CO-WRITTEN WITH JESSICA WAYNE

VISIONS OF DEATH

VISIONS OF VENGEANCE

VISIONS OF TRIUMPH

CURSED HEARTS: THE COMPLETE COLLECTION

THE GRIMM BROTHERHOOD

CO-WRITTEN WITH KEL CARPENTER

REAPER'S BLOOD

REAPING HAVOC

REAPER REBORN

UNDERCOVER MAGIC

HINT OF DANGER

FACE OF DANGER

WORLD OF DANGER* *PRE-ORDER*

ANTHOLOGIES

THE MONSTER BALL YEAR 2

CONTAINS UNDERCOVER MAGIC PREQUEL NOVELLA, SHADE OF DANGER, WHICH TAKES PLACE AFTER EVENTS IN THE KEEPER'S VOW

ABOUT THE AUTHOR

Meg Anne has always had stories running on a loop in her head. They started off as daydreams about how the evil queen (aka Mom) had her slaving away doing chores; and more recently shifted into creating backgrounds about the people stuck beside her during rush hour. The stories have always been there; they were just waiting for her to tell them.

Like any true SoCal native, Meg enjoys staying inside curled up with a good book and her cat Henry . . . or maybe that's just her. You can convince Meg to buy just about anything if it's covered in glitter or rhinestones, or make her laugh by sharing your favorite bad joke. She also accepts bribes in the form of baked goods and Mexican food.

Meg loves to write about sassy heroines and the men that love them. She is best known for her adult fantasy romance series The Chosen, which can be found on Amazon.

Made in the USA
Coppell, TX
19 December 2020